ALSO BY ZACH COLE:

Jeremy Walker series:

BLUE MOON

Titans Unleashed

The Titans' Children

Jeremy Walker side story:

Kaiju Epoch

Project Arachne novellas:

Tsuchigumo

Chimera (2018)

Standalone Novels:

Legion (2018)

Lovecraft (2018/2019)

Anthologies:

The Experiment (2018)

Attack of the Kaiju

Gfantis vs...

THE TITANS' CHILDREN

A Jeremy Walker Thriller

(Book 3)

Zach Cole

THE TITANS'
CHILDREN

Prologue:

Ancient History

Thel-Shuum, pilot of the last remaining Mechanike, and the last of the Anterkian race, piloted the robot Prometheus into the docking bay where it would stay until it would be needed again. While the damage Prometheus sustained throughout the many battles waged over the last few months would heal thanks to nano-bots covering the mech's body, the injuries inflicted upon Thel's body wouldn't. He could already feel the last of his energy, his life, slipping from him.

Even as he was about to die, he was proud. He had followed the order given to him by Dal-Un before she was taken by the Plagueonian monsters. He had protected humanity from the Vexnoxtuqe. He had imprisoned the Titans and their children and fought off the creature that had wrecked Atlantis, locking the creature within the city as it sank beneath the waves.

"Your life signs are critical," Prometheus' artificial intelligence said. "My life support systems are offline. I am unable to help you."

"There is no need. Our job is done," Thel-Shuum told the AI.

"No, it is not. The Vexnoxtuqe aren't dead. They could come back."

"And if they do, someone will find you. They'll complete what I couldn't. You will determine if they are worthy to take the mantle as your pilot."

"Are you sure?"

"Yes, I have faith it will happen."

"I am a construct. I do not know faith."

"Just trust me."

He disconnected from Prometheus, the helmet lifting away, up toward the dome that held the AI's core at the top of the head. Darkness surrounded him. He could feel the cold air rushing into the cockpit from where the head was breached during the battle with the Atlantis monster. Pain radiated from his gut. Something was lodged in his stomach, he knew; blood was flowing from the wound.

Too much blood.

He was losing a lot. He felt cold. He knew he wouldn't last much longer. He was dying.

His thoughts drifted to the one he was supposed to protect: Dal-Un. The Anterkian princess. He remembered the day the Plagueonians took her, the memory burned into his mind.

It was during the early days of the Titanomanchy. Plagueonian ships clouded the skies above Greece, preparing to leave, but they weren't leaving without something…without Dal-Un.

Thel-Shuum, piloting Prometheus, the name given to the robot by the Atlantian known as Hercules, was fighting against the Titans alongside the Titans' children, what the humans referred to as 'gods'. Divine beings of great power. In a way, they were right. The Vexnoxtuque were capable of great power, but they were far from divine.

Thel-Shuum sent Kronos sprawling to the ground, turning in time to see a beast with a flaming head pluck Dal-Un from the ground. He rushed forward, not letting the black skinned monster take the one being that mattered to him. The monster saw him coming, roaring a challenge.

He drew his sword, it extending from a compartment in the robot's palm, and swung, intending to lob off the monster's hand. The Vexnoxtuqe twisted, avoiding the strike and bringing its flaming tail around, slamming it into Prometheus's side. One moment the robot was on its feet and the next it was on the ground. The flaming monster roared a challenge, its skull-like face locked on its opponent, hand still holding Dal-Un.

"Unhand her!" Thel-Shuum yelled at the beast.

A menacing chuckle echoed in his head. A chuckle he had heard before and thought he'd never hear again.

"There is nothing you can do to stop me, Anterkian," the voice that chuckled said.

"Impossible. It can't be you. I saw you die!"

"I nearly did because of that damn Maruian. But my mother saved me. The only downside is having to be this repulsive creature."

Thel-Shuum growled, getting Prometheus to his metal feet, sword still in hand, and shook his head. "I won't say it again. Let her go, now!"

"Thel, don't," another familiar voice entered his mind. Dal-Un's voice. "You know who he is. Plague. One of the deadliest and most brutal warriors of the Plagueonian army. You'd be risking Prometheus, humanity's only hope against the Vexnoxtuqe, if you continue to try to save me."

"I can't leave you!"

"You must! Just…I order you to stand down."

He did as he was told, lowering his sword. It took all his strength to do so. Plague straightened and huffed, satisfied that he was in control of the situation.

"Just promise me…no, I order you to protect humanity against these monsters. Save them, Thel. For me."

He watched in anger as Plague turned striding toward the massive Plagueonian mothership that had descended from the sky to collect the monster. Once he was aboard, it ascended out of the planet's atmosphere, the other Plagueonian crafts following suit.

11

He turned back to the battle between the Titans and the gods, the Vexnoxtuque he was ordered to take care of.

And he did.

At the cost of his life.

He sat in the chair of Prometheus' cockpit as his life faded away.

"Goodbye, Thel," Prometheus said.

He smiled with the last ounce of his strength. "I did it, Dal. I defeated them and saved the humans, just like you wanted."

And then he was gone.

While Prometheus was just an artificial intelligence, constructed to assist the pilot and keep the giant killing machine running, he felt…saddened by Thel-Shuum's passing.

For the millennia it would take for his next pilot to find him, he made some adjustments to his core programming. He tried to modify it so he didn't need a pilot anymore, and he could control the giant mech himself. He was only partially successful. He could move the robot by himself in short bursts. However, he still needed a pilot to function.

And, eventually, one did find him.

FENRIRI

MARUGRAH

1

Sierra Nevada Mountains Forest, outside of Bakersfield, California...

I've gained nothing but bad memories from these mountains. Four years ago, my girlfriend Jessica Riley, who I had just proposed to, was attacked and killed by a werewolf named Scarlet, a jealous ex-girlfriend of mine. Two years later, I came back to find the man who had helped me master my werewolf abilities --I was infected during the attack two years previous-- murdered. At first, I thought it was by the same werewolf that killed Jessica, but I came to find out a vampire was responsible.

But I have a good reason to be back.

Over the last year since the Titans had been released and attacked many cities around the world --and were soon defeated, minus Kronos who mysteriously disappeared-- my team was tasked with locating and securing the burial sites of the Titans' children. But with only one more burial site left to secure, with the one in Antarctica off limits to us and supposedly secured on Lance Cole's --the director of the agency I now work for, the Creature Counter Unit AKA, the CCU-- order, we were given a break, also on his order. I don't take breaks, though, so I'm taking the time to search for answers.

During the battle for Rome, we faced the newest leader of the vampire organization known as the Order, Azrael. Right before he was blown to smithereens, he said something about me not being a Lycan, a special type of werewolf that has the ability to transform at any time, like I had been led to believe I was. He said I was something different, a *Fenriri*.

I've had my team recount every detail of the battle that happened during what we are calling my 'freak out' when I transformed into a much scarier, stronger wolf. The ones who witnessed it recall terror etched on Azrael's face at the sight of me.

After hearing everything, Josh --my best friend and team member-- and I came up with a theory. Two years ago, during the whole situation with the Gate, the farmhouse we were hiding in was attacked by vampires of the Order. But, just as I was about to get my head lobbed off, I was saved. By Scarlet in her wolf form, four days after she possibly could have done so. We think that she was the same as me; a Fenriri. We think whatever attacked her and turned her into a wolf is the source, passing down its abilities from it to Scarlet to me.

That's why Sasha, Josh, and I --dressed in black Dress Uniforms to blend in with the night, my dark skin lending me even more camouflage with the night armed as if we were on mission-- are in the forest full of bad memories, hoping to catch the Fenriri and get some answers.

"What makes you so sure it's still here?" Josh's voice comes through my ear piece.

"This is its home." It's been here for years, even before it attacked Scarlet that night. I don't think it's going to leave after one bad incident. No one ever knew that Scarlet was attacked, so it wasn't threatened enough to leave. It's still here.

I search the darkness as I walk through the forest, ready for the Fenriri to jump out from its hiding spot and attack. But it never does. All that surrounds me is darkness and endless trees.

Where are you? I wonder.

"Find anything yet?" I ask.

"Not a damn thing," Josh reports.

Sasha is silent.

"Sasha, have you found anything?" I ask, stopping in my tracks, worry gripping me.

"Sasha, answer me, dammit!"

Static crackles in my ear. "Jeremy, I'm here," Sasha says, sounding out of breath, but finally responding. "You need to come see this."

"What is it?" I ask. "Where are you?"

"Come to Tark's cabin."

"Tark's cabin was destroyed, don't you remember? What the hell are you even doing there?"

"I chased something here. Just trust me. You need to see this."

I have never doubted Sasha before, so I'm not about to start now. I take off through the forest, making my way toward the place where good memories reside…or where they did. Now, or at least the last time I remember, it was a mangled mess of a cabin from the fight between the vampire Volak and Tark. But as I come upon the cabin, sliding to a stop next to Sasha, I see that I was wrong.

The cabin isn't a mangled mess. It's intact, having been seemingly rebuilt. And the lights are on.

Someone is home.

I rush toward the cabin's door, leaping onto the wooden porch, and reaching out for the doorknob. A hand clamps down on my wrist, keeping me from entering.

"Jeremy, wait!" Sasha hisses at me in a hushed, yet venomous tone.

"Someone rebuilt Tark's cabin. I want to know who and why," I hiss back.

"I know, but you can't just charge in blindly. We need to think this through."

"Whoever it is already knows we're here, so what's the point?"

An unknown man's voice calls from behind the door. "W-what do you w-want?!"

"See?" I say to Sasha. I turn toward the door and yell, "We want answers!"

"I have nothing valuable to tell you."

"Well, you can start by telling us why you rebuilt Tark's cabin and are living in it."

The man is silent for a moment before replying again. "You knew Tark?"

"Yes. He was a good friend of mine. My mentor."

I hear the door unlock from the other side and instinctively grasp the grip of one of the modified Desert Eagle hand cannons strapped to my hips, but don't draw the weapon. The door opens, revealing a disheveled man of about fifty years.

"You must be Jeremy," the man says, a warm smile on his face.

"How do you know my name?" I ask, my voice full of suspicion.

"Tark spoke of you often. Please, come in. I'll tell you more." The man motions for us to follow him inside.

It could be a trap. But, it might not be and I might get the answers I'm looking for. I think on it for a moment before making up my mind. I step into the cabin, Sasha not questioning my judgement and following me in, Josh, who had caught up to us when we weren't paying attention, follows her in.

The place is pretty much the same as I remember it. A living room-like area filled with bookshelves, a fire-place at the far side of room that illuminates the space, and chairs sitting in front of it. The man leads us over to the chairs, taking a seat in one that looks exactly like Tark's favorite seat, a comfortable recliner. I recognize the faded green fabric. It looks like it has tears that have been stitched back together.

Tears caused when the cabin was demolished, I think. *It* is *Tark's recliner! This guy must have saved it…*

"I know why you're here," the man says as he sits in the recliner.

"Do you?" I ask, sitting in a folded chair across from him. Josh and Sasha stay standing.

"Well, at least I think I do. There are only two reasons you'd be here. One is to honor Tark. The other is because you found the truth."

"The truth? The truth about what?"

"The truth about your abilities. That you're not a Lycan like you have been led to believe. We worked hard to prevent you from knowing the truth."

"Who is 'we'? You and Tark?"

"Yes. As soon as Tark found out about your ability, he contacted me immediately. You see, I had an incident four years earlier where I attacked a young woman. I didn't kill her, but I did…turn her."

"Scarlet…"

"Was that her name?" he paused for a moment, thinking. "Anyway, she escaped, but she was cursed with the same thing I have been cursed with. The thing that has been passed down through my family for generations."

"You were born a werewolf?"

"No, I am something much worse. I am the descendant of an ancient evil creature. A creature capable of destroying the entire world."

I narrow my eyes at the man, not understanding what the hell he is talking about. He must understand because he continues.

"I am what you are looking for in these woods," he says. "The vampires you have been pursuing the last few

21

years must have found out what you really are and told you, yes?"

"What are you talking about?" I ask, still not understanding.

"You are Fenriri, just like me."

"You are the Fenriri?" I ask.

I'm in awe. I thought the Fenriri was going to be a ferocious beast, not some old man. But it seems the Fenriri is a lot like a werewolf, able to shift from man to wolf. And that they are like a Lycan, able to change form at will.

"Yes, I am. And so are you," the man says.

"I know. Azrael has already told me that," I say.

"You faced Azrael?" The man looks incredulous, maybe even fearful. Azrael was a terrifying creature to behold, and had probably struck fear into all that had encountered him throughout the millennia, that even this man knows him by reputation.

"Yeah, I faced him. He's dead now," I say.

The man looks awed. "Tark said you were strong, but wow. Taking out Azrael is an incredible feat."

"It wasn't all my doing. Most of the damage was caused by me turning into what Sasha here calls my 'super wolf' form." I motion to Sasha who is standing beside me. "But the actual kill belongs to a friend of mine." The memory of Christina Angel's sacrifice flashes through my mind.

"Tell me about this... 'super wolf'." The man turns toward Sasha.

"Uh...well...it was big. Like, bigger than his normal wolf form. It had armor on its arms, legs, head, and back. Spikes jutted from its back and it had black fur," Sasha says, recalling what she had seen of my Fenriri form.

The man puts a hand to his chin, a thoughtful look on his face. "That's not what mine looks like. Maybe what you turned into was a sort of… 'proto Fenriri' form."

"Whatever it was, it was mean. Jeremy doesn't remember turning into it or what happened while he was in that form," Josh says.

"That's…interesting."

"No, it's not interesting. I almost killed Sasha," I growl.

The man holds his hands up in a defensive gesture. "I didn't mean it in that way at all. I just have never experienced that, nor have I heard about it."

I calm a little and the man relaxes, lowering his hands.

"I still don't know your name," I say with a sigh.

The man perks up, excited that I want to know his name. I figure no one ever asks, or is not allowed to know who he is.

It's probably because of what he is, I think.

"My name is Ben. Ben Fulton," the man says with a smile.

"Well, Ben…" I trail off as the squeak of someone stepping on a loose board reaches my sensitive ears.

My head snaps toward the door, and the wooden porch beyond, where I heard the sound come from.

My eyes narrow as I say, "We have company.

2

Sasha and Josh shoulder their weapons, Josh armed with a KRISS Vector submachine gun and Sasha armed with an AA-12 shotgun. They're close quarters weapons, as we figured the Fenriri would come in close to attack, pointing them toward the door.

"Expecting company?" I ask Ben.

He shakes his head no.

Great, I think. I have no idea who could be here and for what reason. Is it hunters that have finally tracked down Ben for what he did eight years ago? Or is it something worse I'm not even thinking of? The only way to know is to confront whoever is outside.

"What are we going to do, Jerm?" Sasha asks.

"What we do is get ready for a fight, but first we find out who is out there and why," I say, standing from the chair and drawing one of my Desert Eagle pistols.

Josh and Sasha nod, inching toward the door. Once we reach it, I yell, "Identify yourself! I know you're out there."

For a few moments, there was silence. Then, the air was filled with the sound of machine gun fire, bullets flying easily through the wood of the cabin's walls and door. We all drop to the ground, avoiding the hailstorm of lead, even Ben.

I bring my pistol up in a two-handed grip, squeezing off three .50 caliber rounds into where I believe the shooter is standing. As the third round leaves the barrel of my Desert Eagle, the gun fire stops.

I get to my feet, gun still raised as I inch toward the shredded door. I listen, hearing nothing but the buzz of insects in the forest.

Was there just one of them? I wonder.

I kick out, shattering the door, throwing splinters of wood all over the wooden porch, peppering a body that has blood rapidly pooling around it. The pale, skull-like face and pointy ears, not to mention the sharp teeth within its mouth, tells me exactly what I'm looking at.

A vampire.

Why is a vampire here? I think, confused. *Unless...
No, it can't be. We stopped them!*

"Jeremy, look out!" Josh yells, taking out a vampire that was charging from around the side of the hut with his KRISS Vector, triggering a rain of bullets flying at us from the darkness.

I drop to the wooden porch as Josh and Sasha jump back into the hut, bullets flying through the air. I catch a flash of muzzle fire and roll to the side as bullets rip into the spot where I was laying just moments ago. I get to my knees as I catch more muzzle flashes, aiming with my gun and fired where I last saw a flash. A thunderous boom fills the air as a .50 caliber round exits the barrel of my hand cannon and, upon hearing the sound of shredding flesh, finds its target.

I wait for more muzzle flashes and aim for them, taking down what I can only guess are vampires, just like the creature lying dead on the wooden porch. Soon, the gunfire stops. I don't know if I killed all the attackers or they realized what was giving them away and retreated to regroup. I'd hope for the latter, but I very much doubt it.

Hearing no more gunfire, Sasha and Josh step outside of the hut, weapons at the ready just in case, Ben behind them.

"What was all that?" Ben asks, his eyes wide. For being a creature that has struck fear into my most powerful enemy, Azrael, he is pretty fearful.

He must have been in hiding most of his life, I think. *He's not used to people shooting at him.*

"They were either here for us, or for you," I say to Ben.

"Nobody knows where I am," Ben says, scanning the surrounding forest.

"And nobody knows we're here," Josh says. "But they were snooping around the hut. I doubt they'd do that if they weren't here for you."

"You don't think they followed us here, do you, Jerm?" Sasha asks.

"It's possible," I say. "But how would they have known what we were after here?"

"They could be monitoring our comms," Josh says.

Shit! I didn't think about that.

I pluck the earbud from my ear and toss it on the ground, crushing it under my booted foot. Sasha and Josh do the same. Now, the Order that we thought we destroyed a year ago in Rome, is blind. They can't hear what our next move is.

"Alright, what now?" Ben asks.

"Now, we get out of here," I say. "The vehicle we brought is at the base of the mountain. We're probably going to have to fight our way to it."

Ben looks skeptical about the plan, but nods, knowing it's the only option we have.

We jump off the wooden porch and sprint into the forest toward the car that we arrived in. We don't get far before rustling leaves and crunching litter catches our attention. Something is following us.

As we run, I do my best to look back and try and catch a glimpse of what is following us, but can't as each time I do, I stumble.

Dammit!

We all continue to run, until a shout stops us in our tracks. We turn to find Ben tackled to the forest floor by a big, black furred dog with giant, almost sabre-tooth-like incisors. A hellhound. I bring my Desert Eagle up and pump a few rounds into the beast. It raises its head and roars at me, chunks of flesh missing from its hide.

Ben shoves up, throwing the hellhound into the air, and rolls to his feet.

"The fuck was that?" he asks.

"A hellhound. A vampire dog," I say.

"There is probably more than one, too. We need to keep going," Josh says, striking out down the mountain again.

We follow him, staying alert for more hellhounds and vampires. A few more feet from where we encountered the first hellhound, we are stopped by another jumping out in front of us. I can tell it's a different one as it doesn't have gaping wounds. Loud snarling turns us around to find the first, injured hellhound, blood oozing from the holes in its body, standing behind us, in a predatory stance. But it never leaps.

"Stay where you are! We have you surrounded!" A deep voice calls from the darkness.

"I only see two hellhounds and hear you. I'm far from intimidated. Especially after taking so many of you out so easily," I say to the deep voice.

Deep voice chuckles in the darkness, the chuckle soon becoming a mad cackle before he says, "Maybe I don't intimidate you, but *it* will."

It? What is he talking about?

Before I can ask the deep voice any questions, an ear-splitting roar fills the air, forcing me to cover my ears. I glance at the others, seeing them doing the same. The roar ends, the forest growing eerily quiet. I also notice that the hellhounds are gone.

Then the forest shakes as something takes a thunderous step. And another. And another. The trees bend and sway as something makes its way through them. Something big.

What in the hell is that?

We watch anxiously as the trees part, a massive head clearing them, revealing our enemy to us.

3

The creature that steps into our line of sight looks familiar somehow, but I've never seen anything like it before. It's hard to tell what color the creature's skin is with it being so dark, but by the way it almost blends in with our surroundings, I'd guess it's gray in color. Its skull-like face stares at us with black eyes, its mouth agape and revealing long, needle-sharp teeth. Slits that are probably nostrils flare rapidly. Its thick, muscly, simian arms end in four fingers, each with long, obsidian claws. It uses its knuckles to walk, like a gorilla, its back legs being short and stocky, ending in four toed feet, also with shiny, black talons. Its body is broad and armored, much like a Kaiju's, with armored plates running down its back. Now that I think about it, its whole body is armored like a Kaiju's.

Is this thing one of the Plagueonian's experiments? I wonder.

A realization hits me like a freight train.

It looks familiar because it is *Plagueonian. Looks like their experimenting didn't exclude their own.*

The Plagueonian ape turns its skulled head to the sky and lets loose another ear-piercing roar, forcing us to cringe and cover our ears again. Once it's done, it locks onto us, its targets…well, more like prey. The creature doesn't look like it's intelligent. It looks like more of an attack dog, following its master's orders.

"Scatter!" I yell as the beast charges, following my own order and jumping out of the beast's path.

"How the hell are we supposed to beat this thing?" Josh asks as he unloads into the monster with his KRISS Vector.

"I think I know of a way," Ben says.

I look over to him, knowing exactly what he is talking about. There is only one way to beat this thing and that is to become monsters ourselves. I've not transformed since Rome, because I have been afraid of turning back into the thing that almost killed my team mates.

But, it looks like I have no choice now.

Ben is the first to change. His face elongates, becoming canine, his teeth sharpening and becoming wolf-like. His eyes glow red. His limbs stretch and his body expands as his clothes peel apart and slide off him. Snow white fur grows over his entire body. Spikes explode from his back, three on each of his sides. Bone-like armor covers his head, arms, and legs.

I gasp. I've seen the creature he has become before. In a dream, a year ago. I had nightmares of the Titans at first, but it soon shifted away from them and toward wolf-like creatures like Ben before me.

I shake out of my stupor at seeing a monster straight out of my nightmares and trigger my own transformation. It's basically the same as what Ben went through, only without the spikes and my fur is black with red highlights and my eyes are yellow.

The Plagueonian ape turns around, finally being able to stop its charge where its girth kept carrying it forward. It roars and tilts its head to the side, confused at the change in form of two of its prey. It didn't stay confused long, though. It digs the knuckles of its oversized hands into the forest floor and pushes, initiating another charge.

Ben and I meet the monster's challenge, leaping into the air when we're within just feet of the creature. We land on the creature's armor plated back. The Plagueonian ape slides to a stop, digging its claws into the ground to help. It thrashes about like a bull in a rodeo as it tries to shake us off. I make my way toward the creature's face, scratching at it with my claws, aiming for its black eyes. The creature bucks and snaps at me as I do. A rip sounds behind me and the creature squeals in agony. I look back in time to see Ben throwing away an armor plate that he tore away from the monster's back.

The Plagueonian ape lurches forward as its foot is pushed out from under it. I catch a glimpse of Sasha rolling away as the beast falls to the ground, the forest around us shaking. Josh unloads with his KRISS Vector into the monster's face, one of its eyes exploding in a gush of gooey grossness. The Plagueonian ape wails in agony before its head is separated from its body as Ben peels another plate from the creature's back and slams it through its neck, the plate cutting through flesh and bone.

"Damn," Josh says, watching the monster's head roll away from its body, stopping against a thick tree. Blood gushes from the Plagueonian ape's neck.

Movement to the right catches our attention. Sasha brings her AA-12 shotgun up and fires a few blasts, seeing something that we don't. A shout from the darkness reports that she hit her target. She rushes toward who she hit and we follow.

We come upon a vampire, trying to crawl away, one of his legs missing. I stop him by placing a clawed foot on his back, an *oof* erupting from his mouth. I flip him over with the same foot.

"You...weren't supposed to be here," the vampire wheezes.

"Expecting to catch an old man off guard?" Ben asks.

The vampire smiles wickedly. "You and I both know you are much more than an old man, Fenriri. You are the cause of our problems." The vampire thrusts his arms at me. "He has been a thorn in our side for the past three

30

years, reducing a once great and feared organization to remnants."

"I'm going to make myself very clear," I say. "No one gives a shit about your 'once great organization'. I just want to know one thing and one thing only."

"And what if I refuse?"

My hand twitches, drawing his attention, my sharp claws rubbing together. "If you refuse, I will make you tell me, as painfully as I can."

The creature's eyes fill with fear.

"Now that I have your attention, what are you bastards planning? Where are you striking next?" I demand.

The vampire scoffs, but squeals with fright as my hand snaps out, the claw on my index finger just inches from his eye.

"Appalachia!" he squeaks.

"Shit. That's the one site we haven't secured yet," Josh says.

He's right. The Appalachian Mountains is the home to the last remaining burial of the Titans' children we have yet to secure.

"There, I told you. Are you going to let me go now?" the vampire asks.

"I don't remember telling you I was going to let you go," I say.

As soon as I finished speaking, Josh pulls the trigger on his KRISS Vector, putting a round into the vampire's head, splattering his brains on the forest floor.

I turn back to the three people around me, Ben back in his human form…and naked. I shift back into my human form, a shout of pain drawn from my mouth. As I said, I haven't changed since Rome a year ago. Transforming is like a muscle. The more you use it, the more it can handle. In my case, the less it will hurt.

Back in my human form, and not naked like Ben thanks to the stretchy pants I wear, I point to Ben. "You, go back to your cabin and get some clothes on."

He nods and heads back the way we came. I have some extra BDUs in the SUV we drove here, so I'm good on clothes. I'll put them on once we get back to the vehicle.

"What's the plan?" Sasha asks.

"First, I'm gonna get dressed. Then, we're heading to the last site," I say.

I turn away from them and take out my phone. I'm going to need my team for what's about to go down in the Appalachian Mountains.

4

Washington, D.C.

Will stood on the roof of the White House, cold air stinging his face as he looked out into the recovering city. It was night, so all he could see was what was illuminated in the dark. One stood out like a beacon, drawing his attention more than anything in the city: the Capitol Building. It was destroyed two years ago during the Plagueonian invasion by a Kaiju known as Wraith. Since then, it had been rebuilt. And just that day, it was finished, two years later.

Which was why he was at the White House. It was a celebration. Not just for the completion of the new Capitol Building, but also for his and his team's success in saving the planet from a cataclysmic event twice now. The rest of his team, including his girlfriend, Ashley Singer, and his best friend, Aaron Smith, were down in a dining room two rooms away from the Oval Office, eating dinner with the President. Will had already ate and wandered away while everyone else was busy sharing their stories.

Well, the whole team except for Jeremy, Sasha, Josh, and. Jeremy was the team's new captain, their former captain, Christina Angel, dying a year ago in the fight for Rome.

Three of the original Gamma team members died in the fight, during what Lance Cole referred to as the "Second Titanomanchy", where four Kaiju known as the Titans were freed from their prisons and ravaged the world. The creatures were stopped by the combined might of Marugrah and Prometheus, a massive mech which Will piloted himself. The deaths of Alicio Brice, Jake Walker, and Christina Angel hit the surviving members of the team hard. They were all like family. And while Will, Ashley, and Aaron may have been new members to the team, they still considered the soldiers' family as well.

It was the only real family Will had had. He was an only child and his dad left when he was little. His mom worked two jobs just to pay the bills. The deaths hit him hard, especially Angel's. She was like a mother to him. More of a mother than his ever was…

Even a year later, the wounds of their loss are still fresh.

When Jeremy first informed the team that he was going somewhere and would not be attending the dinner, Will's first thought was that he had found a lead on the man he was obsessed with finding, a man named Holdsworth. The team was told about what happened to Jeremy two years ago, just before the Plagueonian invasion, and during it, when he was captured and almost had his head mounted on a wall, all ordered by Holdworth. As far as Will knew, he hadn't had a lead on the man since then.

"Where are you going?" Will had asked.

"I have some questions that need answers," was his only reply.

Will knew that his answer had nothing to do with Holdsworth and more to do with something more personal. He didn't ask Jeremy anymore questions after that.

"Beautiful, isn't it?" A voice came.

The voice made Will jump. He turned, finding President John Scott walking toward him, a Secret Service Agent who he knew as Derek Collard following close behind. The rest of the agents were by the roof entrance door, probably where they were ordered to stay by Scott.

"The city has recovered so much since two years ago," Will said, turning back to the view.

"I suppose so. Just the main things are being attended to at the moment. Like the Capitol Building, which as you can see, is finished, and the Washington Monument, which still needs a ton of work," Scott said, looking out towards the once 555-foot-tall obelisk. It now stood half as tall as it was knocked over during a brutal Kaiju brawl between Marugrah, Drakonah --whom Will was controlling at the time-- Wraith, and Vishlari. Vishlari was crushed beneath the obelisk. "Those and the houses that were affected. I want to get people back into their homes. We have most of them done, but we still have more to attend to."

Will smiled. The President had changed a lot since the battle for Washington, D.C. He wasn't a coward, afraid of dying and always wanting to flee. Now, he would stay and fight if he got the chance. That battle changed him. Maybe it was seeing everyone else fighting for their lives. Maybe it was seeing people suffering. Will had no idea what it was for sure, but he really didn't care. He liked the man Scott had become.

"And what about the other cities that have been decimated by Kaiju?' Will asked.

"Same thing. Airports and homes are a priority. The rest will come next. I heard that the airport in Tokyo that was ravaged by that giant spider-squid creature has almost finished reconstruction. LAX is about halfway reconstructed, but its moving much faster than you'd think," Scott said, still gazing out into the city.

It was all good news to Will, but he had a feeling something bad was going to happen. And whatever it was, it was going to happen soon.

"I wish your new captain and his two friends came. I would've loved to meet him. I've heard a lot about him," Scott said. "You know he was the reason the CCU was created right?"

Will tore his gaze away from the lit-up Capitol Building and looked at the President with a confused expression.

"Well, it was more of what he fought. The chimeras in Fresno, he was the one who fought them. If he wasn't there to encounter those creatures, the CCU would've never been created and we might not be standing here today. Earth might've been a ruined wasteland or a new home for the Plagueonians with humankind an extinct species," Scott explained.

Will nodded, understanding what Scott was getting at. Everything had been connected from the start. And Will feared it was leading up to some big conclusion.

A ring startled them both. Will reached into his pocket and pulled out his cellphone. He was surprise to see who was calling. He swiped the bar, answering the call, and put the phone to his ear.

"Jeremy? You find something?" he asked, no greeting, just knowing something was wrong, and wanted to get down to business.

"You're damn right I did," Jeremy answered. "We got problems. I need you and the team ready for deployment ASAP."

"They're not going to like it. We're on break, remember?"

"Either they start to like it or the world ends. We encountered what's left of the Order. They're planning on releasing the Titans' children."

Damn! I knew something bad was about to happen, Will thought.

"What's our destination, boss?" Will asked.

"The Appalachian Mountains. Site Artemis. I'll meet you there," Jeremy said.

"Roger that."

The line went dead and he turned to the President.

"Looks like we'll have to cut this party short, sir," Will said with an apologetic smile.

"More Kaiju?" Scott asked, fear creeping into his voice.

"Not yet."

"But there will be?"

"Only if we don't stop them from being released…like last time."

Scott put a hand on Will's shoulder. "Then what the hell are you waiting for? Get your team, and go save the world again."

Will looked up into the President's smiling face and gave him a smile of his own and a nod.

They made their way down from the roof and toward the dining room Gamma team was all sitting in. The room was alive when they walked in, people laughing and eating. But, all eyes turned in their direction, knowing something was wrong.

"What is it, Will?" Damen Hlad asked, standing from his seat.

"Listen, I know we're all supposed to be on break right now, but something has come up," he said.

He didn't say anything for a few moments, waiting for someone to complain. No one did. Not even Aaron. So, he continued.

"Jeremy just called me. The Order is still kicking somehow and they mean one final push. They want to release the Titans' children. If that happens... well... it's just like with the Titans. They'll eradicate every human on Earth. Jeremy is heading to the Appalachian Mountains, the last burial site we have yet to secure. He says that's where the Order plans to strike first. Party time is over, my friends. Now it's time for war."

His team mates nodded, understanding the magnitude of the situation and what was at stake. They quickly piled back into the vehicles they arrived at the White House in and headed back to the CCU headquarters and geared up.

They were on a plane an hour and a half after Jeremy's phone call, heading to the Appalachian Mountains to stop a god from awakening from a long slumber and exacting its fury upon the world.

5

New Hampshire...

One of the perks of being a CCU agent is that you can get anywhere you want to go just by flashing your badge. Since the Plagueonian invasion two years ago, the CCU has become quite a big deal, even more so with the emergence of the Titans last year. We're allowed to go where we want, whenever we want. All with good reason, of course.

So, getting a ride from Bakersfield, California, to Coos Country, New Hampshire, wasn't too hard. We hike from Coos Country to the Carter Dome…which is right where the coordinates of the last remaining burial site we have yet to secure have led us to.

It is also the Order's target.

But there's not a soul in sight. Well, besides my team waiting on me. Other than them, all that surrounds us is snow-covered terrain with the occasional strand of green grass breaking through the white.

I meet up with my team at the base of Carter Dome, snow crunching under my boots. Sasha, Josh, and I now wear CCU standard issue body armor over our black BDUs. We didn't have any extra armor, as we didn't plan on picking up a stray, so Ben just wears the clothes he dressed himself in after the fight in the Sierra Nevada Mountains: a beanie cap, a heavy coat, some jeans, and a pair of hiking boots.

"Are you sure they plan on attacking here?" Damen Hlad asks as Sasha, Josh, Ben, and I step up to them.

"Heard it straight from one of the bastard's mouths," Josh says.

"He could have been lying," Jessica Evangeline, who prefers to go by Eva, says.

"Not with the way I…persuaded…him to talk," I say.

The whole group, minus Sasha, Josh, and Ben, look concerned at my statement. Mikayla Jones opens her mouth, probably about to ask about how I persuaded a vampire to talk, but Ben steps out from behind Sasha, Josh, and I, where I told him he should stay until I sorted things out with my team, gaining her and the rest of the team's attention. They grip their weapons tighter.

"Stand down!" I bark before they raise their weapons and blow Ben away.

"Who is he?" Will asks, suspicious of the strange man I've brought with me.

"The answer to my questions," I say.

They relax their stances, loosening their grips on their weapons. I now have their attention. But before I can speak, Ben does.

"Yes, the answer. I am what he is. Well, the source of his…ability, I suppose," Ben says.

"You're a Lycan?" Damen asks.

"No, I am Fenriri."

Will's head snaps toward me. "Azrael called you that in Rome."

I nod. "Josh and I figured we might find the source in the woods Scarlet was attacked in. She was bitten first, after all. Then me. The Fenriri abilities were just passed down."

"And diluted," Ben says, sniffing the air twice.

"What are you talking about?" I ask.

"Your weapons, they carry silver tipped projectiles, yes? You can be hurt by silver?"

I nod, not quite understanding what he is getting at.

"Shoot me," he says, looking first at me and the two people next to me, then to the other six we just met up with. "Any of you wanna?"

"Gladly," Mikayla says, bringing her side arm up, a Sig Sauer P226, and firing off a shot.

My mind barely registers what just happened until I see blood flying through the air…from Ben's leg.

"What the fuck!" I yell. "Why would you ask someone to do that?!"

"Take a close look at the wound," he says, showing no pain at having just been shot…by a silver bullet.

My eyes go wide and dart toward his wound. No steam. Usually, a monster's flesh, most having a weakness to silver, burn and steam when it touches their skin. That didn't seem to be the case with Ben…with the *Fenriri*.

"You're immune to silver?" I ask, incredulous.

He just nods, a smug smile on his face. "It seems that once the Fenriri curse is passed on from a pure blood, it mixes with the vampire DNA locked within you, giving you a weakness to silver."

"Wait, back up… We have vampire DNA inside us?" Eva asks, disgusted.

Ben nods. "Yeah. Gross, huh? They used their own DNA to create humanity, which also lead to the creation of monsters."

"And how were the Fenriri made?" Ashley asks.

"First, you must know what we Fenriri are," Ben says, turning toward the young brown haired woman. "Do you know who Fenrir is?"

She shakes her head 'no'.

"Does anyone know?" he asks, looking to the rest of the people.

"A giant Nordic wolf that is supposed to bring about Ragnarok, the end of the world," Josh says, standing beside me. "I know what you're getting at. I spotted his name right away. You're a descendant of Fenrir."

"You're smart," Ben says. "I like you. And yes, I am a descendant of Fenrir. If you want, I can tell you how we came to be. It is rather gross, though."

"Maybe later," Will says, his voice sounding urgent. "Listen, we made it here before the Order, unlike last time. We have the upper hand. We need to secure the area and fast."

"Will's right. The Order could be here any minute. Break off into teams and scout around. Make sure there are none of the assholes watching us," I order.

They all nod, breaking off into teams of two to cover more ground. Will with Ashley. Aaron with Eva. Mikayla with Damen. Sasha and I start off, leaving Ben with Josh. The ten of us spread out around the big lump of land that rises 4,832 feet into the air at Carter Dome's highest point, snow crunching under our feet, weapons up and sweeping.

We check the surrounding forest, looking for ambushers, but find none. Unless they are deeper into the forest, but I'm not taking the chance of getting lost and not being able to get back to Carter Dome in time to stop the release of an unstoppable super weapon. Well, it *is* stoppable. *I* just can't stop it. There are only two things on earth that can stop a Kaiju. Either another Kaiju, like Marugrah, or Prometheus, a giant robot designed for the purpose of fighting, and killing Kaiju that Will found in the Gate of Tartarus a year ago.

"Reports," I say into my throat mic.

All come back the same: "Clear."

"Regroup at the base of the Dome," I say.

Moments later, we're back where we started.

"Maybe the asshole blood sucker was just fucking with you," Aaron says with a shrug.

I shake my head. Something isn't right. I know that vampire wasn't lying. His terrified eyes had told me that much. They held no deception.

"Do you guys hear that?" Sasha asks.

"Hear what?" Mikayla asks.

I close my eyes, focusing on what I can hear. I hear the wind blowing, rustling trees and snow falling from them… and also a low hum that seems to be growing louder.

What the hell is that? I wonder, making no sense of the noise.

"No, it can't be," Will says, his head snapping toward the sky.

I do the same, scanning the sky, but find nothing.

What does he know that I don't?

The hum grows intense, as if whatever is making it is right over us.

I look up, seeing nothing.

"Why are they here?" Will asks.

"Why is…who…here…" I say, trailing off as a massive object materializes out of nowhere above us.

6

"That's a Plagueonian ship!" Aaron yelps.

I stare up at the massive object above us in awe, remembering images I saw of the alien ships that were seen around the world, accompanying the Kaiju they used as tools to eradicate the populace. But, this one looks different. It looks…reinforced. While it still retains the whale shape, it looks spikey, almost Kaiju-like in appearance with overlapping plates covering its hull and spikes jutting from its sides. Other than that, it is still recognizable as the same Plageuonian ships as two years ago.

"Don't we have a truce with them?" I yell over the loud hum of the ship.

"We may have a truce, but nobody said anything about them visiting," Will says.

Ropes descend from the sides of the ship. I relax, expecting a friendly encounter, but it isn't eight-foot-tall alien beings that descend from the ship above us. It's vampires of the Order.

"What the hell!" I growl, jumping back, drawing one of my Desert Eagles and attacking our descending enemies.

The rest of my team does the same, raising their various weapons and opening fire. Vampires drop from the ropes they were sliding down from to the snow-covered ground, dead. Yellow bolts of crackling energy rain down at us from the underside of the ship, sending us scattering and searching for cover which there is very little of, besides the surrounding forest.

We run for the forest, our bodies shielded by the thick trunks of the trees. The energy bolts weren't meant for us, I realize. They were just meant to scatter us and give the Order troops time to rappel down from the ship.

"Why do the vampires have an alien ship?" Mikayla asks over the comms. We all ran for different parts of the forest.

"A gift, maybe?" Will suggests, standing behind the tree beside mine. "The Order and the Plagueonians were allies at one point."

"Yeah, but that was thousands of years ago," Ashley says, a few trees away. "That ship would have to be millennia old. That's not the problem, though. If they had it before, why are we only seeing it now?"

"Are you suggesting that there actually are Plagueonians on that ship?" I ask.

"It's a theory. There is no way to prove it unless they show their ugly mugs."

She's right. But if there are Plagueonians on Earth, why are they helping the Order? Two years ago, they turned against their queen and helped humanity beat the Kaiju they sent to destroy us. Did they have a change of heart? As always, all I have are more questions and no answers.

I peek around the tree I'm hiding behind to see the Order vampires advancing. The sun is covered by the clouds, but they still wear black protective armor from head to toe. It looks different than a year ago. Instead of the beekeeper looking garb, the armor they wear is form fitting, with oval helmets, looking almost alien-like with glowing green accents and a mechanical look. But what bothers me more than the advanced alien armor is what they hold in their hands. The silver, symbol-engraved objects are undoubtedly Plagueonian energy weapons. One of the vampires sees me peeking out at them, shoulders the alien weapon, and fires, a bolt of crackling yellow energy erupting from the tube-like structure that is the weapon's muzzle.

I duck back behind the tree, the bolt striking the trunk and taking out a chunk of the tree's bark.

Bollocks! That was close!

I draw both of my Desert Eagles. Normally, trying to fire both high powered pistols would break someone's wrists, but with the wrist braces I wear, designed for a Delta operator that favors the big handguns, I can fire both of the hand cannons without fear of that happening. Thanks to the CCU's military connections, I was able to snag a pair. I am not the only one that has been able to snag one. A CIA agent also has a pair. I think his name was Kane.

If they go up against the threats I do, the Desert Eagle certainly has the stopping power necessary... Unless it's against a Kaiju.

I take a deep breath and lean out from behind the tree, firing off .50 caliber rounds into the advancing horde of vampires armed with alien tech, armor and weapons. But, no matter how advanced the armor is, it seems it was designed more for protection from the sun and not bullets as the rounds punch through the armor and the vampire's bodies, blood spraying in the air. But then I notice a few of the bullets melting upon impact, light flickering around them.

Energy shields! Shit!

Click. Click. Click.

My guns run dry. I take cover back behind the tree and quickly reload. My team members fire on the encroaching horde. I look to my side seeing Will firing his M4 carbine. Further down from him, Ashley fires her KRISS Vector submachine gun. A vampire slips around the tree I'm hiding behind, thrusting an energy knife at me.

I jump back, pressing a button next to the magazine ejection button on my Desert Eagles. I feel gears whirl inside of my weapon. With the help of the CCU's techie, which is surprisingly Ezekiel, the ghoul that helped Sasha, Josh, and I thwart the Order's attempt at opening the Gate of Tartarus two years ago, I was able to modify the weapons and allow them to do what they are about to do. The handles swing out, bringing the guns into upright positions, the barrels pointed into the air. A section of the guns in front of the triggers slide forward and up, locking themselves just below the barrels. Next, a silver blade extends from the sections that just locked themselves below the barrels, turning the guns into swords.

My inspiration you may ask? Well, the show RWBY of course. "It's also a gun" is my favorite line, and my inspiration. Of course, unlike Ruby Rose's Crescent Rose, which starts out as a scythe and turns into a gun, mine starts out as a gun and turns into a sword. I've always had a special place in my heart for anime.

I deflect the blade of crackling energy with my silver blade and fling it away from my attacker with one sword and use the other to decapitate the monster. The helmeted head flies through the air where it rolls to a stop at Will's feet. He just looks at the head with disgust as he finishes reloading his weapon and then kicks it away and continues to fire into the horde.

Laser bolts strike the tree I'm behind, throwing chunks of bark in my face.

"There's too many of them! We're pinned down!" Eva growls through the comms.

A roar cuts through the air. The vampire horde stops, turning toward the source. Ben, in his Fenriri form, rushes from the forest, pouncing on the nearest vampire, tearing into it. Blood sprays and guts fly.

The other vampires back away in fright, firing their alien weapons at the new monster, most of their shots missing. More bolts rain from the ship hovering above us, all aimed at Ben. While Ben has the Order vampires distracted, I run from cover, stabbing the nearest vampire in the chest with both of my guns-turned-swords. And because they are also guns, I can do this.

I wink at the vampire, who I can't see behind the smooth, black helmet, a holographic green visor where its eyes should be, and say to what I assume is a stunned and pained face, "It's also a gun." I pull the triggers, two .50 caliber bullets punching holes in its chest. The vampire falls to the ground, leaving behind its blood on the silver blades of my gun-swords.

I turn to my next target just as they are raising their weapon. I lash out my sword, cutting its hands off, they fall onto the snow-covered ground still clutching the alien weapon. The vampire looks at its bloody stumps, probably a look of horror at its missing hands beneath the helmet it wears. It looks up at me just as I put a bullet in its face. It falls to the ground, red staining white.

A chop reaches my ears. I search the sky, only seeing the massive ship hovering above us. Twin explosions appear on the other side of the ship. The alien craft pitches to the side, allowing me to see the lone Black Hawk attack helicopter, the hardpoints located on the aircraft's stub wings smoking. More Hellfire missiles fire from the hardpoints, exploding on the Plagueonian ship's hull. Its shields flicker as it rockets away, leaving behind the vampires it deployed.

Without the big ship blocking its way, it turns its sights on the vampires around Carter Dome. It opens fire with its GAU-19 gatling gun located on the aircraft's nose, mowing down the vampires with 12.7mm rounds. In a matter of seconds, all the vampire lay dead in the snow.

The Black Hawk finds a clearing and descends, its rotors kicking up a tornado of snow. I walk toward it, seeing the CCU logo printed on its side.

"We're either in trouble or…" Will says, but never gets to finish.

He's bashed in the back of his head by a vampire that had been hidden in the forest when the Black Hawk was raining down lead on its friends. I act fast, bringing my gun-sword around. The vampire jumps back, the tip of my silver blade scraping the vampire's chest armor. I bring my other gun-sword around, maneuvering the sword around so the grip hits it in the head, knocking it to the ground and hopefully unconscious. And since it doesn't get back up, I know I did what I intended.

Ashley helps Will, who is rubbing the back of his head, up as the team gathers around the unconscious black and green armored vampire.

"What should we do with him, boss?" Damen asks.

"Cuff him. We finally have ourselves a live prisoner," I say with a slight smile.

We make our way to the Black Hawk, Damen carrying our vampire prisoner. I'm surprised when Ezekiel steps out of the chopper and greets us with a wave. The soldiers behind him raise their weapons as Ben approaches, still in his Fenriri form, but I hold my hand up and snap, "Hold your fire!" Ezekiel looks at me questioningly, but repeats my order.

"Ezekiel," I say upon reaching the ghoul, "what are you doing here?"

"Cole noticed your team leaving and had me track you down using GPS locators in your armor, and told me to come get you," he tells me.

"It was lucky you did."

He nods. "Cole isn't too happy about you guys taking off, though." He points to my ear, silently telling me I should get ahold of the man.

I sigh, switching from short range comms to long range comms and say, "Cole."

"Damn it, Jeremy! What the hell were you thinking running off like that!?" Cole screams into my ear, making me cringe.

"Listen, Lance. If we hadn't have done this, we'd be facing a Kaiju right now," I growl, my patience wearing thin. I haven't liked the man since I met him a year ago and him yelling at me and ordering me around, even if he is my boss, pisses me off.

He's silent for a moment before saying, "Go on."

I recount everything that has happened from the Sierra Nevada Mountains to Ezekiel showing up in an attack helicopter, saving our asses. I even include the possibility of Plagueonians being accomplices to the Order vampires and the fact that I managed to capture one if the vampires alive.

Cole is silent as I finish, probably taking in everything I just explained to him.

"Get back to HQ," he finally says. "We'll talk about what we are going to do next then."

"Roger that, Walker out," I say, turning off my comms.

"Who's the white wolf?" Ezekiel asks as I turn back to him.

"He's a friend," I say bluntly. "His name is Ben Fulton. He's a Fenriri."

Ezekiel's eyes widen the tiniest bit, trying to hide his shock, but I notice.

"I'm a Fenriri, too," I say.

"So you found out," he says.

"I've known for a year. Azrael shouted it at me."

He stares at me for a moment before doing an about face and turning back to the chopper. We follow him, all of us piling into the chopper, our prisoner included, and Ben, now in his human form. The Black Hawk ascends into the sky, two more descending toward Carter Dome, where they will set up a perimeter, establish a camp, and keep watch over the site as we head back to the CCU headquarters in Washington, D.C.

7

Washington, D.C. ...

The Black Hawk's wheels hit hard on the landing pad on the roof of the Creature Counter Unit's headquarters jolting the aircrafts and us inside. It's a tall building constructed like a hotel in Buzzard Point. The side door is pulled open, revealing a gray robotic figure. We obviously don't have any robots here at the CCU. The figure before us is a soldier in an Iron Man inspired suit of armor known as TALOS (Tactical Assault Light Operator Suit). The suits were used by my team in

Rome and since seeing their effectiveness, the suits had been mass produced, the CCU receiving several dozen of them.

A skinny man in an expensive looking business suit, my boss Lance Cole, steps out from behind the hulking gray soldier, his face surprisingly welcoming. I was expecting an expression of rage and pissed-offness.

Ezekiel pushes our prisoner toward the TALOS encased soldier, who grabs the vampire's armored, hand cuffed arms and whisks it away. I step out next, Ezekiel right behind me.

"Great job. Both of you," Cole says, an uncommon smile on his face. It almost unnerves me.

I just give him a nod. Ezekiel, however, gives the man a salute, obviously having more respect for him.

"I'm sure we can get some useful information out of him. However, there is one more matter to take care of," Cole says.

A soldier, dressed in regular black body armor, walks up beside Cole. I'm momentarily confused. *We don't have another prisoner…* I notice Cole looking past me…toward Ben.

"Hold on a minute," I growl, but don't get to finish what I was about to say.

"It's just a precautionary measure, Mr. Walker," Cole says. "He is not a prisoner and won't be treated as such, unlike the prisoner you did bring."

I say nothing. The anger etched on my face says it all for me.

"Look, Jeremy, I know what he means to you," Cole starts, but I cut him off.

"How could you know?" I growl.

"Ezekiel left his comms on. I heard all that was said about Ben Fulton."

I flash an anger filled look at Ezekiel. He fumbles with the earpiece he wears, a confused look on his face as he glances over at me. He gives me an apologetic smile as he finds his comms still active and transmitting.

"I get it. He's a friend of the man who helped you control your abilities," Cole says. "And he is also the cause of what you are now. But it is just procedure. We can't have every stranger that enters this facility just wandering around. After some questioning, he is free to do as he pleases."

I open my mouth to counter, but a hand on my shoulder stops me. I look into the face of Ben, a man I hardly know. I don't know why I feel so protective of him.

Fenriri kinship, maybe? I think.

"It's okay, Jeremy. I'll do as he wants. I want to help. And if this is what it takes, I'll do it," Ben says to me, a smile on his tired face.

I frown deeply, but nod.

"Just follow Matthews," Cole says, watching Ben trail after the soldier. Once they enter the building through the roof access, he turns back to me. "You did good. You stopped a Kaiju from being released and brought back a prisoner."

"Yeah, but I have a feeling this is only the beginning," Will says, standing beside me suddenly.

"Is it because of the Plagueonian ship you saw?" Cole asks. "Are you sure that there were Plagueonians aboard? Or did the vampires just have it to haul around troops?"

"It's hard to tell," I say. "We didn't see any aliens. But like Ashley said, if the ship was a gift from the Plaguconians' first visit to Earth, we would have seen it before now."

51

"So, what? A rogue group of Plagueonians that are ignoring the truce and are continuing in the path of their Queen?"

"Whatever it is, we need to prepare ourselves. Double security around the burial sites. Keep an eye out for any weird looking aircraft sightings."

"I'll get people on it."

Cole turns, about to head back inside the building, but stops, turning back to me and my team. "Mr. Hlad. You may want to start getting yourself settled in soon," he says.

Damen nods, "Yeah, I know. Full moon tonight."

Cole nods, continuing inside the CCU headquarters.

"So, you going to help me still?" Damen asks, looking at me.

"Of course," I say. "I've helped you the last twelve months. You're getting better." I flash him a smile.

He nods, making his way to the roof access, Eva, Aaron, Ashley, Will, Mikayla, and Josh following him.

"Sorry about that, Jeremy," Ezekiel says when they disappear inside the doorway. "I really didn't know it was still on."

I sigh and turn toward the man...ghoul. I sometimes forget what he is. He's just so...human. He flinches as I turn toward him, getting a chuckle out of me.

"Calm down, it's okay. I understand, man. You may be smart, but I get that things slip through that big brain of yours," I say.

He relaxes. "We good then?"

"Of course." I hold a fist out to him.

He fist bumps me with a grin that is close to the one stitched to the piece of cloth around his neck that he uses as a mask. At first, I thought it was to not allow anyone to see his face when he kills or was on secret missions, but I have caught him wearing it when he was working

52

on reports or tech. I asked him about it once and he told me "I work better when people can't see my face." Whatever that means.

"So, what are you going to do now?" Ezekiel asks.

"Now, we're going to rest," Sasha says, giving me a stern look.

I relent. "Yeah. That."

Ezekiel gives me a wink and a smile. "I'd give anything to have a lady like her. She knows what's best for you, even if you don't think it's the best idea."

He walks off, disappearing into the roof access doorway.

"He's right. I know what's best. You've slept maybe eight hours in the past week. You can't keep doing that to yourself. And if something is about to happen soon, you need your strength," Sasha says, gripping my arm.

"Yeah, yeah, I know. I'll rest, I promise," I say.

I'm agreeing with her, for once. Well, I agree with her more often than not. But she is right. If something is coming, something big like Will thinks, then I need to rest and get my strength up as much as possible.

8

Lance Cole stepped into the dimly lit room that only held a hanging lamp, a table, and two chairs, one of them occupied by a heavily chained figure. Cole shut the door behind him and moved deeper into the room, not fearing the creature chained head to toe, all attached to the reinforced floor. He took a seat in the chair, rested his elbows on the table, and clasped his hands together.

The vampire, now stripped of its advanced alien armor, slowly looked up at Cole with menacing red eyes, its sharp teeth bared, its pointed bat-like ears twitching in agitation.

"I'm not telling you shit," the creature spat.

Cole chuckled. "Oh, you will."

The vampire snorted. "No. You'll get nothing from me. I can hold out until I am rescued."

"Why are you so sure you will be rescued?"

"Because, I'm important."

"Yet, your friends in the ship abandoned you. Left you to die."

"That was because they were under attack. The ship is much too valuable to lose." The vampire's eyes widened a touch and then he clamped his mouth shut, knowing he had said too much already.

"Your friends in the ship," Cole said. "They're Plagueonian, aren't they?"

The vampire just glowered at him, saying nothing. Cole sighed in frustration as he thought of a new question to ask.

"What's your name?" he asked.

The vampire squinted at him, but finally said, "Valok."

Impossible, Cole thought in confusion.

"I see the confusion in your eyes. No, you're thinking of my brother, Volak, who was killed at the Gate of Tartarus three years ago," the vampire, Valok, explained.

Ah. That makes more sense.

"Well, Valok, I am Lance Cole, Director of the Creature Counter Unit," Cole said, introducing himself. He was trying to be friendly in an attempt to get information out of Valok.

"I know exactly who you are. You're at the top of our hit list," Valok sneered. "No matter what you do, whether it be trying to be buddy buddy with me or torture me, I will never tell you what you want to hear."

Cole squinted at Valok as he slowly took a pair of sunglasses from his pocket and put them on.

"What are you doing?" Valok asked, confused.

Next, Cole took out a small remote from the same pocket and showed it to the creature.

"What does that do?" Valok asked, fear creeping into his voice.

"Imbedded in the walls of this room are hundreds of ultra violet lights. All I have to do is click this big red button to activate them. It won't kill you, but it'll hurt like hell," Cole explained, a smirk on his lips.

Fear crossed Valok's face, but it soon reverted back to defiance.

Cole sighed.

"Just remember, I gave you a chance to talk," he said and pressed the button.

The room exploded in a flash of violet. At the end of the flash, Valok was screaming, yanking at the chains attached to his arms, legs, torso, and neck, his flesh sizzling and burning. Cole winced at the smell of it.

"Ready to talk now?" Cole asked.

"Ne-never…y-you pathe-thetic m-m-monkey," Valok said between spasms of pain.

Cole frowned and pressed the button again, the room erupting in another flash of violet. Valok's scream became high pitched, his flesh blistering and peeling from his body, some of it falling away to ash.

"F-fine! I-I'll t-talk!" he yelled, pain oozing from his voice.

"What is the Order planning to do next," Cole demanded.

Valok scoffed, his lips still quivering with pain. "We aren't the Order anymore. There are too few of us left to even be considered the same organization and all our leaders are dead. Typhon. Azrael. My brother would have been a leader if he wasn't killed. Azrael was third in line. Now it's me. We are but remnants of the Order. We are the Remnants. They will come for me."

Cole looked at Valok, realizing what the vampire was telling him. Not only did they have a live prisoner of the enemy, he was the leader of the Order…the Remnants. And his followers were coming for him.

BREACH

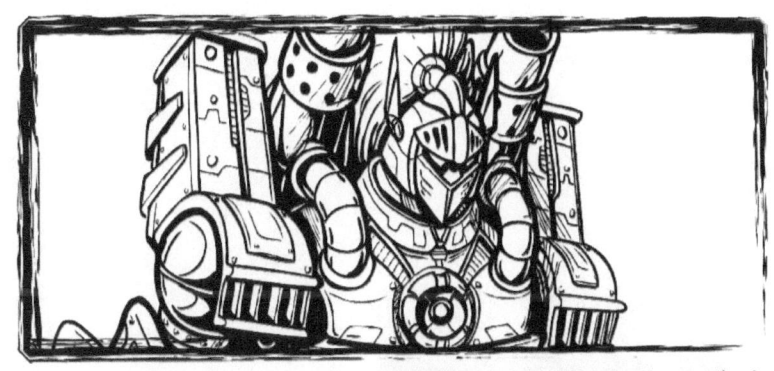

PROMETHEUS

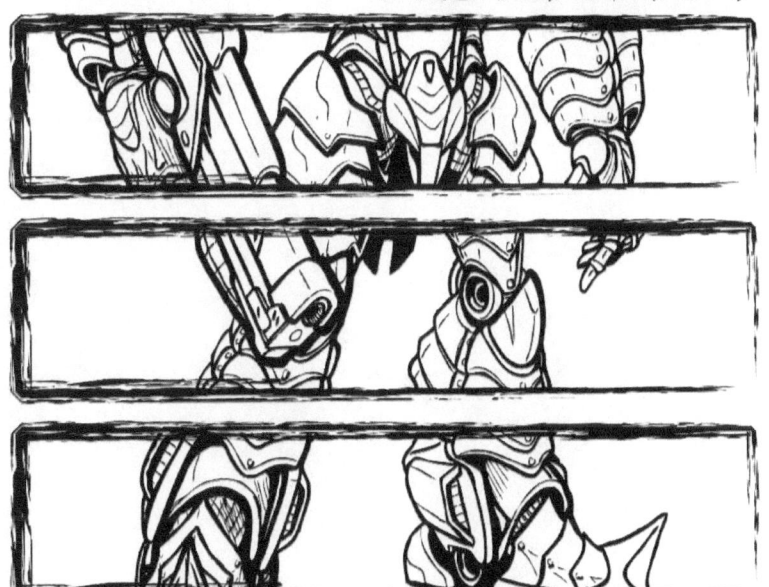

9

My eyes snap open. They quickly adjust to the darkness thanks to my enhanced vision, allowing, me to see in the dark. The ceiling of my room within the CCU headquarters fills my vison. I look to my side, finding Sasha in the bed with me, laying on her side, her back to me. I look to the nightstand beside me, an alarm clock sitting upon it. It reads 11:17 pm. I've only been asleep for a few hours.

Good enough, I think. *I have things to do.*

I roll out of bed, careful not to wake Sasha, and silently make my way to the door of our room. I slowly open the door, slide out into the hallway, and slowly close the door behind me. It latches shut with a click. I make my way down the hallway, toward the elevator at the end. A door opens, stopping me in my tracks. I watch as Josh exits a room that's not his.

I chuckle, gaining his attention.

"Um…hey…Jeremy," he says nervously.

"What were you doing in Mikayla's room?" I ask, a grin on my face.

"Uhh…things."

"Like things to her, or things with her?" I laugh.

His face turns bright red. "We didn't do anything sexual. We were just…talking."

This is the first time I have ever seen Josh, the man who is basically my brother, and the biggest flirt I know, act even the slightest bit shy about anything or anyone. He's had his flings with girls, but those haven't lasted long and he's never been serious about a girl before.

He must really like her, I think.

"I see," I say. "Carry on, soldier." I give him a wink.

He gives me a mock salute and moves across the hall, sliding into his room.

I continue to the elevator, pressing a button. The doors slide open and I step inside. I press the button for the second floor and the doors slide closed. The elevator jolts and then descends. Seconds later, the doors open. The first thing that reaches my ears is snarling and growling. The second is the sound of voices, none of which I recognize.

I step into a hallway much like the one my room is on, except that instead of being lined with doors that open up into rooms, it's lined with barred cells. Most of them are empty, but I come to one near the middle of the hallway that is occupied, but it's who's inside that makes me stop.

Ben lays on a cot, one that is much cushier than the ones in the other cells, asleep. A book lays on his chest, a TV illuminating his sleeping form. A half-eaten steak lays on a plate on the floor beside his cot. A pile of books sits beside that. He snores, a smile on his face.

Cole wasn't lying about not treating him like a prisoner, I think.

I try the cell door, finding it locked, and frown.

I continue down the hall, the snarling and growling growing louder as I grow closer to my destination. I come to the cell at the end of the hall, a black hulking figure inside.

"Damen," I say, the figure whirling toward me, yellow eyes blazing with anger, sharp teeth bared.

Upon seeing me, his eyes soften and his furry lips cover his sharp teeth. His bulky wolf body relaxes.

"Remember what I've been teaching you," I tell my teammate.

His ears twitch and he closes his eyes. He sits like a dog on the cell floor, meditating like I have been teaching him the last year. I cross my arms over my chest as I watch him. It's several minutes before Damen opens his eyes again.

"It worked," he says, his voice deeper than usual due to him being in his wolf form.

"You've gotten a lot better," I say with a smile.

He cocks his head to the side, giving me a weird dog smile.

My head snaps up as an alarm echoes through the hallway and red lights flash. I quickly realize what it means.

The enemy has infiltrated the CCU HQ.

I take off down the hall, back toward the elevator at the end. I skid to a halt, punching the call button. The doors immediately slide open and I jump in, frantically pushing the button for the second floor from the top, where the control room resides. There is always someone there monitoring the facility.

The elevator jolts and ascends. Seconds later, it jolts again and the doors slide open. I rush into the hallway, sprinting toward the Control Room at the end. I slide into the wall at the end as I attempt to stop and stumble into the Control Room to see the security team already in the room, looking at several screens.

"Is it the Order?" I ask.

"No idea. We don't see anything on the monitors," one of the security officers, dressed in standard issue CCU body armor, says.

The building shudders as if from an explosion. I stumble to the side, catching myself on a console.

"Jesus Christ! Did someone set off a bomb?!" another security officer shouts.

"Not an explosion. Look at that thing!" the security guy at the monitor exclaims, staring at the screen with wide eyes.

I walk up behind the man, seeing what he was seeing.

Oh shit!

A Plagueonian ape, what I now have come to call a 'Plape', --I know, it's a dumb name, but it's about the best I could come up with-- stands in the lobby area, the door behind it, from which it entered, a mangled mess. The Plape is smaller than the one I encountered in California, probably designed for the tight hallways of the facility. It sniffs the air, looking around the lobby as dust plumes around it.

"We need to get down there, now!" I shout, turning toward the door to the Control Room.

I exit the room, sprinting down the hallway, toward the elevator. When I stop and hit the call button, I'm happy to find the four security guards had followed me. The doors slide open and we all pile inside. I hit the button for the lobby and the doors slide close. The elevator jolts and descends.

That's when I realize I don't have any weapons.

I look at the security officers around me, which are just CCU soldiers tasked with night guard duties, --different teams are tasked with it each week, my team even having done it a few times-- each armed with various assault rifles, probably loaded with the highest caliber rounds the guns can fire.

Shit. Should have brought Yin and Yang with me, I think, cursing myself for not doing so. Yin and Yang are what I call my modified Desert Eagles. The encounter in Carter Dome was actually the first real combat that they saw. Yeah, I've tested them before that, but that was just to make sure the transformation worked.

The elevator jolts and the doors slide open. Dust fills my nostrils as we step out of the elevator and into the lobby, making me cough. The lobby fills with the sound of gunfire as the security guards --Tango team I think

64

they are-- engage the Plape. The massive creature's roar follows.

I rub the dust from my eyes as it all settles on the ground, getting my first look at the battle in front of me. The Plape swings its big, thick arms at Tango team as they fire at the monster with their high caliber rifles. The bullets don't hurt the creature, which I figured, the rounds just embedding themselves in the monster's thick skin. The Plape brings one of its ape-like fists down on a member of Tango team, crushing the man with a sickening crunch, while batting away another guard. The soldier crashes into the faux service desk, obliterating it. Somehow, I know the man is dead, too, just like the one that was crushed.

I rush forward to help the two remaining members of Tango team. I may be weaponless, but I am far from useless.

I leap into the air, delivering a kick to the Plape's face, which snaps to the side, the creature stumbling to the side. As my feet make contact with the ground, I lunge forward, grabbing the monster's thick arm and pull it out from under it, like Sasha did to the one in California. The Plape falls to the ground with a ground shaking thud and a growl of frustration.

The two remaining members of Tango team continue to pump round after round into the creature, having no luck at all…still.

We need a new plan of attack, I think as I watch the Plape slowly get back to its feet.

10

While the humans were occupied with the Vexnoxtuque he brought with him as a distraction, Thorath snuck away from the battle unnoticed, mostly thanks to the camouflage system in his armor that bent light around him and made him virtually invisible. The same technology was used in Plagueonian ships.

Thorath crammed himself into the human elevator, his eight-foot height and bulky armor barely fitting inside. Through his time on Earth since the invasion two years previously, he had studied the languages, mainly English as it was the most common for his…purposes. The attack on the CCU headquarters was just stage one of his plan. The Vexnoxtuque above was a distraction to keep the humans from stopping him from reaching his destination and enacting stage two of the plan.

He looked at the buttons, finding the one labeled 'Labs' and pressed it. The doors slid closed and the elevator jolted. Thorath could feel the device descend toward his destination. Moments later, the elevator doors slid open.

Faces of surprise and horror greeted Thorath as the doors opened. Maybe it was the fact that he was Plagueonian, or maybe it was the armor he wore -which resembled the creature the humans called Zorax. The helmet he wore looked like the creature's fearsome armored head. Plates of armor ran down his back, covered by a cape that resembled the Vexnoxtuque's wings. Spikey armor covered his arms like the monster's own arms. Each piece of armor covering his body resembled a piece of Zorax. Why? Because that was the Vexnoxtuqe he was tethered to. The Vexnoxtuqe he was *assigned* to. He became fond of the killing machine. The creature's death was painful for him, both physically, because of their link, and emotionally. He didn't experience love for the creature, but he felt as if they were close.

The humans' surprise could also be a combination of the two. He didn't care what it was. He only cared about his mission…his plan.

He squeezed out of the elevator, the human scientists panicking. One of the creatures was so bold as to pull out a gun and pop off a few shots at Thorath. The energy shield surrounding him deflected the metal projectiles and kept him from harm. He raised his weapon, putting a smoking hole in the human's head. The scientist's body fell to the floor, lifeless.

"Anyone else want to try something that stupid?" he growled.

Most of the scientists, which there were seven of, originally eight before Thorath blew a hole in his face, were silent as they sat in the staging area, a long table before them. A familiar creature's head sat on the table. A hallway wrapped around the staging area with more doors lining it.

"Where are they being kept," Thorath demanded, his weapon pointed at the humans.

The scientists said nothing. Thorath growled and prodded his weapon forward.

"T-they're in t-the fourth d-door on the r-right," one of the scientists spoke up.

"Thanks," he said with a sharp-toothed smile. He aimed his weapon and shot off seven shots, each laser bolt punching a hole in a separate scientist.

With the humans dead, he headed down the right side of the hallway wrapping around the staging area, counting down to the fourth door. He grabbed the handle and pulled, the door ripping from its hinges.

Two humans in black armor appeared in the hallway, coming from another hall that led deeper into the basement. They raised their guns, firing at him. Thorath scoffed, raised his blaster, and fired, putting holes in their unarmored faces.

He turned back to the task at hand, stepping into the cold room. Two bodies laid on tables. He took out a vial filled with an orange liquid from a pocket on his waist, uncapping the bottom that held a needle. He jabbed the needle into the half-melted corpse, and depressed the plunger, the orange liquid entering the body. Immediately, the melted parts of what was once his Queen began to reform. A smile stretched across his face.

Echidna's eyes snapped open, her arm lashing out and catching Thorath by the throat. She leaned in close, a growl erupting from her throat, quickly fading. A look of confusion crossed her face. She let go of Thorath and looked around the room she was in.

"Thorath? W-where am I?" she asked.

"A human base," Thorath told her, rubbing his throat.

"The last thing I remember…the Maruian," she said, still confused. It was to be expected. She had been dead for two years now.

"That was two years ago, my Queen. You have been dead that long."

"How am I alive now, then?"

"Since you died, we have studied the Hydra and synthesized a way to bring you back using its regenerative abilities."

"You have the Hydra?"

"No. But it's in this building. Actually, it's in the next room. I have plans for it."

Echidna looked over at the second body in the room with them with a frown.

"Do you want to bring him back as well?" Thorath asked.

Echidna just nodded.

Thorath pulled out a second vial, injecting the second corpse with the orange liquid. The mangled body immediately began to pull itself back together.

"Excuse me, my Queen," Thorath said, stepping out of the room.

He continued down the hallway, past the dead human soldiers, and down the hallway they came from. He exited the hallway into a vast room containing a giant, clear container, a familiar creature curled up, asleep, within. Scientific equipment surrounded the container along with lights illuminating it and the creature inside.

A flash from the darkness confused him until the crackling bolt of energy hit, throwing him into a wall. His shields flickered and died, the generators unable to take the energy surge from the laser bolt fired at him. He caught a glimpse of something small running toward him, a glint of sharp metal in its tiny hands. He kicked out, his foot finding his attacker and throwing off their attack. His attacker tumbled to the floor, giving him a clear view of them.

He smirked.

"A Maruian, huh? You must be Marudon, Queen of Maruia," he said.

Marudon got to her feet, a human KABAR knife looking like a sword in her tiny hands.

And you're Thorath, a Plagueonian general. Not to mention, once upon a time, the handler of Zorax, Marudon said with a snarl inside his head.

Thorath punched the wall and growled in anger at the mention of Zorax. He was beyond furious at the slaying of his prized pet. He calmed and stood up straight... with a smile.

"I could kill you...but I think we have other plans for you," Thorath said.

Before she could process Thorath's words, a fist connected with the back of her head, knocking her out.

"Now that she's out of the way, what are you doing… Oh!" Echidna said, her look around the room settling upon the glass container containing the Hydra.

Thorath gave his Queen a wicked grin and walked toward the Hydra, producing a third and final vial. Unlike the ones containing the orange liquid that he used to resurrect Echidna, this one held a blue liquid.

He reached a console and tapped a few buttons, unlocking and opening the container. The Hydra, who was laying down, lifted its seven heads with a huff, irritated with the disturbance until it saw what was happening. It jumped to its feet and gingerly stepped out of the container.

"Sit," a deep, raspy voice said.

Like a dog, the Hydra did as it was told, looking toward the creature that commanded it. Thorath looked to find a tall, lanky creature covered in wriggling snakes.

Typhon.

Thorath approached the Hydra, the cap popped off and the needle ready. Thorath stopped as the Hydra fidgeted at his approach.

"Do not fret, my pet. This…will make you better," Typhon said.

The Hydra sat still, allowing Thorath to get close enough to jab the needle into its skin and inject the blue liquid.

Thorath quickly jumped away as the Hydra roared in agony. Thorath could already see the beast starting to change as it lumbered for the pull up door. It crashed through the frail metal door and into the city as armor grew on its body and it began to increase in size.

"I can feel its changes," Typhon said, a smile on his face.

"What do we do with the Maruian?" Thorath asked, motioning toward Marudon's unconscious form.

"We take her with us," Echidna said, looking from Marudon to Thorath. "What's next?"

Thorath smiled. "Next, we finish what we started two years ago."

11

The building shook, throwing Sasha from her bed. She groaned as she rose from the floor, rubbing her head, where she had hit it on the nightstand. Her hand came away tacky with blood.

"Shit," she muttered. It was a minor cut, but it still hurt.

She ran for the door, flinging it open and stepping into the hallway. Ashley was in the hallway, a phone to her ear. She pulled it away and grumbled angrily.

"What's wrong?" Sasha asked.

"Will won't answer his damn phone," she growled.

"What's going on?"

"We're under attack."

Under attack? Sasha wondered, but immediately knew by who.

The Order is here.

She ran down the hall, heading for the elevator. She jammed her finger on the call button several times before turning back toward Ashley.

"Keep trying to get hold of Will," Sasha said as the elevator opened behind her with a ding. "We'll probably need all the help we can get."

She jumped into the elevator, the doors closing. She pressed a button, knowing exactly where to find more help.

The doors opened, the hallway before her lined with barred cells. She made her way to the first occupied cell.

"What's going on?" Ben asked.

"We're under attack," Sasha replied.

"Let me help."

"Planned on it."

Sasha grasped the bars of his cell and pulled, ripping the barred cell door away and leaning it next to the opening.

Ben stepped out and asked, "What's your plan?"

She looked down the hall. "We have one more person to get."

She made her way down the hallway, stopping in front of the only other occupied cell.

"What's going on?" the black furred creature asked from within the cell.

"We're under attack, Damen," Sasha said, watching as he got to his wolf feet and approached the cell door.

"I can help," Damen said, his voice deeper than when he was in his human form.

Sasha doesn't budge, hesitating.

"I know you're skeptical," Damen said, gripping the bars with his long boney finger, immediately letting go when they sizzled from contact with the silver that coated the bars. With a shake of his hands, he continued. "I have control of my wolf form. I won't go berserk."

Sasha sighed. "Either way, we have no choice."

She gripped the bars, the silver stinging, but not harming her like it did Damen. With a yank, the door came free. She set the door down as Damen stepped from the cell.

"Let's go," she said, running for the elevator.

An armored fist descends toward me. I'm barely able to leap to the side and avoid what would have been a crushing blow. I've seen what it did to a human being. It would have hurt like a sonuvabitch. It may have even killed me.

My hands twitch and contort, growing hair and claws. I'm momentary confused, then awed. I smirk and run at the Plape, slashing my claws at its thick, armored arm. I jump away, inspecting the damage I inflicted.

"Shit," I say, seeing only superficial lines carved in the thickly armored arm. I faintly hear a ding behind me.

The Plape huffs and charges. I prepare for the impact. A white blur comes out of nowhere, throwing the Plape to the ground. Ben, in his Fenriri form, stands atop the Plape's ugly head. He turns to me, gives me a wave and jumps away as a black blur descends, tearing into the Plape's face.

Damen?

A hand grips my arm, spinning me toward them.

"I brought some help," Sasha says with a grin.

"I can see that," I say.

Sasha turns toward the scene seeing it for the first time. "Is that…?"

"Yeah," I say.

The Plape throws Damen away. He lands next to the Tango squad soldier that was flung into the desk. He sees the soldier and I can see the anger in his eyes. Ben jumps into the air, landing on the Plape's armor plated back as it got to its feet. The Plape bucks wildly until it is met with an uppercut by Damen hard enough to make it topple backwards. Ben jumps away as it lands on its back.

Damen pounces on the creature's underbelly, ripping and tearing at the soft flesh. The two remaining soldiers of Tango team back away, standing on either side of me and Sasha, watching Damen tear away at the Plape as it wails in agony.

73

Minutes go by before the wails stop, the crunching of bones and the slurp of tearing flesh filling the silence.

"Damen, stop," I say in a commanding voice, taking a step forward.

Damen whirls toward me with a snarl, purple blood coating his black furred body. His muscles tense and coil as he prepares to pounce. Upon seeing me, however, he relaxes. He bounds over to me, sitting in front of me like a trained dog.

"I...I got it," he says, giving me a salute.

I wave off his salute and say, "Yes you did. Good job."

My head snaps toward the elevator as it dings and opens. Ashley rushes out, panic etched on her face

"What is it?" I demand.

She catches her breath and says, "Outside... something's happening outside!"

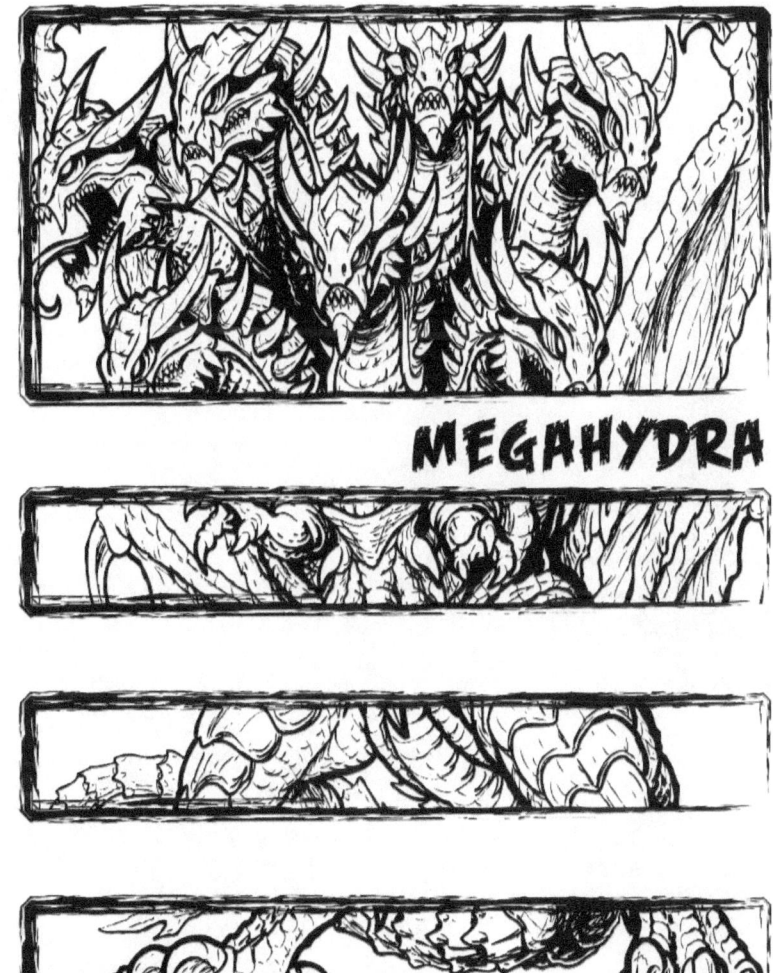

MEGAHYDRA

12

Will pulled the SUV up to the gate and waited. The guards would arrive soon, he knew. He'd been there several times since joining the CCU.

"Wow. I can't believe the President asked us to come have dinner with him!" Nicole beamed, sitting beside Will in the passenger's seat of the SUV.

"Well, you have been doing a great job helping relocate the people who lost their homes during the Kaiju attacks we've suffered," Will said, watching as the guards approached. He rolled down his window and leaned out, giving them a wave. He'd been to the White House enough that the guards knew who he was.

The guards smiled and waved him forward as the gates opened. He pulled the vehicle around the North Lawn, stopping it in front of the White House entrance. He was about to open the door and get out when his phone began to ring. He picked it up and looked at the screen.

"Aren't you going to answer it?" Jamey asked, leaning into the front from the back of the SUV.

"It's just Ashley. She's probably calling to see how I'm doing, because I can't be away from her without thinking I'm going to have a panic attack or something," Will said, setting the phone back down with an irritated look on his face. "She makes me feel like a kid sometimes. Like I always need to be supervised or some shit."

"She's just worried," Nicole said.

"Well, she worries too much."

Will opened the door and stepped out as Nicole and Jamey exchanged concerned looks. They were just as worried about their friend. He held much more than they could ever imagine on his shoulders.

As soon as Jamey and Nicole exited the SUV, the ground shook as an explosion lit up the night far in the distance.

That was toward the CCU headquarters! Will thought, lunging for his phone.

Ashley was still trying to call him. He swiped the green call button, accepting the call.

"Finally you answer!" Ashley growled angrily.

"What's going? What just exploded?" Will asked, ignoring her anger.

"There's a Kaiju," she said, "And it's coming right for you, assuming you're at the White House by now."

"I am. I'll take care of it," Will said.

"Just...be careful."

Will smiled. "Of course. Love you."

"Love you too."

He ended the call and turned toward his friends. He pointed at the White House behind them. "Get inside! It's the safest place for you right now."

"What's going on?" Jamey asked.

"There's a Kaiju heading this way."

"And you want us to just hunker down and wait for it to arrive and flatten the building?" Nicole asked.

"It won't make it here. I'm going to stop it."

"And just how-"

Jamey's question was cut off as Will activated the device on his wrist, teleporting from Washington, D.C. to a secret island facility. Darkness surrounded him, but he knew exactly where he was.

He was in a sitting position, his body resting in a chair of sorts. A helmet settled on his head, linking him with the massive machine he sat inside of.

Will. I have been expecting you. If you hadn't arrived within a few more seconds, I would have summoned you myself, Prometheus said, greeting Will.

"Hello to you too," Will said.

We don't have time for hellos, Prometheus countered, annoyed.

Will had been training with the massive mech over the past year since its discovery. In that time, Will had noticed that the AI was much more human than it should have been. It had a personality.

And not a very likable one, Will thought.

What is not likeable? Prometheus asked.

Will waved him off and said, "Engage teleportation."

Teleportation in 3…2…1…

In a flash of light, they left the island Prometheus had been stored on and appeared in Washington, D.C. Will looked down, finding them standing on the South Lawn.

"The President isn't going to be too happy about us messing up his lawn," Will joked.

That's hardly our most significant worry at this point in time, William, Prometheus grumbled.

"It's always all work and no play with you," Will sighed.

The Vexnoxtuque is almost upon us, Prometheus declared.

Will turned his attention Southeast as the Cocoran Gallery of Art crumbled under the weight of a massive behemoth.

"Holy… is that what I think it is?" Will asked, imagining his mouth agape.

The Hydra, Prometheus said, equally surprised.

The Hydra, once sitting on four powerful legs, resembling a modern dragon, now looked like a wyvern with two powerful back legs, the front legs having devolved into two T-rex-like arms on its weird, ropey, armored chest. It dropped to its wings, using them like arms, as its seven heads launch down, devouring anyone it saw to continue its growth spirt. Its twin armored tails

79

snapped around behind it as it gorged itself, the tails ending in jagged, three pronged spikes.

It's not just the Hydra anymore, Will thought. *Now it's a* MegaHydra.

"The Hydra is immortal. How the hell are we supposed to take it out?" Will asked, watching the MegaHydra gorge itself.

There is only one way, Prometheus said.

Information flooded into Will's brain, showing him what he needed to do.

"Makes sense," Will said, taking a step forward, further ruining the South Lawn.

The MegaHydra stopped its feast, raising its fearsomely armored heads. Seven pairs of eyes locked onto Prometheus. MegaHydra rose to its powerful legs ending in three clawed toes, stretching its wings out in a display of aggression as a roar emitted from its seven jaws.

"Get ready to deploy the sword," Will said.

Roger, Prometheus said, going about the task.

The MegaHydra charged.

"Now!" Will shouted.

The hilt of the sword shot from the robot's palm. Will plucked it out of the air via Prometheus's arm. He pressed a button, the hard-light blade flickering on. He swung the blade as the MegaHydra got within range, slicing off the beast's right wing. Wails erupted from its seven mouths as blue blood sprayed, raining gallons of it upon anyone in the vicinity that had yet to get away. But as quick as the limb was severed, it began to regenerate.

Will attacked again before it finished regenerating, swinging the sword at the Kaiju again, this time connecting with the dragon monster's chest. Flesh and blood flew as the beast wailed in agony once more. But it was used to pain. It had dealt with it its entire life. It locked onto its enemy and attacked.

The MegaHydra thrust its seven heads toward Prometheus, head-butting the massive mech with its armored heads, the robot stumbling backward with each hit. A compartment opened on Prometheus' left forearm as Will deployed the robot's rotary cannon. He aimed it at the MegaHydra's chest and fired, the hard-light rounds pushing the monster back.

The MegaHydra growled in frustration. Will brought up Prometheus' leg and kicked out. The metal foot connected with the MegaHydra's gut, pitching the beast forward. Next, Will brought up Prometheus' knee, the spike that adorned it punching through the bottom of one of the Kaiju's heads. Will pulled the spike free with a slurp and a spray of blue.

The MegaHydra spun, lashing out with its twin armored tails, catching Prometheus in the chest, causing the mech to spin. Will dug Prometheus' metal feet into the South Lawn, bringing the mech to a stop…facing away from his enemy. The MegaHydra plowed into Prometheus' back, throwing him to the ground.

Will rolled Prometheus to the side as the MegaHydra pounced. The ground beside him exploded under the Kaiju's mass. He rolled Prometheus to his feet and readied his sword.

I suggest superheating the blade before attempting that, Prometheus said.

"I forgot you could read my mind," Will grumbled.

It's a good thing I can, too. If you attempted that course of action before hand, the Hydra would have grown more heads.

"Right. Superheat the blade."

Done.

The blade in the robot's hand glowed brighter, green flames radiating from it, attracting the simple minded killing machine's attention. Its seven heads roared in unison as the beast blindly charged forward. Will instructed Prometheus to swing the sword toward the charging Vexnoxtuque. The sword connected with the front outer neck, the blade slicing through, searing it closed in the process. The severed head flew, landing just feet from the White House.

The MegaHydra stumbled back aghast as it looked at the severed head with its remaining six heads. It turned back to Prometheus, its eyes burning with anger.

"Bring it on," Will said.

As if it heard him, the MegaHydra charged. Will readied the sword, preparing to swing when the MegaHydra did something unexpected. It opened its wings, the one Will severed earlier fully restored, and pumped, lifting itself into the air and slashing out with its clawed feet. The Kaiju's claws carved gouges in Prometheus' metal chest.

The robot staggered backward and swung out with its sword, slicing off one of the MegaHydra's feet. The Kaiju roared in pain and tried to fly off, but Will reached out with Prometheus' hand and caught it by its leg, slamming it to the ground with a *boom*.

Will swung the sword down, chopping off another one of the MegaHydra's heads. The MegaHydra brought up its twin tails, wrapped them around Prometheus' arm and pulled, throwing the robot on its back. The monster rose, trying to stand its ground, but it was missing a foot. It fell back to the ground. Will got Prometheus to his feet and swung out with the sword, severing another head. He swung out again, severing another head. He swung repeatedly until all the heads were removed from the MegaHydra's body. The beast fell still and lifeless.

Only one head wriggled, reminding Will that the beast was immortal and would never truly die.

13

The ground beneath my feet shakes as the immortal head of the Hydra, having been mysteriously turned into a Kaiju, falls from Prometheus' hand in front of the CCU headquarters.

"It was a distraction," Cole says, stepping up next to me.

"The Plape?" I ask.

"That's the stupidest name ever. Of all time." He shakes his head. "But yes. A distraction to get to the Hydra. The Kaiju Hydra was also a distraction. Even though Prometheus and the MegaHydra's battle took place in front of the White House, it was attacked while the robot was distracted."

I turn to him, knowing where he's going. "The President? He's...?"

"Missing. The Remnants took him. Echidna and Typhon's bodies are missing as well. Valok is gone, too. I'm not sure it was just a rescue mission for the head of The Remnants. No...this is just the start of something much bigger."

"You're right," I say. "You better think of increasing security around the burial sites of the Titan's children."

"Already happening. Attack helicopters and tanks are en route."

"Copy that." I turn away from the MegaHydra head and head toward the ruined entrance of the CCU headquarters. "But it's hardly going to be enough."

"Then what do you suggest?" Cole asks, irritation in his voice.

"A Prometheus at each burial site is what we need," I say, walking through the ruined doorway.

I hit the elevator call button. I take a look around the faux hotel lobby. It lays in ruins. The bodies have been cleaned up, including the Plape's.

Cole's right. I need to think of another name for them...

I shake my head as the elevator doors open and I step inside. I take the elevator down where my team is gathered in the basement, looking for clues as to what happened while we were distracted by the intruder.

The doors slide open and I step out into the lab, red stains marring its white surfaces. The bodies of the soldiers and the scientists have also been carted away.

I sigh and continue around the staging area, making my way to the back where the Hydra was kept. My team, minus Damen who is still wolfed out and back in a cell, and Will who is still piloting Prometheus, is gathered around the containment box that housed the Hydra, its door now open.

Ashley sees my approach and walks toward me.

"Marudon is missing," she says as she reaches me. "I've checked everywhere she would be and have found no trace of her."

"When was the last time you saw her?" I ask, continuing toward the gathered group.

"Um, earlier. I accompanied her..." She stops talking, realizing something.

I stop walking and turn toward her. "What is it?"

"I accompanied her down here," she says.

"Then we must assume she was abducted by The Remnants," I say, continuing the last few feet to my team.

"Found anything?" I ask as I reach them.

"Aside from Marudon missing, some laser scorching and some weird blue liquid, not to mention Echidna and Typhon's missing bodies, no," Eva says, turning toward me.

"Blue liquid?" I ask.

"Yeah," Aaron says, motioning to the floor.

I squat, inspecting the droplets of blue on the ground. I stand back up and say, "It's probably what they pumped into the Hydra to turn it mega sized."

A flash of blue light makes us jump.

"Damn it, Will," Ashley growls, stomping toward him.

"Hold it," I say.

She whirls toward me with an angry glare.

"You can scold him later," I say. "Right now, it's time to work."

She sighs and nods.

"Thanks," Will says.

"Don't thank me. She's gonna rip you a new asshole later."

Will laughs nervously and asks, "So, what'd I miss?"

"We were attacked," Aaron says.

"By The Order. Though, now they call themselves the Remnants," Eva adds.

"What'd they want?" Will asks, joining the group.

"To distract us," I say. "Echidna and Typhon's bodies are gone. Valok is gone. I think that's what they were after here. And the Hydra was a distraction to take the President."

"Wait, the President is missing?" Will asks, growing frantic.

"Yeah," Ashley says, seeing his panic, her anger melts away.

Will turns toward Ashley, "I left Jamey and Nicole back at the White House."

"They're fine," I say quickly. "In fact, they're on their way here."

Will relaxes.

"What about Walt?" Aaron asks.

"He couldn't make it," Will says.

Aaron nods.

"So, what do we do now?" Sasha asks.

"There is nothing we can do to stop what's coming next," I say. "Except fight."

14

Antarctica…

Doctor Christopher Ouellette stepped from his metal cabin into the cold Antarctic night wearing a thick coat and snow pants that he hurriedly threw on. His attention was immediately drawn beyond the small village of metal structures that housed the other scientists also stationed in Antarctica. That was where what they were there to study laid. The corpses of the Kaijus of the past hovered high over anything else around them, snow collecting on them.

Ouellette shivered, remembering why he stepped out of his warm cabin in the first place. He heard a noise. It wasn't uncommon for him to hear noises. The wind howled. Snow and ice pelted his metal cabin. And occasionally Antarctic wildlife wandered into the village of metal cabins.

But none of that is what he heard.

He thought he heard a scream.

He scanned the cluster of metal cabins surrounded by snow and ice, some having snow on their roofs. Nothing seemed out of the ordinary…until one of the cabins shook.

What the hell? he wondered, his eyebrows creasing in confusion.

Another scream pierced the night, but was silenced just as quickly as it began. Ouellette slowly backed into his cabin and quietly closed the door. He slowed his rapid breathing, calming himself.

Something's in the camp!

He walked over to his desk and grabbed the rifle mounted above it. Every cabin had one for protection, mostly against polar bears.

Whatever was in the camp now, however, was *not* a polar bear.

Polar bears can't open doors and sneak into these cabins...

He pulled back the charging handle on the M-16 assault rifle, hoping it'd be enough to stop whatever was attacking the other scientists. He turned off all the lights and the heater, all powered by a generator, and crouch walked over to the only window in the cabin, right beside the door.

He peeked through the window, immediately darting back down as a shadow passed by. It was big, hulking, and definitely not human.

A voice caught his ear.

"We have cleared all of the other structures and eliminated the human threats, except this one," a deep, inhuman voice said, just feet from his cabin.

They're talking about my cabin, Ouellette realized, panic setting in. *I'm going to die...*

The door to his cabin was kicked in, embedding itself into the far wall. Cold air and snow blew into the cabin, chilling Ouellette. He took aim with his weapon, holding it awkwardly as he had had no training. He pulled the trigger at the first hint of movement, the recoil jarring him.

87

He recomposed himself quickly as a figure entered the cabin, but didn't get the chance to pull the trigger again as the weapon was batted from his grip. He was lifted into the air by strong, inhuman hands.

"This one is a fighter," the creature said, a sick grin on its gray, alien face. It wore a helmet that covered most of its face, a clear glass visor showing its eyes, nose, and mouth.

Another armor encased creature stepped up next to the one holding Ouellette in the air. "What do you want to do with it?" it asked.

The first creature smiled again. "Let him watch the resurrections."

Resurrections?

Before Ouellette could process what was just said, he was dragged from his cabin by the gray monsters and into the howling Antarctic night. The journey was jarring and the constant shaking made him unable to see where they were going until he was thrown to the snowy ground. The gray creatures stood above him…their backs to him.

Huh?

He peeked around the alien standing front of him and jumped back as he caught a glimpse of the lifeless, armored, snow covered face of Zorax.

"The General would love to bring this one back," the first creature said.

"You know who we're here for, though," the second one countered.

"Yes, I do know," the first one said, turning down the row of dead monsters.

Ouellette followed the alien's gaze, finding the creature it was looking at.

Oh no…

The first alien grabbed Ouellette by the hood of his coat, obscuring his vision, and dragged him along as he and his friend made their way toward their target.

"It's sure to be frozen solid by now. You sure this will work?" the second alien asked.

"General Thorath guaranteed it," the first alien said.

Ouellette fell from the alien's grasp, face planting into the cold snow. He pushed himself up, spitting snow from his mouth. He reeled back at the proximity of the frozen, lifeless face. He'd been up close and personal with each of the Kaijus' bodies, but their sheer size unnerved him. The situation he was in made it much worse.

The first alien stepped toward the skull faced corpse of Plague, prepping some sort of giant, metal syringe full of orange liquid. Ouellette watched as the alien probed Plague's neck. Finding whatever he was looking for, he jabbed the needle into Plague, the orange liquid pumping into the Kaiju's corpse.

As soon as the liquid finished pumping into Plague's neck, his head began to glow. The alien that injected Plague jumped back as the Kaiju's head ignited. The Kaiju shook and rose into the snow filled air, his body steaming as the heat from his enormous body melted the ice and snow that covered his body. Plague roared as he got to his feet, swiping at the air around him.

"Plague!" the first alien shouted.

Plague continued to swipe at nothing.

"Plague!" he shouted once again.

The Kaiju stopped its attack on nothing and looked down. Plague leaned down with his eyeless, flaming face, getting a better look at the creature yelling his name.

"Brother," the alien said and Ouellette realized what the aliens that tortured him were: Plagueonians. "We have brought you back to finish what we started two years ago. To help us conquer Earth!"

As soon as the Plagueonian finished speaking, a ship appeared in the sky above Plague. The flaming Kaiju stood up, looking up at the ship.

The Plagueonian mumbled something to itself…or so it seemed. Ouellette realized it was an order to the ship as a laser shot from it, striking a glacier hundreds of feet behind the Kaiju graveyard. The laser struck and the glacier and ground crumbled as if it were hollow.

And as a horrifying creature rose from the newly formed pit, Ouellet screamed in fear.

The Plagueonians laughed.

"Human…meet Zeus!" the first Plagueonian said, picking Ouellette up again.

"And you," the second Plagueonian said with a fiendish grin, "are going to be his first meal in millennia."

The last thing Christopher Ouellette saw were blazing yellow eyes and gigantic, sharp teeth.

ARTEMIS

Interlude I

"Now for the brood," a voice said, booming through the vast cave.

Thel-Shuum turned Prometheus' head downward, finding Hercules standing by the open Gate of Tartarus. He gave the Atlantean a thumbs up, a gesture he learned from the alpha species on this planet: humanity. He picked up the rock slab, the back coated with an Atlantean metal know as orichalcum, the front carved with an H, and affixed it to the hole the Titans were thrown in. With that, he stomped off, letting Hercules do the rest. He engaged the teleportation system, one moment inside the cave, the next being outside, on the island of Corfu.

"We have a target Vexnoxtuque?" Thel asked.

Scanning, Prometheus replied.

The first known Vexnoxtuque is in a mountain range not too far from here. Across the ocean, Prometheus reported after a few moments.

"Lock in the coordinates and take us there," Thel commanded.

Roger, Prometheus said. *Locking in coordinates and engaging teleportation systems. Weapon systems will be reduced to stage one.*

They disappeared in a flash of blue light, reappearing in the same manner, surrounded by lush green trees, vegetation, and big hills. The mountains Prometheus spoke of.

It didn't take him long to find the beast he sought.

It stumbled forward on its seven armored legs, one of them a cybernetic. Its metal tail dragged behind it, gouging out chinks of earth with each step. It stopped its trek, turning toward him, its eight black eyes on him, panting. It was weak, as predicted.

Easier to take out, Prometheus clarified. *Target confirmed as Artemis.*

Thel-Shuum deployed the hard-light sword, getting a hiss from the 'nature goddess'.

What is this Thel? A feminine voice asked, her voice snake-like, a hiss to her words. He knew the voice belonged to the creature before him. *We helped you with your cause. We had a deal! You dare betray us!*

"I'm sorry," Thel said, "but I cannot allow you to wipe out Humanity just because that was who you were…conditioned…to fight. You should turn your rage to the Plagueonians!"

The Plagueonians have left! The humans are our purpose in life! Artemis hissed, turning toward him, mouth agape, saliva dripping from her split maw.

"The Plagueonians will return," Thel said, desperate to talk sense into Artemis. "All you need to do is…be patient."

Artemis snorted. *Patience? Really? You think we can do that? With what they did to us? They made us monsters! All we know to do is destroy! And that is what we must do… Starting with you!*

Thel raised the sword as Artemis charged. Her movements were sluggish, but filled with purpose. A purpose to destroy her former ally. She leapt into the air, using a mountain as a spring board, clawed legs reaching for him, jaws agape.

Thel swung the sword, the blade striking flesh. He was aiming for the creature's unarmored underside, but rockets on her cybernetic arm engaged, propelling her out of danger, losing half of a mandible instead. She hit the ground, crushing trees and vegetation, squealing in pain. She whipped her head toward the robot with a deep

94

hiss, blood flinging from her severed mandible. The metal tail snapped up, yellow lasers firing toward the giant robot. Prometheus stumbled back each time a laser bolt struck his metal skin.

Why are you hesitating? the robot's AI asked.

"She didn't ask for this," Thel said, instructing the robot to avoid the barrage of laser bolts. "None of them did."

If we don't fight, we will be destroyed.

"I know…but maybe we don't have to fight."

What are you thinking?

"Tranquilizers."

The AI was quiet for many long moments as Thel avoided claw strikes from Artemis, the creature in a frenzy, saliva pooling from her maw.

Cryo-missiles armed, Prometheus finally said.

"Cryo-missiles?" Thel asked.

It makes for a more…long term solution without killing them. The only way they'd be brought back is if sunlight hit their skin. So, once they are hit with the cryo-missiles, you'll need to act fast and bury them. Preferably very deep.

"Gotcha!" Thel smiled, happy he didn't have to kill to take care of the threat. There had been enough bloodshed the past years he'd been on Earth.

You know, I don't agree with this plan of action, Prometheus said. *I still think we should kill them all.*

"Whether you agree or not matters not to me," Thel said, a bit annoyed. "This is what I believe is right."

The AI mumbled insults, but Thel ignored it, prepping the missiles, facing down Artemis. The spider beast emitted a deep hiss, her jaws wide…giving him the perfect opportunity. Missiles launched from their cells on Prometheus's shoulder pylons, racing toward

Artemis, entering her mouth and exploding upon contact with the back of her throat in a brilliant blue light.

Artemis squealed, stumbling backward on her eight legs. She shook her head back and forth, confused as to what was happening to her.

What...did...you...do to me?! Artemis snarled.

"Doesn't matter," Thel said. "All you need to do now is sleep."

Artemis shook her head, stumbling all over the place as she fought the effects of the cryo-missiles, but it was too strong for her. She stumbled to the side and fell, unmoving.

Hurry, bury her, Prometheus said.

Thel nodded and used Prometheus's mighty metal hands to begin digging a hole for the creature in the middle of what he knew was a forest.

You realize we will have to do this with every Vexnoxtuque, right? Prometheus asked.

"Yes," Thel said.

As Thel-Shuum dug the hole using a giant robot, the AI was quiet, intrigued, yet infuriated, by his pilot's compassion toward the enemy.

The dig was made in silence, along with the burying of Artemis, the burial site eventually becoming Carters Dome as life continued on.

15

Carters Dome, Appalachian Mountains, Site Artemis...

Commander Gabriel Gregory yawned as he leaned against the M1-Abrahms tank he stood beside in his winter combat gear. He hadn't been stationed to Site Artemis long, only about two days, but he could already tell it was going to be a boring assignment. He looked up as an Apache attack helicopter flew overhead. Security was increased around the site for fear of an attack on the site. Gregory knew exactly what laid under Carters Dome and understood why they did. But even with all the commotion around the site, he was bored.

Honestly, a little action wouldn't be all that bad, he thought.

"Why the hell are we stuck with the shit job?" he said aloud, speaking to no one in particular.

"All wars have stopped. All the money and focus is being put toward rebuilding efforts. No war means we are put on jobs like this," a voice said from atop the tank he was leaning against.

Gregory looked up into the face of Corporal Frank Parr leaning over the side of the M-1, peering down at the man in charge of Site Artemis.

"It was a rhetorical question, Frank," Gregory said with a grin.

"I know. I just like the sound of my own voice," Parr quipped.

Gregory laughed and stood up.

"If you ask me, I rather stuff like this than facing down a Kaiju," Parr said. "Or even being blown up by suicide bombers or shot at. Just think, we're getting paid for sitting on our asses and watching a hunk of dirt. Sure, it may be cold out, but it's like getting paid for taking a vacation. I mean, look at this place. It's damn pretty."

Gregory smiled. "I suppose you're right. It's better to enjoy this than mope about it."

Parr nodded and smiled at his Commander.

Parr's smile fades.

"Hey, you see that?" Parr asked.

"See what?" Gregory asked.

Parr pointed out into the surrounding forest. "Something moved out there."

"It was probably just some animal."

"No, I don't think so. Its shape…it didn't look like any animal I've ever seen before."

Gregory's mind shifted gears. He gripped his rifle tighter and scanned the forest. Shadows shifted from within the darkness. Shadows that were too big to be anything native.

Gregory toggled his throat mic and quietly spoke into it, "All personnel stay alert. Watch the forest. We may have incoming."

He watched as the soldiers around him shifted from relaxed to on alert demeanors. They gripped their rifles tighter, ready to snap them up if need be, and straightened their postures. They searched the forest, seeing the same thing he and Parr did.

"Should we advise command?" Parr asked.

Gregory just nodded and walked off, toward the command tent closer to the base of Carters Dome. He entered the tent, heading for the woman at the radio. Gregory was a single man and since he was stationed here, he figured he try to get to know Erica Haven a little better. He grinned. Ok, he wanted to get to know here *a lot* better. She was a beautiful woman for her age…not that she was that old. She saw him coming, giving him a smile that told him she was equally interested in him, but it quickly disappeared as soon as she saw his serious face.

"Something happen?" she asked him.

"Movement in the forest. I think they're here," Gregory replied.

"Shit. Want me to radio it in?"

He nodded, jumping as gunfire and screams filled the air.

"Fuck," he muttered, heading for the tent entrance, Erica speaking quickly into the radio. The cold wind hit his stubble covered face as he stepped out of the tent, gunfire grating on his eardrums. The camp had been thrown into chaos. Helicopters fired their chain guns into the forest, as did soldiers and the chain guns atop the tanks, engaging an unknown enemy.

No...we know exactly who we're up against.

The ship that materialized above them confirmed it. The Remnants were here...with friends.

"Target the ship!" Gregory ordered, but was too late.

A yellow laser bolt shot from the underside of the spikey ship, blowing a chunk out of Carters Dome, followed by two more. Missiles fired from one of the Apache helicopters hit the Plagueonian ship, the shield around it protecting it from the explosives.

A roar cut through the air, seemingly silencing the war raging around the Dome. Gregory slowly turned toward the Dome as a massive, spindly, metal leg emerged from the hole created in the dome. Another, armored, spikey, spider-like leg emerged next. Both legs grasped the side of Carters Dome, lifting the creature within, revealing a horrifying, eight-eyed face. Mandibles twitched, one mangled and scarred. Its bottom jaw looked like it was split in two, lined with sharp teeth. Its armored face was covered in spikes. The creature's body was lifted from the Dome, revealing more armored spider legs, an armor

99

plated back and an abdomen with a robotic tail attached to it.

The beast, which was undoubtedly the goddess Artemis from which the site was named after, roared again. Missile explosions pocketed the kaiju's maroon flesh, leaving nothing more than black scorch marks behind. Tank rounds hammered the beast, Artemis didn't even flinch. Her metal 'tail' snapped up, the end glowing yellow. The glow increased in intensity before a laser erupted from it, blowing an Apache out of the sky. The flaming ball of metal crashed into the tank Corporal Parr was in, which also erupted in a ball of flame.

Artemis seemed mesmerized by the destruction, watching the flames roll into the sky. The kaiju barked gleefully and went into some kind of berserker state, twitching its robotic tail and letting loose laser blasts, quickly dispatching half of the battle tanks stationed at Carters Dome. The surviving tanks futilely pump round after round into the kaiju with thunderous booms.

"What are we going to do?" Erica asked, falling into Gregory's arms.

"There's nothing we can do," he said, watching Artemis leap from Carters Dome and land in the forest. One of her many armored legs twitched out, sending a tree flying. Gregory tossed Erica away as she screamed his name.

JUDGEMENT

16

"Sir, it's site Artemis."

My head snaps toward Hanna Boyd at the radio. I already know what she's about to report, and I have no doubt Cole does too, but he asks anyway.

"What do they want?" Cole asks.

"Sir...they're under attack. By The Remnants. I could barely hear her over the gunfire."

"Get a helicopter ready," I say, getting a nod from a man at a console.

"Where do you think you're going?" Cole demands.

"Site Artemis. I need to--"

"You won't make it in time."

"Then I can save any survivors..."

Cole shakes his head. "You and I both know if that Kaiju was released, then there are no survivors."

I grind my teeth and mutter a few curses. I know he's right. Like the Titans, these things are merciless. They won't stop until every last human on Earth is dead. It's what they were made for. *Designed* for.

"Sir, we can't make contact with our Antarctic research facility," the man sitting next to Boyd says.

"Shit. Were they hit too?" Cole asks.

"I think it'd be best to assume so."

"So...Sites Zeus and Artemis are compromised."

"Site Ares is under attack," another person says.

"Site Poseidon, too," says another.

Before I know it, six more sites have been named off as attacked...six more kaiju have been unleashed upon humanity.

"Get me images, damn it!" Cole commands.

"Yes sir!" A man says, working his fingers across his keyboard. "Nearest one I can get Sat footage is Site Artemis."

"Pull it up."

With a few more taps of his keyboard, the footage appears on the big screen at the far side of the room. It's a grim sight. Tanks and choppers lay in flaming heaps. Bodies litter the ground, some dead, some dying. A Plagueonian ship hovers over the site. Carters Dome has chunks blown out of it. A woman kneels next to a body crushed under a flung tree…before a laser bolt from the ship vaporizes her.

And then there's the Kaiju.

The spider beast known as Artemis makes its way through the snow topped trees of the forest, heading God-knows-where. Probably to a populated city where it can get a quick meal.

I shiver at the thought. A lot of people are going to die. Horribly.

According to Typhon, --that's Dracula's real name-- the gods and goddesses are different from the Titans. They were born. Soon after their birth, however, they were augmented. He never really clarified how they were augmented, though. But now, I understand.

"Prometheus can't take on eight Kaiju by himself," I say. "Will may have been practicing with the mech, but he'd be overwhelmed fast."

"Even with Marugrah at his side," Cole says.

I nod my agreement.

"Follow Artemis," Cole commands. "Figure out where it's going and have the military meet it there. Get me eyes on the other seven."

I watch as the Plagueonian ship turns and follows the Kaiju.

Having seen enough, I exit the room, making my way down the hallway toward the elevator. So much has happened in a matter of hours. The attack on the CCU headquarters. The MegaHydra. Typhon and Echidna's missing bodies. The President and Marudon kidnapped. And now, eight Kaijus released upon the world.

It's a lot to have to handle…but we have to. And we will.

Lost in my thoughts, I barely noticed that I entered the elevator and arrived at my destination. I step out of the elevator and into the hallway leading to my room. I can feel the frantic energy radiating from the rooms, from my teammates, as I make my way down the hallway. I open the door to my room to Sasha, Josh, Ashley, Will, Aaron, and Mikayla sitting inside.

"Oh, is it gossip time?" I quip, a slight smile on my face.

Josh, who is sitting on the bed, facing away from me, leans back, craning his head back, looking at me upside down, a dubious grin on his face, and says, "We're just talking about how cute you are, Cappy."

I wave him off, failing to hide my smile.

"What's the situation?" Mikayla asks, killing any playfulness left in anyone.

"Well," I say, my smile gone, "the situation is FUBAR. We have eight Kaiju on the loose and the President and Marudon are missing, kidnapped by the Remnants."

I notice Will tense up, his jaw clenched together. He feels responsible for the President. He was there. But he had no idea the MegaHydra was a decoy meant for him and Prometheus so the Remnants, and the Plagueonians, could sneak in and grab the President. Ashley and I have repeatedly told him it wasn't his fault.

"So, what's our next move?" Sasha asks.

I shrug and shake my head. "Until Cole deploys us, we have nowhere to go. We have no idea where the Order took the President and Marudon and we have no way to combat the Kaiju…well, no one but Will."

Will glances at the device on his wrist. I can tell he wants to teleport off to Prometheus and battle the kaiju, but he's outnumbered. The fact that Prometheus hasn't manually teleported Will to him means that the mech knows its outnumbered as well. Or that its flustered with the Kaiju so spread out.

Which is good.

We need to strategize a response instead of running blindly into the fight.

"If anyone has any good ideas on how we can take on eight Kaiju scattered around the world, let me know. Until then," I say, pausing for a heartbeat, "we wait."

17

Somewhere…

Marudon's eyes snapped open, the air around her cold and sinister. She tried to move, but was restricted, held down by something she couldn't see. And she couldn't see much, considering the room she was being held in was pitch black, but her eyes were adjusting. She felt a presence in the room next. Then she heard a groan.

"What…?" a voice said. "What the hell is this?"

Then she felt multiple presences, the sound of a door whooshing open and closed reaching her ears. She quickly shut her eyes, feigning unconsciousness.

"Oh good. You're awake," a sinister voice said, speaking to the other person in the room. "I was afraid those blood sucking idiots knocked you into a coma."

"Wh-what do you want from me?" the other voice, who was most definitely human, asked, his voice full of fear.

The sinister voice, which she knew was a Plagueonian, chuckled. The clang of metal on metal announced the presence of the Plagueonian near her.

"You're horrible at faking," the Plagueonian said, seeing through her ruse.

She opened her eyes, the room brighter, light glinting off the Plagueonian's armor. It was the Plagueonian that she had fought in the CCU headquarters basement. The one wearing the Zorax-themed armor. She didn't know his name, but she was sure he was the one bonded to the Vexnoxtuque Zorax.

The Plagueonian leaned in close, a sharp toothed smile on its face. "The last, non-Vexnoxtuque Maruian," it said. "This certainly is a delight."

She glanced to the side, seeing the human they kidnapped, finding the President.

Of course, she thought.

What are you planning to do with us? she asked the Plagueonian.

The Plagueonian stood up straight with a chuckle. It motioned toward the President. "He is what the humans would call a…hostage. You however…heh, heh, heh… you are my personal play-thing."

The smile on the Plagueonian's face told her exactly what he planned to do with her. And it was nothing good. Plagueonians were never known for 'good'.

He wants to torture me, Marudon thought.

The door swooshed open behind the Plagueonian, two more creatures step in the room behind him, one very recognizable. Marudon's eyes opened in disbelief.

Echidna, Marudon snarled.

"Marudon," Echidna said, a wicked smile on her face. "What a pleasure to see you again."

I can't say I feel the same, Marudon spat.

Echidna chuckled. "Of course not. I destroyed your home planet. Killed off your species. You're the only living, non-Vexnoxified Maruian left…for now."

Marudon squinted at the revived Plagueonian Queen. *For now?*

Another chuckle. "We have big plans for you, Marudon. Your guardian, Marugrah, is strong. Stronger than we ever thought a Maruian Vexnoxtuque could be. It would be the ultimate conquering weapon. We want one." She looked at Marudon sternly, a kind of hunger in her eyes. "And we shall have one."

The Zorax armored Plagueonian clapped his hands excitedly.

The President had wisely stayed silent…until now. He started laughing, gaining Echidna's attention. She turned toward him, a scowl replacing her smile.

"What's so funny, human?" she asked with a snarl.

"You'll fail again, just like last time," the President said.

The smile returned to Echidna's face. "Your kind's resolve is admirable, but it's misplaced. You may have won before, but there is nobody to help you this time. No traitors to turn against me. You're on your own."

The President simply chuckled, as if he knew something nobody else in the room did. Echidna looked unnerved by it, but said nothing as she stood up straight. She looked over at the cloaked figure still standing at the door. It nodded at her and she nodded back.

"Alright then," Echidna said, turning back toward Marudon and the President. She undoes the restraints holding the President down, plucking the man from the table he was strapped to. While they were all distracted, she lifted her tail, pressing a button on her specially made, form fitting black suit, activating the SOS transponder embedded in the suit.

She looked to the Plagueonian and said, "Thorath, I'll let you get to work now."

"Gladly," Thorath said with a chuckle.

As soon as Echidna, holding the President, and the cloaked figure left the room, Thorath began cutting.

18

The Puerto Rico Trench...

Marugrah opened his eyes as a giant, primeval shark swam by. However, it wasn't what woke him. It was a feeling. A feeling of others like him. A lot of them. He could sense their evil intents. Their corrupt souls. They hungered for the destruction of humanity.

That was something he could not allow.

He rose from the trench, leaving the colder waters and entering the warmer, tropical waters, heading toward the closest creature rampaging through Westbrook, Maine, making its way toward Portland. He entered Casco Bay and rose to the surface. He spotted his enemy not too far off, a spider-like monster with mechanical parts.

He bellowed a roar and surged forward, ready to do battle with his enemy.

Washington, D.C. ...

My eyes snap open as blaring klaxons wail and lights flash. I look around. The TV is on, a weird Syfy movie about sharks in a tornado is on. Light streams in through the windows of my room. I'm the only one in the room.

I must have dozed off, I think, rubbing my eyes.

I rub my eyes, and jump out of bed. I make my way toward the door. Before I can reach out and open the door, it swings open, nearly hitting me.

"Shit!" I say groggily, still waking up.

"Sorry," Sasha said, having to shout to be heard over the blaring klaxons.

"What's going on?" I ask, also having to shout.

"Marugrah has surfaced. He's taking on Artemis."

That sobers me up, waking my mind up. We run down the hall, jump in the elevator and take it up. The door opens and we run out, making our way to the control room at the end of the hall. As we enter the room, my eyes immediately fall upon the large screen at the far side of the room. Marugrah stomps through Portland toward his enemy, Artemis, who has just entered the city, her mandibles twitching as she sighted in on the Kaiju charging toward her.

Marugrah stops, just shy of the University of Maine School of Law. Artemis stops as well, standing over Capisic Pond. Marugrah bellows a roar and charges. Artemis matches his roar and charges. Before the creatures collided, Artemis jumped in the air, landing on Marugrah's back. Artemis may be massive, but she's still smaller than Marugrah, being only two-hundred-feet tall and three-hundred-feet long. Artemis leans her massive head down and digs her sharp teeth into Marugrah's armored shoulder. The Kaiju-dragon roars in pain as the teeth slip past armor and find soft flesh. Marugrah tries to reach back and pluck Artemis from his back, but his arms don't allow him to reach that far. So instead, he pounds on the spider-Kaiju's head and claws at its armored face, his obsidian claws peeling away armor. While clinging to Marugrah's back, Artemis's spinnerets go to work, crafting a thick yellow web, trying to wrap the dragon Kaiju in it.

110

"Such terrible, yet magnificent creatures," a voice says, making me flinch from its proximity.

I look to see the owner of the voice: Ezekiel. I was so mesmerized by the screen that I failed to notice who all was in the room.

"Watching them fight is certainly something," I say, turning back to the screen.

Marugrah's claws dig in deep, Artemis's jaws opening, a pained shriek erupting from her throat. Marugrah pulls the spider-Kaiju from his back, throwing her at his feet, on her back. Her legs kick and her body thrashes as she tries to get back to her many feet. Marugrah snarls, raises a web covered leg and slams his clawed food onto Artemis's underside. She roars in pain, her legs snapping closed on Marugrah, the spikes on the end of her legs digging into his armored flesh. Marugrah lifts his leg and tries to shake Artemis off, but she doesn't budge. He roars in frustration and unleashes his crackling emerald flames upon his enemy.

Artemis shrieks in pain and leaps away, landing on her eight legs. Her mechanical tail snaps up and fires bursts of yellow lasers at Marugrah. The lasers strike Marugrah's torso, the larger Kaiju unfazed by the attack. The sides of Marugrah's mouth lifts up, revealing his sharp teeth as he sneers at her. Artemis presses her attack, firing laser bolts from her prosthetic tail as Marugrah takes a step toward her. And then another. And another.

Artemis, seeing her attack having no effect on her opponent, quits firing lasers, backing away from the approaching Kaiju. But she isn't fast enough. Marugrah thrusts out a foot, catching Artemis, and sending her flying. Artemis lands, crushing the Evergreen Cemetery and its associating Duck Pond. Her legs kick in the air as she tries to get back to her many feet, Marugrah stomping toward her.

Marugrah knows she's vulnerable on her back, I think. *He's smart...*

"He's got her now," says another voice that makes me flinch. Will had snuck up on the opposite side of Ezekiel.

But the Goddess of Nature proves Will wrong as she rolls to her feet, surprising Marugrah and lunges at the bigger kaiju. She bites down on his thigh, her teeth digging deep as her mechanical tail snaps up and fires laser bolts into Marugrah's face. Marugrah, who is severely pissed off, reaches down, grabs the robotic tail and squeezes. Artemis wails in pain, her teeth slipping from Marugrah's flesh, as the robotic tail is crushed and torn away from her body. Purple blood sprays into the air as she stumbles back, whimpering, her body convulsing as agony sweeps through her body.

Marugrah drops the now useless prosthetic tail and closes in on his injured enemy who shrinks away from him, trying to retreat to the ocean, but Marugrah is a relentless and unmerciful beast. He lunges at Artemis, lifting her up as the spike tipped legs poke at his armored skin. The laser cannon on her robotic arm activates, firing laser bolts at Marugrah. He growls, biting down on the leg and pulling it away from Artemis's body as she shrieks in pain. Marugrah brings his leg up into her underside, the spike on his knee impaling the arachnid monster. He pulls it free and repeats the act twice.

Blood gushes from three gaping holes in Artemis's underside. I can see the life fading from her black eyes as she suffers from blood loss, soon falling still in Marugrah's grasp. He drops the dead Kaiju and turns his gaze north, sensing something. Another Kaiju probably.

He starts walking, making his way back toward the ocean and his next target.

"He's got the right idea," Will says.

"Huh?" I ask, tearing my eyes away from the screen to look at him.

"If we fight the Titans' children one at a time, we may have a chance. Sure, it may take longer then amassing them in the same place and taking them on, and more people are likely to die, but it's our only chance of winning against them," he explains.

I nod my agreement. Why we didn't think of this earlier, I have no idea. It's almost a no-brainer solution.

"Alright then," Cole says, stepping up to us. "Will, I'm sending you to Japan to take on Hestia."

19

"Is there any word on the President?" I ask, stepping up behind Boyd.

Will had stepped out just minutes ago, teleporting off to his giant robot to do battle with the goddess Hestia. It's up to Marugrah, Will, and Prometheus to take care of the Titans' children. My team and I are tasked with finding both the President and Marudon and rescuing them.

Boyd shook her head, but stopped mid-shake.

"What is it?" I ask.

"I'm picking up Marudon's SOS transponder," she replies.

"Where?" Cole asks, turning to Boyd.

"The Nevada desert, over Bald Mountain, sir," Boyd replies.

"Right. Jeremy, get your team ready. I'm sending you in," Cole tells me.

I nod, turning toward the door, but am stopped as Cole speaks again. "Marudon was working on something. Special goggles in case another alien race came to Earth or the Plagueonians returned. They'll allow you to see objects that are cloaked. Take them. There is no doubt the ship is cloaked and that's why we've not been alerted to their presence in Nevada. They're not far from Area 51, a heavily armed military base, after all."

I glance at the screen, seeing Marugrah wading back into the ocean and nod before stepping out of the control room, making my way down the hallway toward the elevator that will take me to the armory where my team waits. I press the call button and step in the elevator when the doors opens. It's a brief ride as the doors open again. I step into the armory, a blue flash floods the room, causing me to stumble.

The hell…

"The hell was that?" I ask.

"That was Will," Ashley says, walking toward me with Sasha by her side. "He came down here to see me before he left."

I nod, understanding. He's rushing off to fight a Kaiju god with no guarantee of winning. He might not come back. He came to see his girlfriend before he teleported off to fight it.

I look around at the rest of my team, most of them still recovering from last year's fiasco with the Titans and the loss of three of their members, including their leader, a role I have now taken. Aaron and Eva are at the shooting range, looking as if they are competing against each other. Hlad, Josh, and Jones are sitting on the benches, looking over weapons or watching news footage of the Kaijus rampaging across the planet.

I turn to Ashley. "Get Josh and Eva. We have a lead on the President."

She nods and heads off to get her teammates. I head toward the three on the benches, Sasha at my side, not saying a word, which is unusual. We've been through a lot together the past three years since we met, and eventually hooked up. Usually she's talkative and cracking jokes, but now, after the hell we've endured, including herself being turned into a half human, half-vampire known as a 'Halfbreed', she's quiet and probably plagued by many things. An inner struggle she hasn't talked to me about, maybe? I'll have to ask her about it later.

We reach Hlad, Jones, and Josh, getting their attention. Hlad offers a nod that I return. The others, after giving us a quick look, go back to watching television and cleaning their guns. When Ashley, Eva, and Aaron step up next to me, I clear my throat, getting their attention again.

"Listen up," I say, pausing to make sure I have their attention. Satisfied that I do, I continue. "Marudon activated her SOS transponder over Bald Mountain in Nevada. Cole believes that's where the Order and the Plagueonians are keeping her and President Scott."

"So we're going in?" Eva asked.

I nod.

"Their ship is probably cloaked. We'll never find them," Hlad says.

"Well, Cole gave us permission to use something special Marudon has been working on. It'll allow us to see the cloaked ship," I say.

He looks skeptical, but says nothing.

"Right then. Gear up. We leave in fifteen."

I walk away, already dressed in armor and armed, my modified Desert Eagles strapped to my hips, an MP5 slung across my back. A hand on my shoulder spins me

115

around once I'm ten feet away from the rest of the team. I have to refrain from lashing out at the person.

"You know I hate being snuck up on," I say, relaxing, smiling at my girlfriend.

"Sorry, babe," Sasha says, smiling apologetically, but it disappears just as quick as it arrived.

"What's wrong?" I ask.

"What's wrong?" she asks, suddenly growing angry. "We're going to be boarding an alien ship. We'll be behind enemy lines. It'd be a miracle if we all came back alive!"

I put my hands on her shoulders, relaxing her. "I know. It's not the best idea, but-"

"Uh, boss," Josh calls, his voice saying something is wrong.

I walk toward him, Sasha at my side, our quarrel forgotten for now.

"What is it?" I ask when I reach him.

His only response is pointing up at the televisions hanging from the ceiling.

Sasha gasps.

I grind my teeth in anger.

Echidna, the Plagueonian leader I was told was dead, and now looks very much alive hunches over President Scott who is strapped to a blood-stained table. He looks unharmed, but the table was surely used for nefarious purposes.

"Hello, Earth," Echidna says, a wicked smile on her skull-like face. "I have a proposition for you."

HESTIA

INTERLUDE II

Ancient History…

Thel-Shuum looked down at the hill created by burying Artemis through Prometheus' 'eyes'. He had dug deep, imprisoning the beast deep within the Earth.

"Search for our next target," Thel said.

Are we just going to repeat Artemis over and over again? Prometheus asked.

"Yes," Thel said. "And once they are awakened again, the Plagueonians shall have returned and they will take their rage out upon them instead of humanity."

How can you be so sure?

"I have faith."

Your faith will only get you so far.

"Maybe."

After a few moments of silence Prometheus said, *Scanning for Vexnoxtuque signature.*

Thel waited as Prometheus searched for their next target.

Target acquired, Prometheus said.

"Take us there," Thel commanded.

Engaging teleportation system, the AI reported.

Then they were gone in a flash of blue, reappearing a moment later, standing in a body of water, looking inland, their target ravaging a village.

"Where are we?" Thel asked, watching as the dragon beast unleashed yellow flames upon the shacks that made up the village.

A place called Japan, Prometheus replied. *Hestia showed just moments ago, attacking the humans.*

"Apparently they are eager to start their work," Thel said solemnly.

It would seem so.

Thel brought Prometheus ashore with a mighty step, getting Hestia's attention. She turned toward him, her yellow eyes widening in surprise.

Thel? Hestia asked, her voice feminine, yet different from Artemis's, deeper and with less of a hiss to it. *What are you doing here? And why can I not feel Artemis anymore?*

Thel said nothing.

Hestia's brows furrowed, eyes squinting, figuring out what was going on.

I see, she snarled. *A double cross, huh?*

"I'd try to talk sense into you, but that didn't really work well with Artemis," Thel said.

Talk sense…? Oh, I see. You want us to stop trying to destroy humanity.

"Just because you were conditioned to do so by the Plagueonians doesn't mean you have to do it. You're not like your parents. You're intellect, not instinct, like them."

You don't understand how it feels! She stomped one of her front legs, shaking the ground and crushing a hut, along with whoever was inside. *We were made to destroy. It's hard to ignore your purpose; the reason you exist.*

Thel deployed the hard-light sword, grasping it in Prometheus' mighty hand. "I couldn't agree more."

So, this is how it's going to be then? Fine!

She charged with a roar, her jaws agape, her wings spread in aggression. He brought the sword at the ready, watching his former ally gallop toward him. Once she was close, he swung the sword…and missed. Hestia had ducked, veering to the side, avoiding the potentially fatal strike. She spun, bringing the silver ball device attached to the end of her tail, glowing yellow energy spikes protruding from the projectors that covered the device.

120

Prometheus flew backward, holes in his metal stomach, splashing back into the water he arrived in.

She's much more energized than Artemis, Prometheus observed.

"I noticed," Thel said, the robot rising from the ocean, water pouring from his metal skin, a hand to its injured stomach. It wasn't a necessary act, but it felt as if he himself was injured instead of the robot, minus the excruciating pain. It was more like he knew he was injured instead of feeling that he was.

Only I'm not the one injured, he thought.

"Status report," he ordered.

Hull breached in lower extremities, but nothing major was damaged, sir, the AI reported.

"Good." He looked up in time to see Hestia take to the air with a roar and glide toward him. He lifted the energy sword from the water, ready to slash it at the incoming Vexnoxtuque.

Yellow flames washed over the robot as Hestia breathed them upon him. They didn't hurt the Mechanike as it was flame proof, though Thel did feel a little warm inside the metal shell. It did obscure his view, however, allowing Hestia to hit him with her energy spike covered mace, striking Prometheus a little higher than before, throwing the robot back again. Water washed over him. He laid on the soft ground, underwater, looking up.

"Activate thermal vision," Thel said.

His vision erupted in shades of blue, a shape in various shades of red circling above him. He activated jets on Prometheus' legs and back, his back and the cannons that sit upon it scraping against the soft ground as he moved deeper into the body of water that covered most of the planet's surface. The shape, Hestia, followed him as he moved even deeper, soon coming to a deep pit. He deactivated the jets, maneuvering himself so that his head was just below the surface of the water, Hestia just above him. The robot began to sink, its mass much too heavy to float. He waited until he was a few hundred feet from the surface, making Hestia think he just sunk. She still hovered above him, her massive wings beating, keeping her in the air.

Thel kicked on the jets, setting them to full blast, rocketing him upward. He burst from the water, a surprised look on Hestia's dragon-like face. He wrapped Prometheus' metal arms around Hestia's armored neck, the jets powering off. The added weight pulled her from the sky, both of them splashing into the water. Hestia struggled, desperate to free herself.

Got something for you, Prometheus said, startling Thel, the AI being quiet for so long he forgot about it being a piece of the robot he controlled. *Opening compartment.*

A compartment on Prometheus' leg opened. He pulled out its contents, pulling it to his face to see what it was with one hand, the other having a hold on Hestia. He was about to ask what it was when Prometheus answered for him.

Press the button on top and shove it in her mouth.

He did as the AI said, pressing the button with Prometheus' thumb and thrusting the robot's hand forward, shoving it down Hestia's throat. He pulled it out, his hand now empty. Hestia gagged and hacked, the sounds garbled as they were underwater. A torrent of blue-tinged bubbles erupted from her throat as the device detonated.

"A cryo-grenade?" Thel asked.

Mmmhmm, Prometheus said, sounding proud.

"Cool." Thel smiled.

Hestia had gone still, the device working, putting the creature into hibernation.

Any ideas as where this one should go? Prometheus asked.

Thel looked down, into the abyss they were slowly sinking to the bottom of.

"I think this is as good a place as any," he said.

20

Tokyo...

Will had seen things in his life that would drive a normal man insane. Technically, he was normal. Well, besides the fact that he was mentally tethered to a giant Kaiju and the pilot of a giant alien robot. But the scene before his was much more than he expected.

Prometheus stood knee deep in Tokyo Bay, looking at what was left of Japan's capital city. Buildings lay in piles of rubble, the coast devastated, the goddess known as Hestia a mile into the city, a path of destruction in her wake. It was released from its prison deep within the Japan Trench, northeast of Japan. The Plagueonians used lights as artificial sunlight to awaken the beast. It made its way toward Japan, surfacing in Tokyo Bay where it started its assault. The Japanese Self Defense Force tried to repel the Kaiju, but most were dispatched easily or ran out of ammo.

The Kaiju resembled a giant armored dragon, a silver ball-like device with what Prometheus called 'projectors' covering it attached to the end of its armored tail. Armored plates ran down its back. A gem adorned its chest, just like Marugrah, glowing yellow. Spike laden wings stretched from its sides. Flames illuminated the night sky, flickering across Hestia's thick olive skin.

Two dragon-like Kaijus in such a short time, huh? Will thought. *Fitting for a robot that looks like a giant knight.*

Prometheus updated Will on the Kaiju's abilities. The projectors on the device attached to its tail could create energy spikes, which it could use as a mace or fire at its target. It also could breathe fire, also like Marugrah.

Will assumed, like with the gem on the goddess's chest, its flames would be a different color as well, probably matching the color of the gem.

"Alright, Eth, what's available to us?" Will asked the AI.

I'm not entirely fond of that nick name, the AI retorted. *As for what is available to us, there's 'Faithful' as you like to call the hard-light sword, plasma rockets, the rail gun and the rotary cannon. Stage 2 weaponry available in three minutes. Stage 3 in six.*

"Roger that," Will said, instructing the mech to step out of Tokyo bay and onto dry land.

The thud Prometheus' feet created when they hit the earth gained the rampaging Kaiju's attention. Its yellow, pupiless eyes narrowed when it saw the giant mech stepping out of the bay, turning toward him.

Doesn't this bring back memories, a female voice came.

"W-who...?" Will stammered.

Forget about me already, Thel? You're the one who imprisoned me!

It took Will a few moments to figure out the voice belonged to Hestia.

If Maru can, why not these guys? Will thought to himself.

"Ready Faithful," Will said to Prometheus. The AI did as it was told.

Too good to talk to me now? Hestia asked, growing even more angry. *Fine! Let's get this over with! This won't end like last time!*

Hestia charged, her claws digging into the earth.

Indeed, it won't, Prometheus said.

Will pushed the robot forward, stomping toward the charging goddess.

125

"Give me Faithful now!" Will said seconds before the two giants collided.

The sword ejected from the robot's palm, the stock unfolding in Prometheus' hand, the green blade flickering to life, radiating energy that looked like green flames. Will dug Prometheus' giant booted feet into the ravaged earth, skidding to a stop, digging troughs in the process, swiping Faithful at the still charging Kaiju.

Hestia was surprisingly fast though, ducking under the strike, headbutting the robot's feet out from under him. Prometheus fell forward, landing on the Kaiju's armored back and with a horse-like buck of its backside, was tossed away. Prometheus landed on his metal face with an earth-shaking *boom* followed by a roar from Hestia.

Hestia is approaching. Get up! Prometheus urged.

Will quickly rolled the robot to its metal feet, bringing Faithful to bear.

That's when the JSDF decided to return.

Missiles streaked from behind Prometheus, heading straight for Hestia. Six Bell AH-1 Huey Cobra attack helicopters took up positions next to the giant robot, three on either side.

"We'll help you out with the monster!" a masculine voice came, sounding like a dubbed character in a Japanese monster movie. Will realized it was because Prometheus was translating their voices from Japanese so Will could understand them.

"Copy that," Will replied. "Keep it occupied."

"Roger. Commencing stalling actions."

The choppers spread out, opening fire with various weapons on the Kaiju goddess.

What are you planning? Prometheus asked.

"Ready the rail gun. Once Stage 3 weapons are online, get the PA Cannon ready," Will said.

Roger. Stage 3 weapons in three minutes.

Compartments on the side of Prometheus' legs snapped open, revealing two pieces of a device. Will plucked the devices from the compartments and snapped them together, forming the futuristic looking railgun. Will aimed it at the kaiju being riddled with explosions and bullets and pulled the trigger. After a brief charge, a magnetically propelled round erupted from the barrel with a *twang*, striking Hestia's shoulder in a spray of green and purple. Hestia howled in agony as she stumbled to the side.

The JSDF changed targets, aiming for the goddess' injured shoulder. Missiles and bullets shredded the wound even wider, opening it up to the bone. Will fired the railgun again, shattering the creature's bone and severing its arm from its shoulder. Hestia reared up on her back legs, squealing in pain, grasping at her armless shoulder spraying purple.

Stage three weapons ready, Prometheus said. *Readying the particle acceleration cannon.*

The giant cannon snapped forward, between Prometheus' head and left shoulder. Hestia's attention snapped toward the mech as the PAC charged. Her wings snapped out to her sides, catching two of the Cobras and sending them spiraling toward the ground where they erupted into balls of fire while the other four managed to get out of the way. The wings were easily twice the size of the creature itself, being 800 feet across each.

"Fire!" Will shouted.

As the cannon fired, Hestia shoved off the ground with her three remaining legs and lifted off the ground as she beat her wings. The blast of energy barely missed the kaiju, the heat tickling its feet. The blast contacted the ground just behind where Hestia was standing, obliterating the already decimated land.

"Dammit," Will growled. "Eth, get me in touch with those...wait."

Jets roared through the air, racing toward Hestia, missiles firing from their undersides, aimed at her thin, veiny wings. The missiles hit the thin wing membranes and detonated. Hestia screeched in pain as she fell to the ground, fifty foot holes in her wings. Will felt the earth beneath Prometheus' feet shudder as the beast hit the earth.

PAC recharged and ready to fire! Prometheus exclaimed.

Hestia struggled to get up, but with her missing an arm, it was impossible to get her mass off the ground.

No...I can't die! I must...win! Hestia rambled

Will felt himself smile as he activated the PAC, feeling no pity for the beast, a massive twisting yellow beam erupting from the cannon. Hestia's yellow eyes opened wide, knowing it was screwed. It attempted to cover itself with its wings, but they couldn't stop the powerful weapon. A hundred-foot hole was carved into her side, bursting out the other side of her body. The dragon kaiju's body convulsed twice before falling still.

Cheers erupted in Will's ears, no doubt coming from the Cobra helicopters making their way toward Prometheus. Will took apart the railgun and put the two pieces in their respective compartments. The PAC shifted from Prometheus' shoulder to his back.

The lead Cobra came right up to Prometheus' helmet-like face, the pilot inside giving Will a nod. Will nodded back with Prometheus' head. With that, the Cobras turned and flew away.

"Alright, Eth, where is the next one at?" Will asked, watching the Cobra team leave.

The closest Vexnoxtuque is in a city known as Hong Kong, Prometheus said, activating the teleportation system.

They left in a flash of blue light, leaving Tokyo to recover from what used to only exist within movies.

21

Washington, D.C. ...

My fists are clenched so tight, my nails dig into my palms, drawing blood. My body shakes with barely contained rage. It's not because I'm pissed about Echidna holding the President hostage or that the Plagueonian Queen is supposed to be dead. No, it's because of the asshole vampire king standing behind her.

Dracula.

Typhon, I remind myself.

He's the reason I'm where I am today instead of finishing college and married to a beautiful woman. He let Scarlet kill Jessica. He then killed Scarlet when she turned on him.

And now he's back...

I didn't get to kill him last time, but I sure as hell will now.

A wicked smile spreads across Echidna's lips. "Hello, Earth. I have a proposition for you. I understand this is the most important and powerful man on your planet. Surrender to us and you can have him back. Unharmed. And we'll call off our...what do you call them...Kaiju?... as well. They are now your *judges*. If you don't take us up on our offer, they will find you guilty and wipe you out. And I don't want to see any

129

kind of rescue team, or I will personally kill him…You have twenty-four Earth hours to make your decision."

With that, the image of Echidna, Typhon, and President Scott blinks off, returning to images of destruction all over the world, including the battle between Prometheus and Hestia.

I turn away from the screen as Prometheus misses hitting the kaiju with his heavy cannon.

"That was Dracula," Sasha says, having seen the same thing I did.

"Yeah, I know," I say, trying to shake away my anger for the moment. "Everyone get ready. We can't believe what that bitch said. No way to know if she really has the power to call off the Kaiju or if she will even hold up her end of the deal. For all we know, the President is being tortured as we speak. Or he could even be dead. The government won't accept her deal. We're President Scott's only hope."

My team nods, readying their equipment as I start toward the elevator.

"Where are you going?" Sasha asks.

"Like you said, we're going behind enemy lines. In order to come back alive, all of us, we're going to need all the help we can get," I tell her.

"And who are you planning to get to help?" she asks.

"Some friends."

I step inside the elevator, the doors closing behind me. I press the button to go to the second floor. The ride is only a few moments before the doors open. I walk out into the long hallway lined with holding cells. I make my way to the cell in the middle of the hallway, the person inside looking over at me through the barred door.

"Hello, Jeremy," Ben Fulton says, standing from his cushioned cot.

130

"Hello, Ben," I greet the Fenriri.

"Come to talk more about what a Fenriri is?" he asks.

I wave my hand at him. "Later. Right now, we have another matter to attend to."

"Right. The aliens and the President." He motions toward his TV which displays the news and the disasters happening around the world.

I nod. "We need your help."

"You're going after the President then?"

I nod again.

He looks to the TV and then back to me. "Cole. He'll never allow it."

"He doesn't have to know."

"I don't," a voice says, spinning me around. Cole stands a few feet away from me. "But it'd save you some hell if you did get my approval."

I wait for the ass chewing I'm sure I am going to get, but none comes.

"Who else do you need?" he asks, surprising me.

"Ezekiel," I say.

He nods. "Done. Just bring the President home. There's no way to know how long he has. We can't trust what Echidna said."

With that, he walks away, back toward the elevator.

He stops and turns around.

"Oh. Here," he says, tossing something to me.

I catch it and see it for what it is. A key. I look up to see Cole enter the elevator and turn around. He nods to me before pressing the button and the doors close. I unlock the door to Ben's cell.

"I've never gotten to do things like this before," Ben says, stepping out of his cell. "I've been in hiding for so long, I forgot what living was like. What *fighting* was like. Now…" He laughed incredulously. "I'm going to be fighting aliens!"

131

I ignore his enthusiasm as I head for the elevator. I hear his footsteps behind me as he follows me. We enter the elevator and take it up to the top floor. The elevator doors open and we walk out, making our way down the hallway toward the end of the hall, past the control room where the stairs to the roof are. We emerge on the roof of the CCU HQ building and toward the transport waiting for us.

Ezekiel turns toward us, stopping mid-step from boarding our transport, a vertical take-off and landing (VTOL) vehicle capable of reaching high speeds. Ezekiel gives me a friendly wave and boards the futuristic looking dropship that lacks any kind of propellers, two big engines on its sides instead. It's not nearly as big as a C-130 transport ship, but its big enough to hold all ten of us. Ben and I board the VTOL and take our seats.

"Alright! Let's go!" I yell into the ship's cockpit.

The pilot gives me a thumbs up and goes to work on the controls. I'm surprised at how silent the dropship is as it lifts off the roof and takes us on our way toward the enemy ship.

I don a pair of headphones that allows me to speak with the pilot.

"We're off, sir," the pilot says.

"That ship isn't going to let us get close. They may even kill the President if they see us coming," I say. "This thing have a few surprises I don't know about?"

"Yes, sir! Thanks to your alien buddy, this baby has cloaking capabilities and cannot be detected by anything, not even them. They won't see us coming."

Well, they're going to be in for a big surprise, I think with a smile on my face.

22

Above Nevada…

Echidna sat on her throne, her mind lost in thought. Thought of her time in the dark place. The land of the dead. She had never felt fear before, but in that place, even the strongest creature was afraid and powerless. But she was out of that place now, and back into the real world, where she did have power. And she would use that power against her enemies.

"My liege," a voice said, snapping her from her thoughts.

She looked up to see a vampire, in black battle armor designed by her best scientists for the blood suckers, kneeling in front of her throne.

"What is it?' she asked.

"We've lost two Vexnoxtuque," the vampire said, lifting his head up.

"How?" Typhon asked, stepping up next to Echidna's throne.

"The robot Prometheus and the monster Marugrah have engaged the attacking Vexnoxtuque," the vampire explained, holding his palm up, a holographic projector device activating, showing the fall of Artemis and Hestia.

Echidna ground her teeth together as anger took hold of her.

Damn nuisances, she thought.

"What do we do, my liege?" the vampire asks.

"Station ships around the remaining Vexnoxtuque," Echidna ordered.

The vampire bowed and exited the throne room, relaying her orders.

133

Once the vampire exited the room, the space filled with laughter. Echidna and Typhon turned to the table sitting a few feet from her throne which held their hostage.

"You can't possibly believe this plan of yours is going to work," the human said.

"It's your species' weakness, the love of their own," Typhon retorted.

"Maybe, but you have no idea how the U.S. government works. They won't surrender our whole race for one man."

Echidna grunted in agitation at the creature's surly tone.

"You know, there might have been a time I would have been absolutely terrified at the situation I am in right now," the human said. "But two years ago, when you came after me in D.C., seeing people fight to protect me as I cowered behind them changed me. Now, it's my turn to save them…"

"Big talk for such a frail creature," Echidna snorted.

"You're pretty frail, too."

Echidna whirled toward the human, standing from her throne, glaring at the man.

He laughed. "Being brought back from the dead has changed you. You're…disturbed. Broken."

"Maybe. But I can still kill you easily," Echidna snarled, taking a step toward the annoyance.

A boney hand on her arm stopped her. She looked into the eyes of Typhon. "Calm yourself, Echidna. We need him, remember?"

She closed her eyes and took a couple deep breaths, calming herself.

The man known as Scott let out a 'hmph' before going silent again.

"They may not surrender," Typhon said. "But they won't just let us keep you. They'll send someone after you. And when they do…" Typhon giggled. "When they do, you will watch them die."

Deep space…

Tsuzar sat in the command chair of the Plagueonian Mothership, watching his crew at the consoles in front of his, working the ship and scanning for the rogue group they had been warring with for two years, who had managed to escape them. He had no idea where they scampered off to, but he was determined to find them…and put them down for good. They were all that was left of what was the old Plagueonian race, the race that waged war on any species they came across and wiped them from existence. They became a problem after they returned to their adopted home planet Atlantia, where everything began. It started with an assassination attempt on Tsuzar himself, escalating to a civil war before the rogue group stole ships and disappeared into space.

The race went against all that Tsuzar believed in. Plagueonians.

He preferred to call his species by their original name: Hestialite. But the group they fought against were still Plagueonians.

"Sir!" a voice called from within the rows of consoles.

Tsuzar stood from his seat. "What is it?" he asked.

"We have a signal, from our spy within the rogue group! Their beacon is coming from…oh my," the Plagueonian speaking paused.

"Where's it coming from?" Tsuzar asked.

"It's coming from Earth, sir…"

Tsuzar sat back in his chair. "I see. Looks like we're going back to where this battle first began."

After a moment of silence, Tsuzar spoke again, looking to the pilot of the massive ship.

"Demestres, lock in the coordinates for Earth and engage the hyper drive."

"Aye, aye, sir," she said, punching in the coordinates into the navigation computer.

Back to Earth, huh? Tsuzar thought, memories of the battle two years ago flitting through his mind as the pilot engaged the hyper drive and they entered slip space, rocketing toward Earth.

ATHENA

INTERLUDE III

Ancient History...

The location they arrived at for their next target was a cold, snowy swath of land, the frozen water coating the ground. It seemed mostly devoid of life. Human life at least. He could see animals scampering around, running from the two giants towering above them. Thel turned Prometheus' head toward his target, seeing surprise on her face. Her orange eyes shifted from the robot's face to the holes in its abdomen. Her brows furrowed, her eyes shooting back at Prometheus' face, eyes squinted.

I see now. That is why my sisters seemed to disappear, Athena growled, her voice commanding.

Thel looked around, confused as to why Athena would come to an unpopulated wasteland like this if her mission was to destroy humanity. Another look at the beast revealed cuts and missing patches of flesh. Wounds from the Titanomanchy. She came here to rest and heal.

What is this, Thel? she asked.

"Your mission is wrong," he said simply.

She put a hand to her hip and rolled her eyes, a very human gesture of annoyance. Of all the Vexnoxtuque he knew, Athena was the most in control, her old self seeping through.

We should have anticipated you turning on us, she said.

"Indeed, you should have," Thel said.

You going to kill me then, like you did Hestia and Artemis?

Thel was about to tell her he didn't kill the other two, but decided she didn't need to know he wasn't going to kill her.

139

I still think you should have killed them, Prometheus said.

"Shut up," Thel growled.

Thel brought up Prometheus' fists. Athena growled at the act. She clenched her solitary fist, her other arm a cannon built into her armored arm. She charged with a roar. Thel stepped one of Prometheus' feet out in front of him, thrusting one of the robot's fists forward. Athena twisted, grabbing Prometheus' outstretched fist and kicked out, throwing the robot's legs out from beneath it. Thel shouted in surprise as Prometheus fell, landing face first into the snowy ground, plumes of it exploding into the air as he hit, the ground shaking violently.

Athena's chuckle echoed through his head as he got the robot's arms beneath it, and with the help of jets on its chest, got Prometheus to his metal feet. As soon as he got Prometheus back to standing, the robot was thrown on the ground, this time on its back. Athena aimed her cannon at Prometheus and fired. The shot missed. She stomped a foot in anger. The ground shook as Athena made her way to the fallen robot. She looked down at him, her orange eyes squinted, steam rising from her body, the heat it produced interacting with the cold and snow filled air.

You're losing, Thel, she said.

Thel just chuckled, her eyes widening before squinting in anger again.

You dare mock me! she roared.

She reared her arm back, hand balled into a fist, thrusting it forward. Thel brought Prometheus' up, their fists meeting. Athena's eyes widened in surprise as she saw what sat upon his wrist.

Oh, sh-

Hard-light rounds shot from the rotary cannon, pummeling her arm. Athena roared in pain, stumbling

140

backward, clutching at the affected arm with her cannon arm. Thel got Prometheus back to his feet, deploying the hard-light sword. Athena snarled, clenching her fist, the arm he shot unharmed, minus a few dents in her armored skin where the rounds hit. She charged, Thel meeting her charge. He swung the sword out as Athena attempted to skid to a stop, instead slipping on the wet earth. She fell backward as the sword's blade leaving a shallow gash just under her chest armor. She punched the ground in anger, rolling to the side to avoid the sword as Thel swung it down at her.

Are you actually trying to kill this one? Prometheus asked.

"No," he said, "just trying to tire her out."

Athena rolled to her feet and charged, swinging out her hooked claws. Thel leaned Prometheus back, avoiding the swung claws, kicking out a metal leg, the booted foot connecting with Athena's soft gut. An *oof* escaped her mouth as she was lifted off her feet from the blow. She fell to her knees as Thel retracted the robot's foot, clutching her gut. She looked up at him, breathing heavily.

"Arm the cryo-missiles," Thel said with a frown.

Prometheus said nothing, going about his task.

Athena's brows furrowed, her eyes squinted.

What are you waiting for! Kill me! she hissed.

Thel shook Prometheus' helmeted head.

She roared, her mouth opened wide. Missiles erupted from Prometheus's shoulder pylons. Her eyes opened wide. She jumped to the side, the missiles missing their target.

"Dammit!" Thel growled, dodging a punch from Athena, the Vexnoxtuque having gotten to her feet and attacked.

141

Thel spun the robot, its foot connecting with Athena's side. Athena stumbled, turning her blazing orange eyes toward him.

"Think you can whip up another of those cryo-grenades?" Thel asked.

Already got one ready for you, Prometheus replied.

A compartment on the robot's leg snapped open. He reached Prometheus' hand inside, his metal fingers wrapping around the device inside and pulling it from within.

Athena charged with a savage roar, thrusting her cannon arm at Prometheus's damaged stomach. She fired the cannon, the blast of yellow energy throwing the giant robot back. Thel activated the jets on Prometheus' back as the mech stumbled backward, keeping it from falling. Athena stomped a foot forward, her legs spread, arms to her side, body leaned toward the ground, mouth open wide, a roar emanating from her throat. Her anger was taking hold of her. Thel rushed Prometheus forward as Athena's roar was about to come to a close. He thrusted the hand clutching the device forward, letting go of it. The grenade sailed through the air, entering her gullet through her open maw.

Athena stood straight up, her jaws snapping closed, confusion written all over her face. Then she furrowed her brows, her eyes squinting at him. Thel made no move, even as she took a step forward. Then another. She stopped with her foot in the air as she was about to take another step. Her mouth opened, blue smoke flowing from within as she squealed in pain. She stumbled back, clutching at her throat. She snarled and took a step forward, her leg buckling beneath her weight as her energy faded. She fell face first into the snowy earth.

He glanced behind him, finding a body of water, knowing exactly where he was going to bury Athena. He grabbed her limp body by her arm and got to work.

23

Canada...

Marugrah rose from the cold waters of Hudson Bay after
inspecting the hole hundreds of feet below him, near the
center of the water. Marugrah waded toward the shore.
He could see his target off in the distance, making its
way to...who-knows-where. When Marugrah's clawed
foot hit the snow-covered soil of Manitoba, Canada, the
Vexnoxtuque, known as Athena, had just reached the
City of Thompson, which was known as the "Hub of the
North", meaning it's the regional trade and service
centre of Northern Manitoba.

   Marugrah bellowed a roar, getting Athena's attention.
She turned toward him, her blazing orange eyes
squinting at Marugrah in annoyance. The creature was
unnerving to anyone looking at the giant beast.
Marugrah could feel it. It was because of the Kaiju's
appearance. It looked...human in stature. The beast was
far from human, though. It stood tall like a person and
carried itself confidently, but its face, while human in
structure, was completely alien. It was thickly armored
and had spikes under its angry eyes and bottom jaw. Its
mouth was filled with sharp, jagged teeth. The armor on
her shoulder, back, and chest were a shining gold, along
with the skull on her right wrist, which was less of an
arm and more of a spiked arm cannon which looked to
be surgically implemented. The rest of the beast was
sky-blue in color. Its right arm was more humanoid,
ending in five clawed fingers. Its legs were armored and
ended in five clawed toes.

   Athena stood her ground, not moving, just staring at
Marugrah as he approached her. He had no idea what the
Vexnoxtuque was planning, but he could sense its

intelligence. She wasn't like Artemis, who was mostly instinct. Athena was intellect. Strategy.

Which makes it even more dangerous, Marugrah thought. *I must be just as cunning and strategic to prevail.*

Marugrah dropped to all fours and charged. Athena stood her ground, raising her cannon arm at the charging Kaiju. After a brief charge, a yellow laser bolt erupted from the cannon. Marugrah hopped to the side, barely avoiding the bolt of energy, exploded soil pelting his armored hide. Athena let loose three more laser bolts, Marugrah avoiding all of them. Athena snarled, as Marugrah roared, still charging.

Athena took a step, and then another, breaking into a charge of her own. Just before the two giants collided, Marugrah dug his claws into the snowy ground, slowing his forward momentum, and spinning, bringing his long, armored tail tipped with a spiked club around, sweeping Athena's clawed feet out from under her. As the humanoid Kaiju fell on her back, Marugrah pounced. He dug his claws into Athena's sides, eliciting a cry of pain from the goddess.

Marugrah opened his jaws wide, about to clamp down on Athena's shoulder, but she lashed out her five-fingered hand and caught him by the throat, his teeth inches away from her blue flesh. Athena got her legs under Marugrah and shoved, throwing the dragon-Kaiju off her. Both Kaijus rolled to their feet, Marugrah standing up straight, sizing each other up.

Marugrah, impatience overtaking him, charged with a roar, slashing his claws at the enemy. The first strike found her armored chest, the second Athena managed to dodge. As Marugrah stumbled forward, Athena sent a fist into his gut forcing the air from Marugrah's lungs. While Marugrah was distracted with trying to regain his breath, Athena sent a spinning kick into the side of his fearsome reptilian face, sending the Kaiju sprawling to the ground with an earthshaking *boom*.

Marugrah's head was spinning, but he could feel the anger building. He could feel the *madness* building. He tried to fight it so it wouldn't overtake him, but he didn't get a chance. Athena grabbed him by his spiked carapace, lifting him in the air and tossing him. Earth exploded in the air around him as he landed after being flung.

Marugrah sprang to his feet, his green eyes radiating oozing anger. A wave of energy had washed over him and it felt...good. Athena let out a 'hmph' as she saw the newly energized Marugrah, still not seeing him as much of a threat.

That's her mistake, Marugrah thought, trying to focus the rage while beating back the madness that was trying to consume him.

Marugrah roared, loud and fearsome. A challenge. After he finished announcing his challenge, he let loose with his green flames. Athena lifted her cannon arm in front of her, the flesh stretching and expanding via an unseen mechanism beneath its skin.

More augmentations...

The arm had become a shield, the hard, armored limb unfazed by the fiery attack. Marugrah ceases his flame attack, slashing at Athena's gut before she can lower her arm. He dragged his claws through her flesh, leaving three deep slashes leaking purple. Marugrah slashed out again a little higher, just below her armored chest. Blood sprayed. Athena cried out in pain and frustration. He was about to slash at her again, aiming higher this time, for her throat, but Athena lashed out and grabbed his arm before he could, spinning and flinging him.

146

As Marugrah soared through the air, he focused his energy on his core, a beam erupting from the gem on his chest, striking her shoulder and blowing a chunk of her blue flesh away. Athena shrieked in agony as purple ichor flowed from the wound. Marugrah struck the ground, creating a crater in the Canadian soil. When Marugrah got back to his feet, Athena was stalking toward him, anger and hate radiating from her orange eyes.

Marugrah tried to breathe his green flames, but all that came out was smoke. He grunted in agitation.

That beam must've drained my energy supplies, he thought, still not understanding his new body after two years of being the way he was.

With his ranged attack depleted, he stood his ground, waiting for Athena to get in close so he could employ his melee tactics upon her.

But she did something that caught him off guard.

Athena jumped in the air, twisting and delivering a kick to Marugrah's snouted face, throwing the Kaiju to the ground, snow puffing in the air around him. Impacts shook his body as Athena fired laser bolts at him from her cannon arm. Fortunately for him, his thick, armored skin protected him from the attacks.

Marugrah slowly got to his feet as his body was bombarded by laser blasts from Athena, anger fueling his resistance. He snarled and let out an earth-shaking roar so angry Athena shrunk back a little, halting her laser assault. Marugrah charged, frenzied. Athena, not one to back down from an enemy, stood her ground.

Expecting more claw strikes, Athena bent her legs, her muscles coiling and ready to spring her out of the way. But that's not what came. Marugrah sprang into the air, mimicking one of her attacks, his clawed foot found her

147

armored chest and threw her back. She stumbled and fell onto her armored, shell-like back.

Marugrah brought his fists down on Athena's leg, snapping it in two as the goddess roared in pain. She knew she wasn't going anywhere with a broken leg. Marugrah could see it in her eyes as she glanced at the mangled limb, her breathing heavy and erratic. She looked up at Marugrah with something like terror in her eyes. That was a split second before Marugrah unsheathed a spike from one of the chambers on his wrists and plunged it into her human-like face, killing her instantly as her brain was skewered. Marugrah pulled the spike from Athena's face, a gaping hole now in her skull. The Kaiju Goddess of Wisdom laid still on the snowy Canadian ground, purple gushing from the hole in her face.

Marugrah huffed, his hot breath condensing in the cold air, before standing tall and roaring his victory to the gray sky above. Two enemies were dead by his hand, one by Prometheus', but there were many more left, scattered around the world. Each one a beacon to him, beckoning him to them. He shook his head, not allowing it to overwhelm him. One of the beacons was engaging Will and Prometheus. It'd soon be dead, the beacon winking out, one less annoyance on his mind.

Feeling a beacon close by, he decided to make his way to that one. He headed back to Hudson Bay, slipping beneath the waves and began the journey to his next battle.

BOARDING ACTION

24

Nevada...

"ETA, ten minutes, sir."

My eyes flutter open from my not-quite-asleep state. I've been in and out the whole trip. I've learned that sleep helps before a battle because you never know when you're going to be able to sleep again. And the battle we're heading into now is one of the worst scenarios a soldier could find themselves in; being behind enemy lines, I mean. And by 'behind enemy lines', I mean aboard their ship. I look around at my ten-person team, all wide awake and ready to fight.

Good, I think. I'm not exactly fond of leading them on this suicide mission, though.

"You sure we can do this?" Sasha asks, sitting next to me.

"We're already here, so there's no turning back either way," I say, glancing at her. "Whether we can, I can't say. But we're sure as hell going to try. Echidna said she could call off the Kaiju, so maybe she has a way of controlling them. If we take out the control unit on the ship, we'll sever her control on the Kaiju and maybe, just maybe, they'll be easier to defeat."

"Or maybe they will be even harder, going berserk without a driving force," Josh says, sitting across from me, beside Mikayla.

"Or that. We'll deal with that conundrum when we get to it, I suppose."

"The Kaiju that are left at least. Artemis, Hestia, and Athena are taken care of," Ashley says.

Everyone readies their various array of weapons in the last minutes of our flight to the cloaked Plagueonian ship. I heard of what the original Gamma team encountered the last time they were on a Plagueonian ship. The biggest of which was a Cyclops Vexnoxtuque. I have no doubt they have more Cercopes waiting inside.

Cercopes are the new name I came up with for the creatures I previously named Plapes. In Greek mythology, Cercopes were mischievous forest creatures who roamed the world and turned up anywhere mischief was afoot. In one of the many myths for the creatures, in an attempt to explain their name ('tail-men' in Greek) Zeus turned them into monkeys. I thought it the perfect name as the damn things have caused a hell of a lot of mischief for us since we first encountered them.

"ETA, three minutes," the pilot's voice comes again.

I stand, looking over my team. "Alright, everyone ready up."

With one last check of their weapons and gear, making sure everything is in working order, they stand with me, ready to disembark the VTOL we are riding in. I pull the goggles --well, something closer to night vision devices-- over my eyes and make my way to the back hatch. The pilots possess similar devices so they can see where the ship we are about to board is. Josh has the fourth and final pair of goggles.

"We're coming up on the ship," the pilot says.

"Roger that," I say.

My stomach lurches as we descend on the ship. I half expect the ship to shudder and the pilot to call out that we've been hit, but that never happens.

"We're attached," the pilot says. "Opening the back hatch for y'all now."

The hatch hisses and opens, revealing the gray, armor-like hull of the ship to me. It hovers over Bald Mountain like a floating Kaiju. Not too far from the mountain is Area 51, a heavily armed military base that has no idea the alien ship is even here. Sandwiched between the two

152

is a now abandoned town by the name of Stone Hill. I heard there was an incident in the town and that's why it was abandoned. It's classified information, though, even for a high ranking CCU agent like me.

"Holy shit sticks, are you sure the ship is there?" Aaron asks, looking out the back hatch.

I forgot he can't see the ship, I think.

"It's there," I assure him, but his face tells me he's still skeptical.

I make my way out of the hatch and step onto the hull, showing him that it is indeed there.

He shakes his head and says, "I'm never going to get used to this crap."

The team steps out into the invisible hull gingerly, some stumbling, their brains not quite understanding the situation. Once we're out, the VTOL, the only thing visible the inside of the hatch, which is slowly disappearing as the hatch closes, zooms off…impossibly quiet.

"How are we supposed to get in?" Wolf asks, ever the soldier.

"With this," I say, pulling out a gun-like device from my chest armor.

He nods, understanding what the device is and what it does. I kneel close to the ship's hull and activate the device. I put it against the cloaked hull of the ship and pull the trigger, a laser cutting through the thick metal. I cut a three-foot in diameter hole in the gray hull of the ship, big enough for one of us to slip through at a time. The three-foot, circular slab of hull falls away, landing with a loud *clang* on the floor, nine-feet below us.

"Fuck," I mutter.

"Welp. They know we're here now," Ezekiel says.

"I'll go down first," Wolf says. "The jump won't hurt me. I'll catch the rest of you."

"Have you forgotten?" Ben asks, an eyebrow raised.

"Oh. Right." He glances at me. "I'm not used to having more non-humans on the team."

"It's alright," I say. "Besides, I'm going first. The rest of you follow. Josh, Mikayla, Eva, Ashley, and Aaron will need help."

They nod their confirmations. I nod back and hop through the hole I cut, landing on the hull piece that fell, my boots clanging on the metal. I move to the side, drawing my modified Desert Eagle hand cannons, scanning the hallway I'm facing with them, luckily finding no targets. I turn around, my guard still up, watching as the rest of my team enters through the hole above. Once Ezekiel, Sasha, Ben, and Wolf are through, Wolf catches the rest as they jump down, Josh being the last since he has the cloak seeing goggles and helping the rest that can't see more than the piece missing from the hull.

"Well, what now?" Mikayla asks.

"I hate to be the one to quote *Scooby Doo,* but I think we should split up," I say. "We'll cover more ground that way and hopefully find President Scott and Marudon faster."

"Is that wise, though?" Ben asks.

"Of course not," I say. "But we need to get them and get out as soon as we can."

"I'm going with you," Sasha says, defiant.

"Fine," I say. "Ashley, Josh, and Mikayla, you're coming with me as well." I point behind me, indicating the path we'll be taking.

"Wolf, you're in charge of Ben, Ezekiel, Eva, and Aaron." I point the opposite direction telling them the path they'll be taking.

"Yes, sir," Wolf says, with a nod. "Good luck."

154

I ignore the fact he called me sir, just because I can't be sure I'll see him again.

I nod. "You too, my friend."

With that, we split off into two teams, each team heading to their designated path into the unknown depths of the enemy ship.

HADES

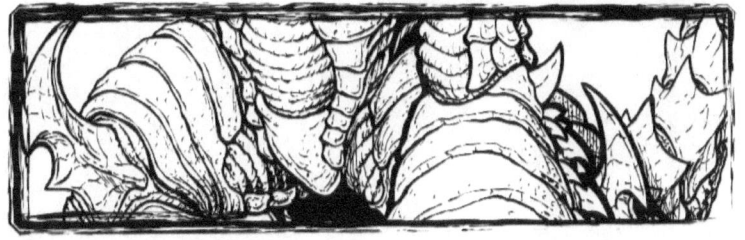

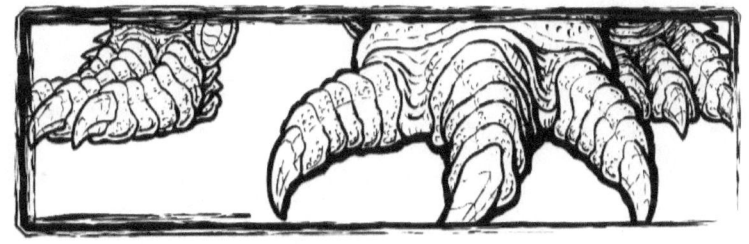

INTERLUDE IV

Ancient History...

Prometheus rose from the water, stepping back onto the snowy earth after finishing the burial of Athena.

Vexnoxtuque detected, Prometheus reported.

Thel-Shuum sighed. After the defeat of the Titans, the remaining children scattered, taking to the ocean, going about their own agendas.

"Take us to it," Thel said, exhaustion taking its hold on him.

No time to rest, he told himself.

The teleportation system whirred, activating. The snowy land disappeared, replaced by a village like the one they saw when they fought Hestia in Japan.

"Are we in Japan again?" Thel asked.

Negative, Prometheus said. *They call this place China.*

Their target stood further inland, engulfed in fire, the buildings around him, and no doubt any unlucky humans in the area, aflame. Catapults fired at the beast from a hill, their attacks ineffective against the giant monster. The beast known as Hades roared. Liquid surged from his throat, igniting, and washing over the catapults, incinerating them.

"Our turn," Thel said, pushing Prometheus into a run toward the hell beast.

Hades noticed their approach, turning toward them with a roar.

Thel! his gravelly voice came. *I should have known it was you. You're the reason for my sisters disappearing, aren't you?*

Just like with Athena, Thel decided to say nothing, letting the creature choose its own conclusion. Hades snarled, most likely thinking they are dead, like Athena did.

Ashamed to admit your deeds? Hades snorted. *Let me be the judge, juror, and executioner for your crimes, then!*

Hades stomped toward Prometheus, who Thel had stopped a mile from the beast, crushing huts and people beneath his massive feet. Thel stood his ground as the beast charged, still engulfed in his flaming cocoon.

"Raise the heat shields," Thel ordered.

Prometheus said nothing, but he knew the AI had gone about its task.

Hades slammed into Prometheus, Thel barely able to keep the mech upright by grasping the monster's arms. The flaming cocoon surrounded both of them.

Heat shields holding, Prometheus reported.

Thel grunted as he held Hades back, the beast snapping at Prometheus' face. He brought Prometheus' knee up, connecting with the unarmored strip of flesh on Hades's stomach. The creature weakened, allowing him to spin around, Hades lifting off his clawed feet, and tossed the beast to the ground.

"We need to find a way to cool him off," Thel said, watching Hades hit the ground and slide, causing more death and destruction. Thel cringed at the sight. *Oops.* His vision shifted past Hades, toward the coast. Water.

That could work, Prometheus said, knowing what his pilot was thinking.

"Let's do it then," he said, walking toward the recovering Hades.

Hades looked up and roared in anger. Thel clenched Prometheus' fists, thrusting it into the Vexnoxtuque's face. Hades fell on his back, dazed. Thel reached down and grasped Hades' thick arm, dragging the dragon beast toward the ocean. Hades moaned, slowly recovering.

Better hurry, Prometheus urged.

"I'm trying," Thel growled, engaging the robot's thrusters, bending its legs and jumping into the air. He landed hundreds of feet away, Hades still in his grasp, his body slamming back to the earth with him. He was almost to the ocean.

Hades roared, the collision with the earth jolting him from his stunned state. He yanked his arm from Prometheus' grasp and rolled to his feet. He snarled, his orange eyes oozing anger.

Thel did the only thing he could think to do…he ran.

You can't run from me! Hades called after him.

Thel could hear the brute's footsteps thundering behind him as the monster took the bait.

Nice thinking, Prometheus said.

Thel said nothing, focused on his objective. Prometheus' feet hit the water, Thel wading the robot deeper. A moment later, a splash sounded behind him, announcing that Hades had entered the water. Thel stopped wading, and turned to face Hades, the creature hip deep in water, his top half still wrapped in his flaming cocoon, the water around him boiling and steaming. Thel stood his ground, Prometheus' fists clenched. Hades stopped as well, looking at him with a skeptical expression.

You decide to accept your fate? Hades asked.

"I don't think you quite grasp the situation you're in," Thel retorted.

Hades hissed, not the brightest of the Titans' children. The females seemed to be more intelligent than the males… not counting Zeus. He's the smartest of them all, hence the reason he was their leader.

Time to finish this fight, he thought.

Hades roared and charged, Thel meeting it. Thel reached out Prometheus' hands, grasping the long,

161

curved horns protruding from the back of Hades' head and pulled. Hades roared as he fell forward, splashing into the water in a cloud of steam.

Thel had Prometheus take a few steps back, preparing the robot for Hades's retaliation. After a few moments of waiting, Hades not rising from the water, Thel took a step forward. The sound of rushing water, coming from behind, stopped him. A three-fingered hand wrapped around Prometheus' helmet-like head, slamming him into the ocean.

Damn! Not as unintelligent as I thought…

Stage 3 weapon systems available, Prometheus announced.

Thel ran through all the stage 3 weapons in his head, frowning. Stage 3 were vastly powerful weapons meant for killing.

We should use the…, Prometheus started.

"No," Thel said adamantly, knowing what the AI was going to suggest. "Vent excess power."

The AI grumbled, but did as it was ordered. Energy exploded from the circular device at the robot's core, slamming into Hades above, throwing the monster away. The robot rose from the ocean, water falling like waterfalls from his body, in time to see Hades splash down hundreds of feet from him.

Back to stage 1 weapons, Prometheus announced.

"Ready all cryo weapons," Thel said, making his way toward the felled Hades.

All cryo weapons available, Prometheus reported.

Thel reached the spot he saw Hades land, dipping Prometheus' metal hands beneath the boiling water. The robot's fingers found the creature, pulling him up by his armored shoulders. Hades' head lolled to the side, the creature knocked silly. Thel grabbed a cryo grenade from the compartment on his leg, activating it, and deposited it into the unconscious beast's mouth. It slid down Hades' throat and detonated, the creature spasming, but not waking.

Any idea what to do with this one? Prometheus asked.

Thel looked further out into the ocean and said, "Of course I do."

25

Hong Kong, China...

The flash of blue faded, revealing Hell on Earth to Will. The city of Hong Kong was an inferno, the Devil himself standing in the middle of the blaze.

No, not the Devil, Will thought. *Hades.*

The demon-like Kaiju roared, the flames looking as if they were emanating from the creature itself. Prometheus got them as close to the Kaiju as possible without landing in the blazing hot fires that had engulfed the city, landing them in the Rambler channel, hundreds of thousands of feet from the monster who was near the Sam Tung Uk Museum, which was now a melted pile of stone.

Zooming in with Prometheus' superior vision, Will could see that the flames were in fact coming from the Kaiju, pores in its red armored skin spewing a liquid that ignited upon contact with the air, turning into flamethrowers. The flames pouring from Hades' pores stopped. Will zoomed out, knowing the beast had spotted them.

He flinched as he found he was right. The Kaiju's blazing orange eyes stared at him, burning with a hateful intensity, his armored brows furrowed.

"I know all the Kaiju you imprisoned hate you, but I sometimes wish I didn't get their hateful glares, too," Will said with a shiver.

It cannot be helped, Prometheus said. *So, suck it up.*

Will frowned deeply, or at least he thought he did, at the AI's rude comment. The more time he spent with the AI, the more...human...it became. And it annoyed him. AIs weren't supposed to be human. They were supposed to analyze data. Help the human operators without the emotion Prometheus showed.

He reminds me of Cortana from the Halo *video game series,* Will thought.

Only I'm not, Prometheus said, Will forgetting that thought was the same as speaking while he was connected with the mech. *I'm real. Not fictional.*

"Right," Will said.

Thel! a deep voice entered his head. *Is that you?*

Will decided not to respond to the beast. To let it think it was Thel-Shuum still at the controls of the mighty machine.

Silence again? Hades scoffed. *Fine! I don't need you to talk to rip you to pieces!*

Hades threw his dragon-like face back and let out an earsplitting roar. Luckily for Will, his ears were protected within the battle mech. Finished with his battle cry, Hades charged.

Will stood his ground, hoping to engage the behemoth in the water where it would be easier to put out his flames.

As Hades stomped his way through the burning and melted city, Will shuffled Prometheus backward, deeper into the water, hoping the beast, lost in the rage at the sight of its imprisoner, would blindly follow him into the water.

To his delight, his plan worked. One three-toed foot after the other, Hades splashed into the water, hellbent on reaching him. Boats bobbed with the waves as Hades sloshed toward Prometheus, the source of his rage. When the God of the Underworld was within reach, Will cocked back Prometheus' arm and shot it forward, the mech's fist making contact with the Kaiju's ugly face. Hades, dazed from the blow to his face, stumbled backward, but didn't fall. The hell beast shook off the blow and growled, his anger growing. He slashed out with his claw tipped, three fingered hands. Will barely avoided the attack, the tips of Hades' claws scraping across Prometheus' metal chest, just below the spinning yellow core.

Spinning around to avoid Hades' attack, Will used the momentum to increase the power to Prometheus' fist as he drove it into Hades' face again. The force of the strike threw Hades off his feet, landing on his armored back with a giant splash. Will used the time it took for the beast to get back to its feet to deploy a weapon. Hades flinched in surprise as Will swung Faithful at him, the crackling green blade barely missing the beast's throat.

Hades snarled, opened his mouth wide and unleashed a torrent of flames from his sharp toothed maw. Will rolled Prometheus to the side, the flames striking the spot the mech was just moments ago, turning water into steam. As Prometheus finished his roll through the water, landing on his metal feet, water draining from his metal body, Will brought Faithful to bear. He looked up at Hades as he closed his jaws, extinguishing his deadly flames.

"You defeated this guy before, what are his weaknesses?" Will asked.

Water, Prometheus said, *as you've already figured out. He has a couple soft spots, too. The throat and stomach.*

Will glanced at the beast's throat and stomach. Both were free of armor.

"A well-placed punch might stumble him enough to finish him off with the sword," Will said, strategizing.

Exactly what I was thinking, Prometheus said, sounding excited.

166

Will pushed Prometheus forward, sword at his side. Hades snarled and took a battle stance, his claws hooked and ready to dig into his oncoming opponent. Will grinned, taking pleasure in the fact that the Kaiju had no idea what was about to happen.

While Hades's eyes were locked onto Faithful, the sword the expected attacker, Will thrusted Prometheus' free hand forward, driving it into the soft flesh of the Kaiju's stomach. Hades pitched forward, a wheezing sound exiting his throat as the air was driven from his lungs. Hades dropped to his spiked knees, holding his stomach in a very human gesture of pain.

Will raised Faithful over Prometheus' head, ready to bring it down and end Hades when a shadow fell over him.

26

Nevada...

Damen Hlad, better known as Wolf, his callsign, had been through a lot in his life, but since joining the CCU, things had just gotten insane. Not only did he fight supernatural monsters, which he was one of, hence his callsign, but also aliens and Kaiju. It wasn't an easy job, but someone had to do it. And now his job was to scour an alien ship in search of the President of the United States, Marudon, and the Kaiju shutoff switch.

He led his five-person team down the large gray and gold hallway of the Plagueonian ship, trying every door they came across. So far, they've not found anything, not to mention *anyone*.

Something's not right, Wolf thought.

"Woulda thought we'd have run into some baddies by now," Eva said, stepping up next to him.

Wolf nodded his agreement.

"There is a large door ahead," Ezekiel stated. "Maybe it holds one of our objectives?"

"Only one way to find out," Wolf said, starting forward, his FN SCAR assault rifle shouldered. "Stay together. Heads on a swivel."

As they came upon the nine-foot-tall by seven-foot-wide door, it slid open, as if expecting them, darkness waiting beyond.

"I don't know about you guys, but I have a really bad feeling about this," Aaron said with an involuntary shiver.

Wolf nodded, agreeing with the young man. But they had a mission to complete, and it could possibly be beyond the door they were standing in front of.

Wolf continued forward, gun raised, his team following close behind him. As soon as they entered the room, the door slid shut behind them. Wolf squinted as the lights snapped on, his superior eyes adjusting quickly. The room was vast, filled with futuristic looking crates.

A storage room, Wolf surmised.

He almost made the mistake of lowering his weapon when a giant crate in the middle exploded with a roar. What Jeremy had come to call a *Cercope* emerged from the wreckage with a snarl. Armed Plagueonians stepped out from behind the crates around the room.

"Oh great, we stepped into a trap," Aaron groaned.

"We were bound to sooner or later," Ben said, speaking for the first time since they began their trek through the ship.

The Cercope's roar triggered the beginning of the battle, the Plagueonians opening fire on Wolf and his team. They dove to the sides, taking cover behind nearby crates. Wolf, Aaron, and Eva behind one crate, Ben and Ezekiel behind another across from them.

"Open fire!" Wolf commanded, aiming his rifle and firing off three round bursts, taking out two targets.

Gunfire and laser bolts flew as more Plagueonians dropped, angering the Cercope. It roared and charged, heading straight for the crate Wolf, Aaron, and Eva hid behind. Wolf, seeing the attack coming, tackled his team mates out of the way as the crate they were previously behind went flying. Wolf rolled to his feet and fired bullets into the Cercope's skull-like face.

"It's like a Kaiju," Ezekiel's voice came from behind the beast's gigantic form, followed by the report of rifle fire from the M-16s he and Ben were given. "Bullets won't hurt it."

"Right," Wolf muttered, slinging his SCAR over his back. He clenched his fist as the beast leaned in close with a snarl and sent it hurtling into its face. The Cercope stumbled back, dazed from the blow to its ugly face.

Wolf watched as Ben launched himself over the Cercope, sending a punch to the top of the Vexnoxtuque's head, sending the creature to the gray floor of the room.

Wolf turned to Aaron and Eva as Ezekiel skirted the Cercope and joined them. "You three take care of the Plagueonians," he said. "Ben and I will take care of the Cercope."

They nodded, taking off around the crates to engage the Plagueonians that had surrounded them.

Wolf turned back to the Cercope, Ben landing blow after blow to the monster's head. The situation reminded him of the last time he was on a Plagueonian ship, two years ago, fighting the Cyclops. Only this time, he wasn't the only non-human.

169

The Cercope hissed and roared in agitation as it tried to reach the nuisance atop its head. Wolf rushed forward, aiming for the creature's back legs. His eyes widened as one of the Cercope's massive arms came down, the monster aiming to smear him across the floor. He rolled out of the way in time to avoid the attack, the limb hitting with a loud clang of flesh on metal.

Wolf rolled back to his feet and continued the course to his target: the Cercope's back legs. He lowered his shoulder, putting all the force he accumulated into it as he struck the beast's knee. Dual crunches rang out through the alien storage room. The Cercope's wail of agony and Wolf's pained shout followed. Wolf jumped back, holding his dislocated shoulder as the Cercope fell to the ground, its knee shattered and inverted. Wolf grinned at the injury he inflicted upon the killing machine.

The rest is up to you, Wolf thought, watching as Ben ripped a spike from the creature's forehead and drove it into its blazing yellow eye. The orb erupted in a gush of yellow and white. The Cercope squealed in pain.

Wolf turned his attention to his dislocated shoulder. *This is going to hurt like a sonuvabitch*, he thought as he grasped the shoulder. He breathed in and out, deep breaths, before yanking the joint back in place with a shout.

"Fuck!" he growled, breathing heavily.

He shook off the pain and turned his attention back to Ben and the Cercope. The Cercope craned its head toward its back, its jaws snapping wildly as it tried to reach Ben, but its neck wasn't long enough to reach the Fenriri. Ben smirked at the beast, cocking his arm back and thrusting it downward with enough force to break through the Cercope's thick, armored skin, the creature's purple blood spraying all over Ben.

170

Damn, Wolf thought, vaguely remembering puncturing the skin of the Cercope that invaded the CCU headquarters. Though, the skin was its softer underbelly, he didn't doubt he could rip through the tougher, armored flesh like Ben just did.

Ben's arm wiggled around in the hole he just punched in the Cercope's flesh, searching for something. Ben's eyes lit up, finding whatever he was looking for, and pulled. The Cercope emitted a high-pitched wail that was cut short by a tearing snap as Ben pulled apart the creature's spinal cord. The creature fell to the ground, its eyes wide, its erratically rising and falling side the only movement from the beast.

The room fell silent. No gunshots. No laser blasts. Nothing.

Ezekiel, Aaron, and Eva stepped up next to Wolf as he held his aching shoulder.

"Damn," Aaron said, eyebrows raised in awe at the fallen Cercope as it breathed its last breath and fell still; dead.

A high-pitched squeal, muffled as if behind a door, caught Wolf's ears.

"You hear that?' Wolf asked turning to his team as Ben, covered in purple Cercope blood, joined them.

Ben and Ezekiel nodded while Eva and Aaron just looked at each other in confusion.

"It came from that way," Ezekiel said, looking past the crates and toward the back of the storage room. "I think I saw a door back there while we were fighting the alien soldiers."

"Lead the way," Wolf said as he heard another squeal of pain.

27

"This has got to be the longest hallway in the history of hallways," Josh groans as we make our way down the gray and gold walkway that leads to who-knows-where.

"Quiet," I growl. We've been traveling down the same hallway for the past half hour, running into nothing and only finding locked doors along the way. I don't mean to be an asshole to my friend and adopted brother, but I'm on edge and feel any noise may trigger an attack.

"Sorry," he whispers.

I turn to apologize for snapping at him when I notice something behind him, just around the curve in the walkway. I only saw a glimpse of it, but I know it's not friendly. Nothing in this ship is.

"What is it?" Mikayla asks, standing next to Josh, seeing that I got distracted by something behind him.

"I saw something," I say, raising my weapons a little higher.

"We're being stalked?" Ashley asks as she and Sasha join Josh, Mikayla, and I.

"Yeah," I say. "Just around the bend."

"Is it a Plagueonian?" Sasha asks.

"No idea. I just saw a blur."

"What do we do?" Josh asks.

"You guys stay here. Cover me. I'm going to check it out."

"Jeremy," Sasha says. "I don't think that's a good idea."

"None of this is a good idea, Sash, but we're still doing it. Cover me." I catch a glimpse of her deep frown and pleading eyes before I turn and make my way toward the bend where a possible enemy awaits.

What's her deal? I wonder, noticing her strange behavior lately. I file that question away for later when

172

we're not on an alien ship and death looms around every corner.

I round the bend, guns raised and ready to fire, but am stopped by a voice.

"Wait! Please do not shoot!" the voice is feminine and the creature has its arms raised in front of it in a non-threatening manner.

Now that I get a good look at the creature, I see its slim and curvy, like a woman, identifying its gender. Its appearance, however, is anything but. It, she, is a Plagueonian. She wears sleek, black armor that closely resembles the armor The Remnants vampires wore. Her face is visible, though. Green lights indicating the armor to be powered. Her left arm, however, is robotic.

"Why are you following us?" I ask. "From what I know, Plagueonians don't stalk. They attack."

"I'm...I'm not a Plagueonian. I'm a Hestialite," she says. "The name's Savernst."

"Savernst?" I hear Ashley say, followed by her boots clanging on metal as she runs over to me and the Hestialite still holding her hands up.

I see relief on her face as her eyes land on...Savernst.

"You know it...uh...her?" I ask her.

Ashley nods. "She was a part of the rebellion against Echidna two years ago."

"Ah, miss Ashley," Savernst says with a smile, lowering her arms.

I lower my guns, still uneasy, but trusting my teammate.

"You still haven't answered my question," I say. "Why are you following us?"

"Surveillance," Savernst says. "Making sure you were not one of...*them*."

"I don't like the sound of that," Josh says as he and the rest of my team joins us.

173

"Them?" I ask.

"Test subjects," Savernst says. "For their experiments."

"They have human prisoners?" I ask, a new objective showing itself to me.

"They're probably not human anymore," Savernst says, shattering any hope I might have had of rescuing those taken by the savage owners of the space craft we are aboard.

"We have to go," Savernst says. "They might have sent them after us already."

"Oh great," Josh groans. "Now we have to worry about people-turned-monsters? Lovely."

"Let's just get moving," I say, turning back the way we were heading before. "Do you know where they are holding President Scott and Marudon?"

"Marudon is near the back of the ship. I believe your friends were heading the right way. They'll find her," Savernst replies. "Your President Scott is in the throne room, not too far from the ship's control room. We're going the right way. Just continue on this path. They're leading you into a trap, you know."

"It had crossed my mind," I say.

We walk in silence down the hallway for another twenty minutes, still finding locked doors and no Plagueonian activity.

We're definitely being led into a trap, I think.

We continue around another bend that leads into a door. I stop and turn to my group, which now includes an eight-foot alien.

"The throne room?" I ask, hitching a thumb at the gray door.

Savernst nods.

"Echidna is behind that door then, huh?" Ashley says.

"And Typhon," Sasha says.

174

"Probably your human experiment pals, too," Josh says.

"They've been on us for the last ten minutes," Savernst says.

My head snaps back the way we came, searching for anything unfriendly looking.

"What are you talking about?" I ask with a growl.

And then I see it. Movement just beyond the bend we rounded to reach where we are. I didn't see much more than a thin, inhuman frame. I barely notice raising my Desert Eagles. The rest of my team, Savernst included, raise their own weapons.

"Why didn't you say something?" I snap.

"I did not want to cause a panic," the Hestialite says.

I kind of understand where she is coming from, but I'd prefer to have known we were being stalked by a pack of ravenous science experiments.

"Everyone get ready," I say.

As soon as I say something, the first creature sprints from around the bend and toward us. It's recognizable as human in shape, but that's it. The rest of it is very non-human. It's covered in thick, black flesh. Its mouth is full of sharp fangs. Its glowing orange eyes are wide and wild. Long obsidian claws extend from its finger tips; its back legs were long and powerful like its arms, the toes also sporting long claws.

I raise my Desert Eagles and pull the triggers, taking off half of the creature's face and an arm. The creature falls to the gray floor, purple blood gushing from its wounds. It falls still; dead.

These creatures might have been human once, but they aren't anymore. Technically, they aren't zombies, but I can only come up with one name for what I just saw: Vrykolaka, the Greek word for zombie and, interestingly, vampire. That's a mouthful, though, so I think I'll go with the shortened version: Vryko.

Vrykos fill the hallway behind the one brazen enough to charge us alone, claws wriggling and jaws gnashing, ready to rip and tear.

"Open fire!" I command.

The hallway fills with the sound of gunfire as we engage the charging Vrykos.

POSEIDON

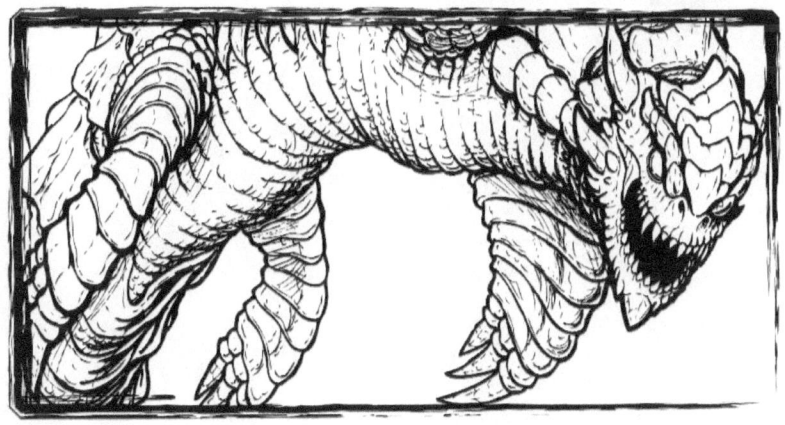

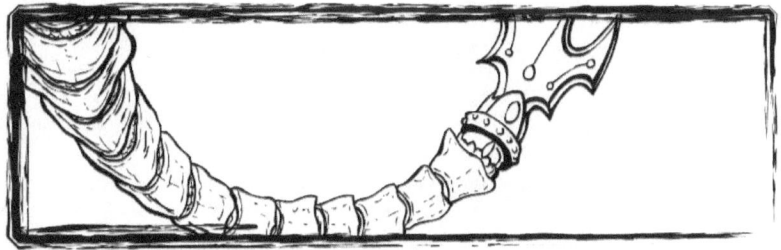

INTERLUDE V

Ancient History...

Thel-Shuum stepped Prometheus onto dry land, what would be known as the Parcel Islands, after burying Hades at the bottom of the South China Sea. He could feel his exhaustion growing. He hadn't slept in days. It's all he wanted.

I can't, he reminded himself. *There is work to be done. Just hang on a few hours more...*

Incoming! Prometheus exclaimed, waking Thel's mind.

"From where...oh," he said, easily finding the fin-like structure slicing through the water, heading straight for him. "Looks like the fight decided to come to us."

The creature leapt from the water, arcing through the air toward him, jaws agape, sharp teeth reaching for him. Thel reached out Prometheus' metal hands, catching the beast.

What have you done with them?! the creature demanded. Thel recognized the fish-like monstrosity to be Poseidon.

"The same thing that's going to happen to you," Thel replied.

Poseidon roared, jaws wide, saliva spattering the robot's face.

That's what you think! Poseidon remarked.

Hull breach! Prometheus reported. *Lower back.*

Poseidon's tail had snaked around, the trident attached to the end of his tail piercing the armor on Prometheus's lower back. Thel set Prometheus into a spin, letting go of the beast and sending the Vexnoxtuque flying, the trident blade ripping from the mech's body. Poseidon splashed down, righting himself in the water and surging back toward Prometheus.

"Ready the tasers," Thel commanded.

Tasers ready, Prometheus said, the devices emerging from a compartment on the robot's arms, locking in place in front of its fists. Electricity sparked between the two prongs at the end of the devices.

Thel reeled Prometheus' arm back as Poseidon exploded from the water, thrusting his arm forward. The taser connected with the side of the fish beast's armored head, electricity shooting into it, eliciting a cry of pain from the beast and throwing him away. He splashed back into the water, disappearing beneath the churning waves.

Thel scanned the water's surface, waiting for Poseidon to surface again. He was surprised to find the attack come from behind him. Poseidon rammed his head into Prometheus' back, where his trident blade had struck earlier, throwing the mech forward. Water washed over the robot as he splashed into the water, sinking beneath the waves.

Prometheus' metal feet hit the dirt covered ground deep under the water. Fish and other marine animals scattered, frightened of the giant robot that had invaded their home. Visibility was scarce; what little light was left in the dusk sky diffused by the water. A compartment on either side of Prometheus' head snapped open, beams of light cutting through the dark liquid, allowing him more visibility. As soon as the lights snapped on, he was greeted by Poseidon's open maw.

Thel shouted in surprise as Poseidon's jaws clamped down on Prometheus's metal head, the sound of rending metal ringing inside of the cockpit he sat in. The spotlights illuminated the monster's gullet. Thel grabbed ahold of the beast's throat, squeezing. Poseidon roared, the sound muffled by the water, bubbles erupting from his mouth, releasing his grip on Prometheus' head. Thel engaged the thrusters, pushing the robot away from the monster. Poseidon glowered at him.

You have no chance, Thel, Poseidon said. *You're on my turf. I have the advantage.*

Thel raised Prometheus' fists, the tasers having retreated into their compartments, useless underwater.

We need to finish this fast, Prometheus urged. *Or at the very least get above water. The head has been compromised. It's only a matter of time before the pressure gets to us.*

"Understood," Thel said. "Any ideas?"

The Ion Can-

"Non-lethal options, Thes."

The AI was quiet for a moment before replying.

Maybe a concussive blow to the head would stun him long enough to administer a cryo weapon, Prometheus replied.

"Alright," Thel said. "Prepare the elbow jet."

Roger.

Poseidon roared, his flipper-like arms and legs flailing madly, his tail whipping back and forth, propelling him forward in a charge. Thel reeled Prometheus' arm back.

"Wait for it," he whispered.

Poseidon surged forward, only a hundred feet away, his mouth open, unlucky sea life being sucked inside as he breathed in to emit another roar.

"Wait for it…"

Poseidon was almost upon them, only a couple dozen feet, jaws open as wide as they could go, ready to crush Prometheus' head.

"Now!"

The jet on Prometheus' elbow engaged, putting more power into the punch that connected with the front of Poseidon's face, the creature's charge coming to a halt. The creature fell still, unconscious.

For now, Thel reminded himself, working fast.

He plucked a cryo grenade from the compartment in the robot's leg, opening Poseidon's maw and depositing the device inside, armed. As soon as he did, Poseidon shook his head and snarled.

What did you just...? Poseidon hissed, stopping, looking confused. His mouth opened, blue bubbles erupting from his throat. *What...is...this...?*

Thel could tell Poseidon was fighting it...and losing. His eyes fluttered before finally closing, the creature falling still. Thel breathed a sigh of relief.

Hurry, Thel, Prometheus said. *We can't endure the pressure much longer.*

"Right," Thel said. "To land we go."

He grabbed ahold of Poseidon's comatose body, taking it to where the beast would lay for all of eternity. At least, that was what Thel had hoped...

28

Hong Kong…

Will turned away from the hurt and still recovering Hades, spinning Prometheus around in time to catch a glimpse of sharp metal being thrust toward him. He dove Prometheus to the side, avoiding the strike, the weapon finding Hades' armored shoulder. Hades roared in pain as the owner of the weapon splashed into the water next to the devil Kaiju, retracting the weapon, which disappeared beneath the water with the rest of the creature.

You fool! Hades hissed at the newcomer.

A massive, horned, armored face slid from the water, eyes glowing a sinister red. Its armor plated back appeared next, a fin-like spike extending from the plate in the middle of the creature's back. Its skin was a vibrant blue. The rest of the beast remained underwater.

Poseidon, Will thought.

Poseidon roared at Prometheus, spittle flinging from his fanged mouth. Poseidon glanced at his brother, sneered, and turned back to their common enemy.

"Think we can handle two Kaiju," Will asked.

You've trained for this kind of situation since facing the Titans, Prometheus said. *You got this.*

"Right."

Will felt himself smirk as he put Prometheus into a battle stance, sword at the ready. Hades got to his feet, stepping up next to his brother, Poseidon. The two Kaijus charged as one. The pods built into Prometheus' shoulder pylons came to life, firing hundreds of plasma rockets at the charging gods. Purple explosions rocked the monsters' bodies, slowing their advance, but not stopping it. The Kaijus continued forward.

Hades continued coming straight at Prometheus while Poseidon broke away, surging around to flank Will. Poseidon reached Prometheus first, the same weapon used to attack him the first time the creature appeared exploding from the water behind the Kaiju. Will caught it just before it pierced Prometheus' side in the mech's metal hand, seeing the weapon for what it was.

A trident.

Makes sense, Will thought. *It's Poseidon's symbol after all.*

Unlike the mythical Poseidon, who carried a trident atop a staff, the trident on the Kaiju version looked to be surgically attached to the end of the monster's tail. Hades arrived next, slashing at Prometheus with his clawed arms. Will blocked the attack with Prometheus' sword. Hades pulled his hand back with a shriek as it struck the energy blade.

Will spun Prometheus, swinging Poseidon around into its sibling. Both Kaijus splashed into the water. Before Poseidon went under, Will caught a glance of his underside. It had four, stocky legs that looked like fins. In fact, Poseidon as a whole was built like a fish.

A true god of the sea, Will thought.

Hades rose from the water with a roar. Poseidon, however, never rose. Will didn't think the creature was dead, though. Water was its domain. It was probably lurking just beneath the surface, waiting to strike.

Hades opened his jaws wide, flames erupting from his maw. Will quickly activated Prometheus' energy shield. The shield protected him from the scorching flames. Seeing his attack having no effect, Hades cut off his attack.

A looming shadow revealed another reason: he was covering for his sibling's attack.

Poseidon's trident found Prometheus' side. Luckily, it didn't strike anything major. Will turned on the beast, yanking the trident from Prometheus' side as Poseidon dug his teeth into the mech's shoulder. Will raised Faithful, ready to use it to pry Poseidon loose, but the robot's arm was caught.

Will struggled to free Prometheus' arm as Poseidon continued to tear into the robot's shoulder, but Hades was strong and held the arm from moving. Two cannons emerged from the side of Prometheus' shoulder pylon, taking aim and firing yellow laser blasts into Hades face. Hades snarled and bucked, letting go of Prometheus' arm to shield his face.

With the arm now free, Will swung out with Faithful. There was a moment of resistance, but the energy composed blade found flesh and passed through, severing the Devil Kaiju in half. Purple blood sprayed and organs flew everywhere.

Poseidon stopped his assault on Prometheus' arm at the sight of his sibling cut in half, both halves landing in the water with a splash. Poseidon wailed in agony, leaping from where it was perched upon Prometheus, landing in the water.

Will tracked the creature's shadow beneath the water's surface with Prometheus' enhanced vision. Poseidon was circling him, trying to find a blind spot. Will didn't take his eyes off the fish-like Kaiju circling him like a hungry shark.

After a few circles, Poseidon exploded from the water, jaws agape. Will dodged the attack, the fish-beast sailing just feet from the robot's metal chest. Poseidon splashed back into the water, just feet from where Hades fell. Will pushed Prometheus forward, the mech sloshing through the water.

"Woah!" Will shouted, surprised.

Hades's top half had sprung from the water, latching onto Prometheus with his powerful arms.

"How the hell are you still alive?" Will growled at the Devil Kaiju.

Will drove Prometheus' fist into Hades' side, the Kaiju holding fast despite being severed in half and losing hundreds of gallons of blood.

It's driven by pure rage, Will thought, seeing Hades's wild orange eyes.

Of course, Prometheus replied. *Rage is what compels the Vexnoxtuques.*

Will rolled his eyes, mentally. *I know. This isn't my first encounter with a Vexnoxtuque.*

The AI remained quiet.

Will delivered two more blows to Hades's side. The pain was evident in the Kaiju's facial expression, but he never let go.

Will snapped Prometheus' head up, realizing Hades was a distraction.

Poseidon's armored fin cut through the water, barreling straight for Prometheus. It slid beneath the water for a moment before the Kaiju exploded from the water again, jaws wide, tail cocked back and ready to thrust the trident at the end into something vital.

Will couldn't move the robot with Hades locking it in place so he did the only other thing he could think of. He held Faithful out, the crackling green blade of energy pointed at the airborne Kaiju sailing toward him.

Poseidon's red eyes widened, realizing what was about to happen before it did. The energy blade impaled Poseidon's face, his jaws still open wide, the creature's momentum continuing to move the creature forward, his teeth reaching the sword's hilt.

Will deactivated Faithful's blade, Poseidon's corpse falling into the water, turning it an inky purple, the sword's hilt folding up and disappearing back inside the compartment in the mech's palm. Will craned Prometheus' head down, looking at Hades' torso still clinging to the robot's legs. Hades roared, trying to sound menacing, but it was weak. The beast was fading, its life limited.

Will reached down with Prometheus' metal hand, latching onto the dying Kaiju's face. Will peeled the creature from the giant robot's legs, its earlier strength sapped. With another weak roar, Hades disappeared beneath the water, dying next to his sibling.

It looks like...you...win..., Hades' voice came.

Will felt himself take a deep breath and let it out slowly.

"Alright," he said. "Where to next?"

ARES

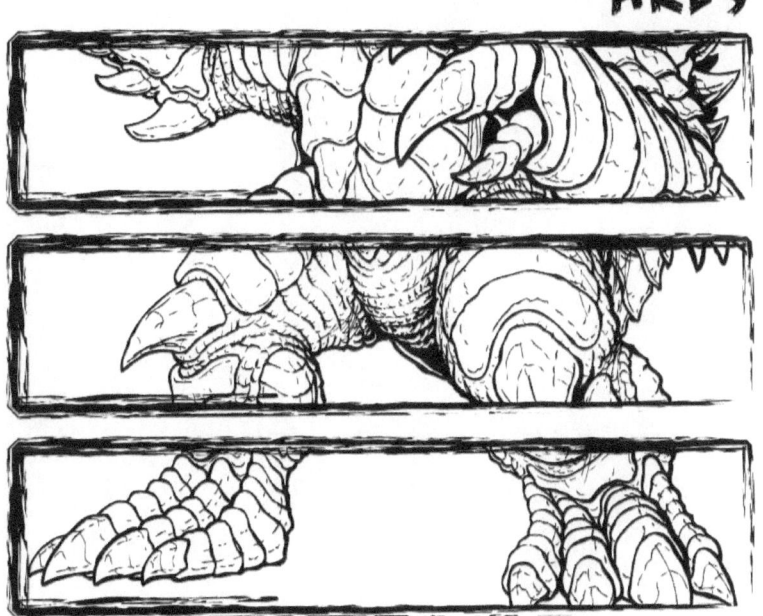

INTERLUDE VI

Ancient History...

The god of the sea was imprisoned on land, an island, far from where Thel-Shuum had fought and defeated the fish-beast. He looked up into the night sky, stars twinkling above him, with a frown.

Home is up there somewhere, he thought. *Destroyed. Taken over. My species extinct...*

Dal-Un...

The thoughts of his homeworld, taken over by the Plagueonians, and the loss of the one he was supposed to protect, saddened him. It's the reason he was in the position he was now, fighting Vexnoxtuque on Earth. He shook the thoughts from his mind, along with the encroaching advance of exhaustion, his body trying to shut down, getting back to the task at hand.

Multiple Vexnoxtuque have been detected, Prometheus reported, displaying a world map with red flashing dots indicating where each beast had surfaced. There were four left.

Almost done, he told himself.

Which one should we go after? The AI asked.

"Surprise me," Thel replied.

Roger that.

A hum filled the cockpit as the teleportation system activated. Then they were gone in a flash of blue light. One moment they were on the island they buried Poseidon, the next they were on a barren, snowy terrain, snow falling from the dawning sky. He turned his attention from the sky to the Vexnoxtuque.

Another barren, snowy land? Thel thought, confused as to why this would be a choice for the Vexnoxtuque to start the extermination of humanity.

He found the answer as he took in the form of the monster occupying the land. Ares, the supposed 'god of war', turned toward him, his green eyes squinting at Prometheus. Chunks were missing from his armored flesh and gashes covered his body.

He came to rest and heal...

Thel? What are you doing here? Ares asked, his voice weak.

When Thel didn't answer, Ares tilted his head to the side, his green eyes still squinting at the robot.

And why have many of my brothers and sisters just...disappeared? Ares asked.

Thel's only response was to draw the hard-light sword. Ares reeled back with a hiss.

I see now, Ares growled, raising his arm, which ended in a surgically attached sword.

They charged at each other, swords raised. They swung in unison, hard-light blade striking metal. Thel was surprised when his hard-light blade didn't cleave through Ares' sword.

What's it made of? he wondered, but shook his head at the question. *A question for another day.*

He had more important matters to deal with.

Ares roared, apparently not as weak as he seemed before, sounding angry. He increased the pressure, the blade of his sword grinding against the hard-light blade of Prometheus', a crackling sound filling the air. Thel felt Prometheus' metal feet slide as the Vexnoxtuque did. Thel twirled the robot to the side, Ares stumbling forward, his sword digging into snowy earth. He whirled on Prometheus with an angry snarl, his eyes blazing with anger.

Go for his legs, Prometheus said.

Thel turned his attention to the creature's legs, powerful and armored, ending in four clawed toes. He knew what Prometheus was suggesting. The creature was bulky, mostly up top, making him top heavy. If his legs were taken out, he'd fall, giving them time to hit him with a cryo weapon.

Thel retracted the hard-light sword and produced a new weapon, it extending, holding it in two hands. A hard-light blade flickered to life at the end of the staff, completing the spear. Ares scoffed at the sight, seeing the weapon as weak and unintimidating.

That's his mistake, Thel thought.

Ares charged, sword raised, ready to cleave off Prometheus' limbs. Thel avoided the creature's attack, spinning and bringing the pole of the spear into the back of the war god's legs. Ares squealed in pain as his knees buckled and he fell to his hands and knees. Thel brought the pole down hard on the base of Ares' head, knocking the creature unconscious. Ares slumped to the cold, snowy earth.

Well, Prometheus said. *That was much easier than I thought it'd be.*

"Indeed," Thel agreed, looking down at the fallen Vexnoxtuque. "Then again, he was severely injured. He was worn out from the Titanomanchy."

True. That could account for such an easy take down.

"Now then," Thel said as he reached down and grasped Ares by the giant spikes protruding from the monster's shoulders. "Time to take care of this guy."

After dragging Ares to the spot he picked as his burial site, he administered a cryo grenade to the beast. Then he began to dig.

29

Anchorage, Alaska…

Marugrah rose from the cold water of the Shelikof Strait, blooming light from the city catching his attention. His target had decimated most of the city since its release from within the Chugach National Forest where it was imprisoned millennia ago, unleashing its rage upon humanity.

Marugrah made his way from the freezing waters and onto the beach that surrounded the city of Anchorage. He felt compelled to roar and announce his presence to his enemy, but the more rational part of his mind told him to keep quiet and surprise his enemy. He obeyed the logical thought and kept quiet, stomping his way toward his enemy. He could see the creature in the distance.

It was bulky and looked to be hunched over. The Kaiju was heavily armored, giant armored spikes jutting from its shoulders. Spikes covered its back, too. Helmet-like armor covered the creature's head, giving it a warrior's aura. The giant, metal sword surgically attached to its right wrist certainly added to the fact that the beast was a warrior.

Not just any warrior, Marugrah thought. *Ares. The Greek god of war.*

Ares' left arm ended in a three fingered, clawed hand, untampered with by the Plagueonians that created him. He stood on two, armored legs that ended in four clawed toes. His thick skin was a grayish-brown in color. He was certainly a sight to behold.

Marugrah entered Anchorage's ruins, sensing no life around him, his massive body steaming from the heat it generated reacting to the cold, Alaskan air. He noticed a tiny snow flake float past his eye. Then another. And another. It had begun to snow.

The frozen water falling from the sky wouldn't bother the massive Marugrah, nor would it affect the coming battle.

Marugrah dropped to all fours, making his way through the ruined city as stealthily as a giant monster could. And, it worked. Ares continued his rampage, unaware of Marugrah's approach. With a mighty roar, Ares swept his sword tipped arm through the city, tearing apart buildings and probably chopping apart whoever was unlucky enough to be in the path.

Once he reached Ares, Marugrah stood on his back legs again, grabbing ahold of the giant spikes jutting from the Kaiju's shoulders. Ares roared in surprise, trying to crane his head around to see his attacker, his jaws snapping as he did.

Marugrah held the spikes tight, bringing his tail around, the club at the end connecting with the war god's armored stomach. Marugrah let go of the towering spikes as Ares pitched forward.

Anger overcame pain as Ares whipping around at Marugrah, swiping his massive sword at the guardian beast. Marugrah jumped back, the tip of the sword grazing his armor-plated stomach.

Ares roared, opened his jaws wide, and thrusted his head forward. Marugrah, seeing the attack coming, lashed out his arm, grabbing Ares by the throat and keeping the Kaiju from digging his fangs into his throat, the war god's intended target. Ares' jaws snapped at Marugrah, eager to dig his teeth into his flesh.

He's not very smart, Marugrah thought.

Marugrah brought his knee up into Ares' gut repeatedly. Drool mixed with purple blood gushed from Ares' mouth, the pain seeping through his rage. Ares' mind started working; thinking. Despite being raging killing machines, once a Vexnoxtuque started thinking, they could be quite smart. And deadly.

Ares snapped his head up, blood and spit dripping from his maw. Marugrah could see the gears turning behind Ares's blazing green eyes.

That's not good...

With his eyes locked on Ares', Marugrah didn't notice the Kaiju move his arm, thrusting his sword into the dragon beast's foot. Marugrah threw his head back and roared in agony. Ares' sword withdrew from Marugrah's foot with a slurp, both beasts back pedaling away from each other.

The two Kaijus sized each other up, snow landing in the crags and folds of their armored skin, melting almost immediately and turning to steam due to the enormous amount of heat their bodies emitted. Marugrah glanced down at his injured foot seeing green blood pulling around his foot. Marugrah sneered, anger seeping into his mind.

Over the last two years being a giant monster, Marugrah had tried to control his rage and the darkness it brought and in some instances, channel it against his enemies.

His fury made him stronger.

He invited the anger in.

Marugrah shifted his gaze from his injured foot to his enemy waiting for him to make his next move. Marugrah sneered at Ares, getting no reaction from the Greek god. His sneer turned into a rage filled roar. Ares met Marugrah's roar. Both creatures charged at each other, teeth bared, claws hooked.

Marugrah ducked as Ares swung his sword at him, the weapon sailing just inches from his armored back. As the sword passed overhead, Marugrah lashed out with his claws, raking them across Ares' knees, scraping away armor and flesh. Ares grunted in agitation, kicking out at Marugrah, catching the dragon beast in the chest. The kick sent Marugrah stumbling backward, trying desperately not to lose his footing. He knew that if he did, Ares would be upon him double time and he'd not stand a chance against the hulking beast.

Marugrah managed to stay on his feet, leaning back to avoid Ares' swung sword arm. He was much more agile than the bulky Ares, almost like a ferret to a human. Ares snarled in frustration, swinging his sword again. Marugrah avoided the strike. Marugrah jumped back, out of Ares' reach. Ares stood his ground, cocking his head to the side as he stared at Marugrah. He could see the wheels turning behind the beast's glowing green eyes again.

A shriek turned both Kaijus' eyes upward. A winged creature circled above them. And then, in a flash of blue light, the creature fell from the sky.

30

Nevada...

Vrykos drop with every pull of the trigger. But with every Vryko that fell, three take its place. They swarm into the hallway, blocking any way of escape.

There's hundreds of them, I think, aiming, and taking down two more Vrykos with my twin Desert Eagles.

My team and I pump round after round into the Vryko horde, dropping countless numbers of the monsters, but so many still remained.

"There are too many of them!" Josh says, yelling to be heard over the gunfire.

"I know!" I growl, dropping six more Vrykos with three trigger pulls from each gun. "We need to find a way through that door!"

"I'm on it!" I hear Savernst say.

I don't take my eyes off the Vryko horde, and only stop pulling the triggers to reload. I just have to trust that Savernst is working on the door. We don't have much longer before the Vrykos overwhelm us. They're getting uncomfortably close. Only feet away now...

Only a few mags left...

"Got it!" Savernst calls out.

"Everyone in!" I yell, emptying my guns' clips and turning toward the door, seeing my team running through the massive door. I run, making my way through the door after my team. Once I'm through, Savernst goes to work on a panel next to the door. Past the door, the Vryko horde closes in. I reload, firing .50 caliber rounds through the door. My team follows my lead, firing their weapons through the door and into the Vryko horde.

The door clunks and slides closed, hundreds of thunks sounding from the other side as the Vrykos try to claw their way through the door to get at their meals.

I sigh a breath of relief, surprised adrenaline hadn't taken hold of my system during the fight.

"That was intense," Mikayla says, hands on her knees, breathing heavily.

"Yeah, it was," I say, holstering my weapons.

I turn around, taking in my team...and the room beyond. Its sizeable and royal looking in an alien way. A... well the only way I can describe it is a throne, gray and gold, decorated with jewels and intricate carving sits on the far side of the room, an armored figure occupying it.

"Echidna," Ashley growls.

A familiar, cloaked figure steps out from behind the throne, smiling wickedly beneath the hood covering its face, teeth sharp, the canines longer than the rest. It pulled its hood back, revealing a pale face covered in intricate swirls.

"Well, if it isn't the Lycan boy and the Halfbreed. This certainly is a pleasant surprise," the figure says.

"Typhon," I growl, my fists clenched in anger.

Typhon smiles wider. "So you found out my real name, huh? That it's not really Dracula?" He laughs.

"Enough talking," Echidna says, standing from her throne. "We all know why you're here."

She reaches behind her throne, sliding something out from behind it. The sound of metal screeching on metal makes us cover our ears and close our eyes. When we open them, we see our objective strapped to a table in front of Echidna.

"Mr. President!" Mikayla exclaims.

"You shouldn't have come for me," he says, looking defeated.

"We couldn't just leave you in their hands," Sasha says, gripping her rifle tighter.

"I know," he says with a slight smile. "You're good people. Even if some of you aren't exactly...people."

"Were my demands not clear?" Echidna says, breaking up a budding moment. "I believe I said for no one to come for him."

"Well, guess what, ugly? We don't listen so well," Josh says, defiant.

"I see that," Echidna says, something moving behind her back. A tentacle-like appendage snakes around from behind her, toward President Scott. The end opens, revealing a mouth filled with razor sharp teeth.

I act fast, drawing one of my Desert Eagles and firing it one handed, the wrist brace I wear saving it from being broken from the gun's kick. The bullet severs the limb, embedding itself in the throne behind it. Black sprays from the wound, coating President Scott.

"Argh!" Echidna roars, hunching over in pain, her breathing heavy. "That…was a…big mistake!"

"Humans," Typhon scoffs, his boney arms crossed. "You act so tough, yet your bodies are so frail."

"It's the only way we survive," I snap at the vampire king.

Typhon chuckles. "Well, you won't be surviving this encounter, I promise you that."

Savernst steps up next to me, laser rifle pointed at our enemies. Echidna's eyes light up at the sight of the Hestialite.

"Ah," she says, a twinge of pain in her voice. "Savernst. It's been too long. I see your *generous* leader Tsuzar has provided you with a new arm." She spits the word 'generous' out in a way that makes me think of as disgust.

"He's done more than provide me with a new arm. He's taught me a great many things, one of which is how to fight," Savernst growls. "This encounter will not end up like our last."

Echidna laughs. "We'll see about that."

Both monsters charge.

I draw my second Desert Eagle and start pulling their triggers, aiming for Echidna's legs. Savernst, seeing what I'm doing, follows my lead. My team opens fire on the charging Typhon. Echidna reaches Savernst and I, clenching a massive fist and thrusting it at us. Savernst and I jump out of the way, barely avoiding the fist as it connects with the gold and gray floor, leaving a deep dent. I roll to my feet and look up just in time to avoid one of her tentacles, mouth open wide, ready to devour me. I draw a knife and swipe it at the tentacle as it tries

200

to pull back, leaving a deep gash in its flesh. Echidna just grunts in pain, her attention on Savernst.

"Last time, I took your arm," Echidna says. "Shall I take your other?"

Savernst chuckled. "You can try if you like, but I guarantee it will not happen."

"You're that confident in your newfound abilities?"

"You're damn right I am!"

Savernst charges at the Plagueonian Queen, pulling the trigger on her laser rifle, sending laser bolts into the abomination. With her back to me, I can see Echidna's tentacles snaking around toward the approaching Savernst, maws open and ready to rip and tear.

No you don't! I think, gripping my knife tighter in my gloved hand as I lunge at Echidna's back. I work fast, slicing apart the bases of her tentacles, screeching sounds emanating from the mouths on the ends. Echidna just growls, used to the pain. However, she doesn't acknowledge me, keeping it on Savernst.

I jump from Echudna's back, turning my attention to my team and their fight against Typhon. Typhon swipes his gnarly arms at Sasha, who avoids the strike, firing a barrage of bullets into the limb. Typhon snarls, showing no reaction to the damage the bullets did to is arm. The rest of my team surround the vampire king, firing at him with their weapons.

My gaze turns back to Echidna and Savernst. Echidna swipes her clawed hands at Savernst who bounds in the air to avoid the strike. She lands on Echidna's extended arm, firing her weapon into the Plagueonian Queen's helmeted face.

There is only one way we're getting through this alive…Wolf, hurry up, my friend.

31

Wolf followed Ezekiel to the door he saw at the back of the alien storage room they had just fought an intense battle in. The screeching grew louder with each step they took toward the door, loud enough for the others of his team to hear it.

"That has to be Marudon," Aaron said.

"Sounds like she's in some major pain," Eva said, sounding extremely pissed. She was the one who had known Marudon the longest, after all. After coming to Earth, Eva was the one who found her. The one who brought her to the CCU. They were like Will and Marugrah. Best friends.

"We can't lose her. She's a vital source to the CCU," Wolf said, rushing forward, the door sliding open when he got close. He stepped through the doorway, rifle raised and trained on a menacing looking figure leaning over something. The rest of the room looked like a jail or holding room, with energy barriers to keep the prisoners locked up instead of iron bars. Wolf couldn't see inside to see if the cells were occupied.

"What is it?" the figure asked, its voice sinister sounding, still focused on whatever it was leaned over.

"We're looking for someone. A small, red saurian creature named Marudon. You know where I can find her?" Wolf asked, a smirk on his lips.

The figure turned toward him, a sneer on its boney face. The armor it wore looked familiar, bearing a resemblance to the Kaiju Zorax. A long cape flowed from his back, looking a little like Zorax's wings.

"I'm surprised, really, that you were able to get past my guards. Especially the Vexnoxtuque," the Plagueonian said.

"It might have been hard if we were regular humans," Wolf replied.

The Plagueonian tilted his head to the side. "No, you're not are you? Well, two of you are. But not you and the other two. What are you?"

Without answering, Ezekiel rushed forward, sword claw formed around his hand. He swung the blood comprised weapon at the Plagueonian, connecting with the alien's armored side. The war monging alien grinned fiendishly.

"So it's a fight you want?" the Plagueonian asked. "You don't even know my name." He plucked Ezekiel from the ground and flung the ghoul as he shouted, "It's Thorath!"

Aaron and Eva opened fire with their weapons as Ben and Wolf charged at Thorath. Wolf caught a glimpse of what he was hunched over when they entered the room: Marudon. She was strapped to a table, her body covered in cuts, gashes and blue blood.

"Watch your fire!" Wolf yelled. "Don't hit Marudon!"

Wolf rushed forward, firing his rifle at Thorath, distracting him. While Thorath had his attention on Wolf, his energy shield protecting him from the soldier's bullets, Ben flanked the Plagueonian. Ben charged, tackling Thorath. The larger Plagueonian's feet slid across the floor, strong enough to match the Fenriri's strength. Thorath smiled, wide and wicked. He heaved, flinging the Fenriri away. Smile still on his face, he turned to Wolf who had stopped his charge, his rifle silent.

"In case you haven't figured it out yet, I'm no ordinary Plagueonian," Thorath said, thrusting his hands in the air as if he were praising the heavens. "I'm like my Queen... evolved. Part Vexnoxtuque."

Awh shit, Wolf thought, grinding his teeth in frustration.

While Thorath might be part Vexnoxtuque, he was nothing like them…well, other than the natural armor and enhanced physical strength.

Which means he'll be harder to take down…

Before Wolf's brain could process it, Thorath's arm shot forward, his boney fingers wrapping around his waist, and plucking him from the floor. Wolf shouted in surprise as he was sent flying through the air. A shock rocketed through his body as his arc through the air came to an end. He fell to the floor, face first, from the energy barrier that arrested his fall and shocked him upon impact. Eva and Aaron appeared at his side, helping him to his feet.

Thorath's chuckle filled their ears, turning their eyes toward the monstrosity. He stood, his fingers twitching with excitement. Ezekiel and Ben had begun to flank the Plagueonian, stopping when his voice boomed through the room.

"Oh my. It's really excited," Thorath says, his face in an expression of ecstasy. "I've not felt it like this since the Titanomanchy! Not even two years ago, during the invasion of Earth was it this active."

He looks around at the five blank faces around him, with a wicked grin.

"You see," he says, "I'm more than my Queen. While she experimented upon herself with the early Vexnoxtuque serum, to make herself more powerful, the serum I was given is different. Even different from what Plague was given. It took me years to fully revert back to my Plagueonian form after my first transformation during the Titanomanchy."

Thorath reached up, lifting the helmet from his head, revealing his bald, skull-like face, smile still wide on his

204

weird alien lips. "I am your judge…your juror…your executioner!"

His eyeballs bulged, bursting from their sockets, held aloft by gross, veiny tendrils. Tentacles, the bottoms covered in sharp hooks, exploded from his mouth as the flesh on his face rippled and distorted.

The hell is going on…?

Thorath's body expanded, revealing more horrific features as his transformation continued. Spikes, armor, a tail, and two weird tentacle-like appendages protruding from his back. Within minutes, Thorath was no longer himself. No longer a Plagueonian. He was something else.

He's a Vexnoxtuque, Wolf thought.

Thorath threw his new ugly face back and roared, terrifying and feral. Next came his voice, deep and throaty.

"I…am…your doom!"

32

I charge at the beast known as Echidna. As much as I'd like to be taking on Typhon, as he is the asshole responsible for ruining my life and leaving me a supernatural being, I know that Echidna is the real threat. Or, at the very least, if we take her out, the Plagueonians will give up…I hope. Echidna's eyes flick toward me for a moment before turning back to Severnst, whom is currently firing her laser rifle at the Plagueonian Queen.

Echidna rips a piece of metal from the wall that she uses as a shield against Savernst's laser bolts. Shielded from one enemy, she turns to me. Her words stop me in my tracks.

"Typhon told me about you," she says. "The Lycan boy. You rattled a lot of cages two years ago, before we arrived on Earth."

They still think I'm a Lycan, I realize. *Let's keep it that way...*

"What's it to you?" I snap.

She smiles, sinister and wicked. "It means that if you scared them, and even took out Typhon, not to mention Azrael, you're strong. And I like challenges."

She shoves, throwing her makeshift shield at Savernst like a Frisbee, the sharp metal meant to cut her down, but she dives out of the way of the flung metal. Echidna turns toward me, fists clenched, ready for a fight.

If it's a fight you want, I think, *it's a fight you'll get!*

I charge at the Plagueonian Queen, drawing my modified Desert Eagles, pressing the buttons that activates their transformation from guns to swords. Echidna shows no reaction to the weapons or my charge, holding her ground. I leap into the air, weapons to my sides, aimed for her exposed neck.

They never make contact.

One of her snakes sneak up on me, now fully regenerated from being chopped off, its snout like a battering ram to my side. I tumble through the air, landing hard on the unforgiving gray and gold floor. I get to my feet, Yin and Yang still gripped tightly in my hands. I stumble to my feet, catching a glimpse of the battle with Typhon. Sasha squares off with the Vampire King, opting to use her bare hands to pummel the abomination. But none of the punches she throws hits their target. Behind her, the rest of the team are caught in a firefight with vampires wearing the same black armor as before, minus the helmets since there's no sunlight to hurt them.

I turn back to my enemy, Echidna, fearing for the rest of my team. I knew from the beginning this mission was suicidal. I just thought we'd stand a bit more of a chance.

I stumble to my feet to find Echidna closing in on me, fist reeled back, ready to shoot forward and turn me into bloody chunks. I dive to the side, barely avoiding the attack. I roll to my feet, body aching, mind sharp.

"You won't be able to defeat us in your human form," Echidna says, pulling her fist from the dent in the metal floor, where I was standing just moments ago. "The weapons in your hands will not hurt me."

"What's your point?" I growl.

"You're holding back. I thought you were going to be a challenge but…it's so human of you. You're ashamed of your other half. Your Lycan form."

"I might have been ashamed of it at one point, but not now. Not anymore. I embrace it."

"Then why are you holding back? Come at me with all your might, warrior!" She squints at me. "Oh, I see. You're afraid of something."

I sneer at her, taking a battle stance, Yin and Yang to my sides, ready to rush at my enemy.

Echidna chuckles. "There's something you're not telling us, isn't there?"

I just continue to glare at her, silent.

She smiles, wide and wicked. "I intend to find out what you're hiding!"

Echidna charges, the snakes protruding from her back writhing with frantic energy, jaws opening and closing. I notice the snakes that make up her toes exhibiting the same behavior as her massive feet pound toward me, reverberating off the metal floor. Laser bolts stagger her as Savernst fires her plasma rifle at the Plagueonian

Queen. I look her way, finding the Hestialite waving me over. I run over to her as she covers my retreat.

"Your weapons do no more than anger me!" Echidna roars.

I slide into the cover Savernst made herself comfortable behind. Savernst aims her rifle higher, pulling the trigger twice. Two yellow bolts of energy shoot from the weapon's barrel, finding Echidna's eyes. She shrieks in pain, clutching at her face.

"You bitch!" she shrieks. "You blinded me. You blinded me, you bitch!" She repeats the same thing over and over as she clutches her eyes.

An unusually large hand on my arm turns me toward Savernst.

"We don't have long," she says. "A fleet of Hestialites are on their way here and when they arrive, they will blow this ship out of the sky."

"How long do we have?" I ask.

"An hour at most. Could be less."

"Damn...alright. Keep her occupied. I'll get President Scott. I just hope the others found Marudon..."

With a nod from Savernst, I sprint from cover as she fires laser bolts into Echidna's face, keeping her blinded for as long as possible.

I only make it three steps before the door we came in explodes and the Vrykos we left in the hallway swarm into the throne room.

IRIS

INTERLUDE VII

Ancient History…

Thel-Shuum stood Prometheus up straight, looking at
his handiwork. Like the others, he had dug a deep hole
and placed the Vexnoxtuque's comatose body inside. He
covered it back up, burying the creature.

A shriek turned his attention skyward.

"Looks like one found us again," Thel said, sighting in
on the beast circling them like a vulture did its prey.

It looked down at them with its armored head, eyes
squinted in anger. She angled herself downward,
dropping toward the snow-covered earth. She swooped
upward with a mighty flap of her wings, her feet
throwing up plumes of snow upon impact. She opened
her jaws wide, a horrific sounding roar erupting from
her mouth.

Thel! a raspy female voice came, the beast before him,
Iris, speaking to him. *What is the meaning of this?! I just
witnessed you burying my brother Ares…*

She was quiet for a moment, staring at him with her
mechanical eyes.

Is he dead? Iris finally asked.

Thel said nothing, as he had done with the rest of the
beasts thus far. Iris hissed, her tongue wriggling in her
sharp-toothed maw. Thel brought up Prometheus' fists,
ready to fight. Iris roared, her wings spread to her sides
in a display of aggression; a threat.

Speak or be destroyed! she demanded.

Thel remained quiet. Iris shook with barely
containable rage. Her fists clenched, blood dripping
from the clenched appendages, her talons digging into
her palms.

Fine! she roared and charged.

Thel stood his ground, avoiding Iris' swung hooked claws. Her eyes were wide, frenzied looking despite them being cybernetics. Thel dodged a strike that left the beast overextended, bringing Prometheus' metal knee into Iris's soft gut. Iris pitched forward, the air rushing from her gullet. Iris fell to her spiked knees, clutching her gut.

Thel clenched Prometheus' metal fist and drove it into the side of the Vexnoxtuque's armored face. With a pitiful wail, the beast fell to the cold, snow-covered ground. Thel was about to have Prometheus ready a cryo grenade, thinking the beast was unconscious, barely registering the motion from Iris's tail. Before he knew it, the mighty Vexnoxtuque slaying robot was falling to the ground, swept off its feet by Iris' tail. Snow exploded in the air as Prometheus hit the ground with an earth-shaking boom, settling on the robot's metal body. Iris rose to her feet, towering over the fallen Prometheus. The cores of her eyes began to light up with color.

Energy build up detected! Prometheus declared.

"Engage the thrusters!" Thel exclaimed.

Thrusters on the robot's feet, back, and chest activated, propelling the robot backwards, away from Iris as twin beams of color burned into the spot Prometheus was moments before. Thel increased the power of the thrusters on Prometheus's back, bringing the robot to its feet. Iris spread her wings wide to her sides.

I must find Zeus and warn him of your betrayal! Iris said, looking toward the sky. *Then we shall gather our brother Phobos and destroy you!*

Her wings lifted before shooting downward, the first mighty flap not lifting her weight much, so she repeated the action, lifting higher with each flap.

"No, you don't!" Thel said, rushing Prometheus forward, grasping Iris's ankle, her clawed toes curling at his touch. She peered down at him with a hiss, her wings flapping madly, struggling to carry her higher with the added tons of weight. She swiped her clawed hand down at the robot's limb locking her in place. She missed, unable to reach Prometheus' hand, her body unable to bend in the way she wanted while flying.

Thel yanked Prometheus' arm downward, bringing Iris with it. Iris roared in surprise as she was swung through the air. Thel threw her to the cold, snowy ground hard on her armored back. Iris coughed, a strange hacking sound, the air driven from her massive lungs. Thel brought Prometheus's metal foot down on Iris's gut, driving the little bit of air that remained in her lungs from them.

Thel leaned Prometheus forward, grasping Iris' lower jaw and pulled it open. He grabbed the cryo grenade he prepped earlier from the compartment in the robot's leg. He deposited it in the recovering Vexnoxtuque's open maw. The device slipped down her throat and activated, an explosion sounding from within, blue steam erupting from her fanged mouth. With one last breath, she fell still, falling into her hybernative state the cryo grenade triggered.

"Looks like you're not telling anyone," Thel said, looking down at Iris' still form.

Alright, Prometheus said, *let's get this over with.*

"Right. Then we only have two more left to go."

Thel reached down with Prometheus' metal hands and grabbed Iris by the ankles, getting to work in burying her.

33

Anchorage…

Prometheus fell from the sky after tackling the goddess
Iris in the air, landing in a destroyed swath of the city.
Iris squealed in pain as they hit the ground, the giant
mech landing atop the beast, cushioning his fall. Will
rolled Prometheus off the winged devil and onto his
booted feet. Iris stumbled to her feet after him, turning
toward him with a snarl, allowing Will to take in the
Kaiju's every detail.

The first thing Will noticed was her eyes. Instead of
glowing and sinister looking, they were mechanical.

*Most of the Titan's children we've encountered thus
far have had some kind of unnatural modification made
to them by their Plagueonian creators to make them
deadlier than they already were, but this one's definitely
the weirdest,* Will thought. *Why does it have mechanical
eyes? How does that make it deadlier?*

The mechanical eyes were framed by a fierce looking
armored face with a wide maw full of sharp teeth.
Jagged plates of armor ran from the base of the beast's
neck to the base of its tail where they transitioned into
round plates of armor that ended at the tip of its tail.
Two great wings extended from her sides, a beautiful
array of blacks, blues, reds, and purples making up the
fleshy membranes of the wings. The same went for her
skin, which was mostly black, but the colors flowed
through her skin, as if Will could see the blood rushing
through the Kaiju's body. An aura of the same colors
seemed to surround her body, faint but still there. She
stood on powerful back legs that ended in four splayed
out clawed toes. Her armored arms looked strong and
powerful, tipped with five clawed fingers.

Iris roared, clearly enraged about being used as a meat cushion.

Nice of you to join me, Marugrah said, his voice telepathically entering Will's head.

Will looked in the direction of his friend, finding him grappling with the hulking war god Ares, the Kaiju fifty feet taller than Marugrah.

"I wouldn't want you to have all the fun," Will joked.

Oh yes. I'm having a blast, Marugrah retorted.

Will snapped Prometheus' helmeted head back toward Iris as the sound of massive feet pounding toward him caught his ears. Iris had rushed forward while his attention wasn't on her, already having covered half the distance between them. Will raised Prometheus' arms in front of him, crossing his forearms to protect the mech's body from the blow as Iris slammed into him. Her arms wrapped around Prometheus, claws digging into the robot's back. Will could feel the damage, but it didn't hurt like pain.

Proximity counter measures activating, Prometheus reported.

An electric current pulsed through the Kaiju killing machine's metal skin, making contact with the monster hugging it, fangs just inches from slipping into its side. Iris squealed in pain as she let go of Prometheus, stumbling back from the pain of millions of volts of electricity being shot into her body. Her four-hundred-foot body convulsed and spasmed as her muscles were involuntarily contracting by the attack.

"Good job, Eth," Will said, rushing Prometheus forward, driving the mech's knee into Iris' gut. The Vexnoxtuque pitched forward in pain with the blow, spittle flying from her mouth. Will raised Prometheus' arms in the air, fists clenched, bringing them down on

215

the Kaiju's armored back. The blow sent Iris sprawling to the ground.

"Alright…time to finish this bitch off. Deploy the rail gun!" Will said.

Compartments on the sides of Prometheus' legs snapped open, the two pieces of the rail gun inside. Will plucked the two halves from the compartments, snapping them together to form the weapon. He took aim with the rail gun at Iris's head. He tightened Prometheus' finger on the trigger, the magnetically propelled round erupting from the rail gun's barrel in a flash of light, obscuring his view of Iris for just a moment.

"Oh shit," Will said, surprised.

Iris pulled her armored wings away from her head, the core of her mechanical eyes blazing red with anger, very much alive. Before he could react, Iris beat her wings, lifting off the ground and latching onto Prometheus. With a menacing roar, she bit down on the robot's shoulder.

"Plasma missiles!"

Compartments on Prometheus' shoulder pylons opened, missiles erupting from their pods and arcing around, exploding in plumes of blue and purple on Iris' armored back, a squint of the eyes the only reaction the rainbow goddess showed. Iris jumped away from Prometheus, her eyes glowing brightly.

Energy build up detected! Prometheus announced.

Will dove Prometheus to the side as beams of color exploded from the core of her mechanical eyes. As Prometheus rolled back to his metal feet, Will raised the rail gun and fired off a shot. Iris quickly wrapped her wings in front of her, shielding her from the magnetically propelled round. Will anticipated her shielding herself, though, putting Prometheus into a

216

sprint. As Iris' wings parted, her eyes widened in surprise.

Will drove Prometheus' fist into Iris's gut, pitching the Kaiju forward. Next, Will brought Prometheus' knee into Iris' chin, snapping her ugly head back, stunning her. Will disassembled the rail gun and put them back into their respective compartments, Faithful deploying from the robot's palm. Will activated the energy blade, taking a step toward the rainbow goddess.

Prometheus stumbled back in surprise as Ares catapulted into the stunned Iris, both Kaijus falling to the rubble covered ground. Will looked to Prometheus' side, finding Marugrah had stepped up next to the mech…his eyes locked above them.

Will snapped Prometheus' head skyward, stumbling back a few more steps.

The sky was alive with activity, the aircrafts hovering in the sky very much not human. Armored versions of the Plagueonian ships from two years ago headed toward the two defenders, cannons deployed, ready to support their monstrous weapons.

Then one of them exploded.

And another.

The hell? Will wondered.

More ships appeared in the sky, lacking the jagged armor the others did. Will recognized them from the Plagueonian invasion two years ago. The armored ships turned to their unarmored attackers, seeing them as a more pressing threat. Laser bolts flew.

A third party had entered the war.

THORATH

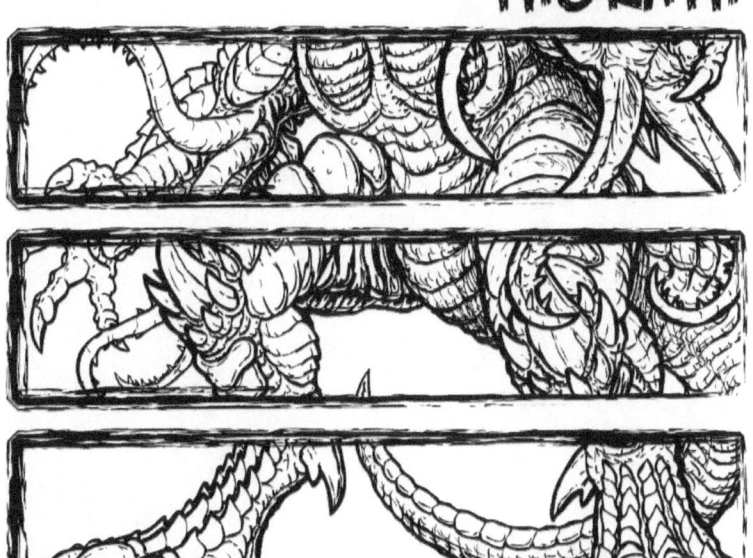

34

Nevada…

"Really, dude? 'I am your doom'? Super cliché villain line," Aaron quipped.

The newly Kaiju-fied Thorath turned to them with a snarl, not amused with Aaron's comment. The creature looked like it leapt from the twisted mind of H.P. Lovecraft. His skull-like face was framed by spikes of varying sizes. Its maw, filled with razor sharp teeth, dropped open, tentacles spilling from within. His eyeballs were held aloft, wriggling in the air by what looked to be his corneas. Armor and spikes covered his back, along with two tentacle-like appendages that ended in a diamond-like structure, the middle what Wolf could only describe as speakers with a fleshy center. His arms were strong, spiked, and armored, ending in five boney, clawed fingers. His legs were also armored and spiky, ending in four clawed toes. An armored tail swayed back and forth behind him. Tentacles wriggled from his sides. He stood hunched over, his fifteen-foot height too high for the ten-foot-tall room. His skin was green, pink, and purple with yellow flecks. His eyes glowed a sinister yellow.

Thorath shuddered, breathing heavily. "Damn. I forgot how much that hurts," he said, his voice deeper and more sinister sounding.

How can we hope to beat…that???

"No, no. No bigger. Just the right size," Thorath said, seemingly talking to himself.

"What do we do?" Aaron asked, standing next to Wolf.

Wolf shook his head. He had no idea what to do. He'd single-handedly taken down the Cyclops two years ago, but the thing he was looking at now was much worse than the Cyclops ever was.

Eva, Ben, and Ezekiel joined Wolf and Aaron, all of them facing down the beast of terror that was Thorath.

"If you guys can get it to stay still, I may be able to blind it," Eva said, adjusting her Barret M82 sniper rifle in her hands.

Wolf put a hand to his face in thought. "Hmm. Maybe if we can blind it, we can find a weak spot."

"Ben and I will flank him," Ezekiel said. "You and Aaron rush it head on."

Wolf nodded. "Sounds good to me."

"Roger that. I'll try and find a good spot to get a shot at him," Eva said. "I need him to stop moving, though."

Everyone nodded, going about their assigned roles.

Wolf and Aaron exchanged uncertain looks, turning back to Thorath. He was mumbling to himself, almost like he was trying to keep something at bay. Ezekiel and Ben snuck up on either side of the beast, Ezekiel with his tail claw, and Ben with his M16 assault rifle.

Wolf, FN SCAR at the ready, and Aaron, a SCAR of his own in hand, charged at Thorath, keeping its attention off the two about to take him down. Thorath's head snapped toward the two charging soldiers, the tentacles slipping back into his fanged mouth as it closed, floating yellow eyes locked on his targets. The charging soldiers squeezed their triggers in unison, three round bursts erupting from the weapons' muzzles. Thorath flinched back as hot lead peppered his armored face, more surprised than hurt.

We're not going to hurt him with bullets, Wolf thought. *But we don't have to hurt him...*

His and Aaron's distraction allowed Ezekiel and Ben to close in on his flanks. Ezekiel struck first, thrusting his tail claw at Thorath's side. Thorath roared in pain as

Ezekiel's tail claw contacted flesh and penetrated, drawing blood. Black blood. Ben struck next, landing a punch to the side of Thorath's face. The Plagueonian turned Mini-Kaiju stumbled to the side, stunned by the blow…but he recovered quickly with a shake of his ugly head.

Thorath chuckled. "My turn."

Thorath snapped his arms out to his sides, grabbing his two attackers in his massive hands, lifting them off the ground and tossing them into energy barriers. Wolf cringed, remembering what it felt like to make contact with an energy barrier.

"What do we do now?" Aaron asked, panicked.

"I'll distract him. Try to get him to stop moving," Wolf said. "You sneak around and get Marudon."

Aaron nodded, agreeing to the plan.

As Aaron walked away, getting into a position to allow him to sneak around Thorath, Wolf slung his rifle across his back and cracked his knuckles.

Thorath threw his head back and laughed. "You think you have a chance, insect?!"

"Won't know until I try," Wolf said, a smirk on his lips.

Thorath sneered, his hand shooting forward. Wolf dove to the side, avoiding the Kaiju-Plagueonian's massive hand from smearing him across the floor. Wolf rolled to his feet and wrapped himself around Thorath's armored arm. Thorath roared in annoyance, pulling his limb back. Once close enough, Wolf leapt from the monster's arm and onto his face. Tentacles spilled from Thorath's mouth, reaching for Wolf. He slipped his knife from the sheath on his chest to defend himself from the reaching tentacles, their hooks itching to dig into his flesh. Thorath roared in pain as Wolf's knife sliced through one of the monster's tentacles, black blood spraying.

As the tentacles retracted, Wolf made his way to the top of Thorath's head, holding on to his horns to steady himself on the creature's shaking head. Wolf looked to his side, seeing movement in his peripheral, finding Thorath's glowing yellow eye looking at him. Wolf gave it a smile and thrust his knife into the orb. Thorath wailed in agony, his eye retracting, head high, as Wolf jumped away from the beast.

"Now Eva!" Wolf shouted as hit the ground.

A boom rang out through the room, blood spraying from the side of Thorath's face. Thorath stumbled back, clutching at his face. His leg caught on something and he tumbled backward...crushing the table Marudon was on.

"NO!" Wolf shouted, rushing forward.

A hand caught his arm, turning him around. He sighed in relief. Aaron stood beside him, Marudon cradled in his arms, bloody and unconscious. Eva, Ezekiel, and Ben stood beside him.

"Right then," Wolf said. "Mission complete. Let's get the hell out of here."

They nodded, turning for the door. Wolf took one last look at the fallen Thorath, who was still, unmoving, before following his team out of the room.

35

All eyes were on the Vryko horde as they entered the room, dozens of them, eyes glowing, teeth gnashing. They're unpredictable, a wild card, uncontrollable, a threat to all. That's why we didn't see any Plagueonians or vampires on our way here to the Throne Room. The Remnant vampires understood this, turning from Josh,

Mikayla, and Ashley to the horde of humanoid monsters. My team does the same, turning and firing at the Vrykos with the vampires.

My eyes shift from my teammates to my love: Sasha. She bounds into the air, avoiding a claw strike from Typhon, aimed for her legs. As she falls back to the ground, she drew her katana, swiping it at the gangly vampire king. Typhon barely avoids the swung sword, lunging forward at my girlfriend.

A roar from Echidna reminds me I don't have time to dawdle. I focus back on my task: retrieving the President.

They can take care of themselves, I think, trying to squelch my anxiety.

However, my worry for my family remains.

In the past year since I assumed command of Fire Team Gamma, I've grown closer with the members, more than I thought I could with anyone besides Josh and Sasha. While Josh and Sasha are closer to my heart than the rest, I do consider them more than my teammates. They are my family. I'd do anything to protect them.

But right now, I have a duty to retrieve President Scott.

"You shouldn't have come," Scott says as I stride up to him and begin to undo the straps that hold him to the table.

I've only met the man a few times, once after the attack of the Titans a year ago, and the few dinners he has invited me and my team to. Will told me the impact the Plagueonian invasion had on the man. Seeing all those people die to protect him. It inspired him to be stronger. To be braver.

"Not my decision, sir. Director Cole arranged your rescue," I reply.

"You are the best the CCU has. They can't afford to lose you," he says sternly.

"I brought some help. Anyway, as soon as we have you, we're getting the hell out of here."

He nods.

I undo the last strap and he falls into my arms, the table a bit too high off the floor for him to slide off without injuring himself. I set him on the ground and turn toward my team, battling Echidna, Typhon, and the Vrykos. I toggle my throat mic, which is set for local communication; the four of my team-members in the throne room.

"Disengage," I say. "Main objective complete. Unable to complete secondary objective."

Affirmatives flood my ear as my team acknowledges my command.

I grab Scott by the wrist and lead him back to the cover Savernst is behind, firing into Echidna's face…just in time for her plasma rifle to run out of juice.

"Shit," she mutters, surprising me. I had no idea aliens shared such a word with humans. "What now?"

"We get the hell out of here," I say.

She glances at Scott and nods. "Hurry. Before she recovers."

I nod and the three of us dash from the cover, heading for the door back into the hallway where my team clears a path through the dwindling Vryko horde for us. I fall behind, letting Savernst and Scott get ahead of me.

We don't make it more than a few feet before I'm snagged by my leg and sent flying through the air. As I do, I hear Sasha yell my name. Echidna's intricately carved throne arrests my fall…hard. I roll down from the seat, the metal floor as unforgiving as the throne. I lift myself up, feet with snakes for toes stomping into my view, identifying who sent me flying.

226

"Where do you think you're going, Lycan?" Echidna growls, her voice full of venom.

I stumble to my feet, glaring up at the monster before me.

She scoffs. "You humans disgust me. You act so tough and fight so hard. But it's all for nothing, you know. You have no chance of winning. Your robot and Maruian can only fight so much before they can't fight anymore. And when that happens…we will wipe them out. And you'll have nothing left to protect you."

"That's what you think," I wheeze. "Those two have more will than any of us. They'll fight to protect everything they know and love." I grin fiendishly. "And Marugah would be pissed to know you abducted his Queen. And you know what anger does to a Kaiju."

Her face momentarily twists into an expression of worry before shifting back to anger. She clenches her fist, reels it back, and thrusts it at me. My reaction time is too slow, my dive to the side sending me flying through the air again, this time at an angle. I bounce off a far wall, feet from the throne I was standing before. Pain rockets through my body as I slam face first into the floor again. My body, being superior to a regular human's, can take a lot of punishment. My temper however…

I jump to my feet, my rage overcoming the pain.

"Ready to give me a real challenge now, Lycan?" Echidna asks, delight in her voice.

"I'm…not…a…fucking Lycan!" I yell, rage overcoming my logical thought process.

Echidna's face twists into a mask of confusion as my body changes. Clothes and armor peel away from my body as it expands, black hair covering my body. A snarling maw full of sharp teeth. Pointed ears. Yellow

227

eyes. Long boney fingers tipped with razor sharp talons. A fluffy tail.

Just when I thought my transformation was done, more pain lances through me as six spikes, three on either side, explode from my back. I notice that my teeth are weird, too. Instead of being canine, they are hooked and serrated.

Echidna barks a laugh. "Finally, a challenge!"

I step up to the Plagueonian Queen, only a foot shorter than the she-beast.

I snarl, surprised that I'm in control of my new form. The last time I transformed into something other than what I thought I was, I blacked out, having no control over my body, driven by pure rage. This one...

I pat my fur covered body, feeling boney armor beneath.

The form from a year ago had the armor over the fur. The spikes were different, too.

Is this the true Fenriri? I wonder.

Half Fenriri, I remind myself.

I hook my claws, and look up at my opponent...only to find two opponents.

Both Echidna and Typhon stand before me.

"I see now," Typhon says. "This is why you're so strong. You're not a Lycan. You're a Fenriri." He laughs.

"Enough talk," I growl, my voice deep and scary.

I charge at my enemies, ready to take them both on at once.

PHOBOS

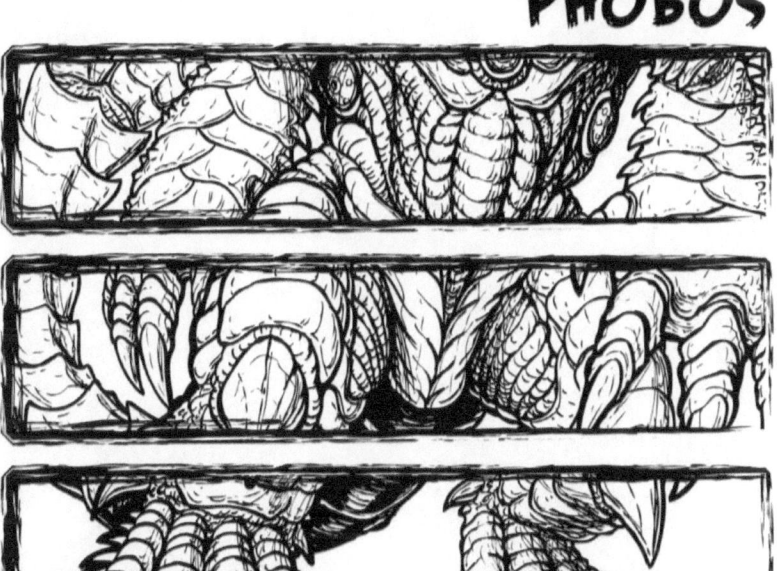

INTERLUDE VIII

Ancient History...

Only two more left, Thel-Shuum thought, looking down at where he buried Iris, farther north from her brother, Ares. His eyes fluttered. He wanted nothing more than to sleep. He was exhausted.

But I can't, he thought. *Not yet. Not until the last two are imprisoned.*

Thel? Prometheus' voice came. *Are you alright? Your vitals are erratic.*

"I'm fine, Thes," Thel replied. "Just...tired."

Maybe you should rest.

"We don't have time for rest."

The AI said nothing, knowing what he said to be true. His concern, though, was not misplaced, Thel knew.

"Alright, take us to our next target," Thel said to the AI.

The AI remained quiet still, the teleportation system whirring in his ears as it activated. The whir grew louder, soon reaching a high pitch before they disappeared in a flash of blue light. The snowy terrain was replaced by a city under siege. People ran in terror as buildings crumbled. Bodies were crushed under rubble or the feet of the beast rampaging through the city. Phobos stopped, looking down at the death and destruction he was causing with an excited bark. His cold blue eyes widened as he looked up, settling upon the robot. His brows furrowed, a growl erupting from his fang filled mouth.

I think he sees us, Prometheus remarked.

"What gave you that impression?" Thel said, the sarcasm oozing from his voice.

Phobos leaned forward, arms spread to his sides, mouth wide, and roared. He charged forward, all primal fury, no questions for his betrayal. He just attacked.

Phobos was always more primal than the rest of the Titans' children, Thel thought.

Thel extended Prometheus' arm to his side, summoning the hard-light sword. It extended from the compartment in the mech's palm, the stock unfolding, the hard-light blade flickering on, crackling with green energy. Thel spun Prometheus out of the path of the charging beast, the blade of his sword finding the flesh on the back of Phobos' leg. Phobos roared in pain, dropping to one knee, his twin tails thrashing wildly. He got back to his feet, violet blood gushing from the gash on his calf. He snarled as he turned toward Prometheus. Thel brought the sword to bear, facing down the 'god of fear'.

I see why they give him that name, Thel thought. *He truly is a terrifying looking beast.*

Phobos's jaws dropped open, his obsidian teeth glinting in the moonlight. A glob of green goo shot from his open maw. Thel knew what it was, rolling Prometheus to the side, avoiding the green lougie. It hit where he stood moments ago, erupting in a puddle of acid, eating at stone and dirt. As Prometheus rolled to his feet, Thel looked up, facing the monster down once more. Phobos sneered, angered that his attack failed.

You can't possibly believe you can subdue a beast such as this, do you? the AI asked.

"I'll only kill him if there is no other option," Thel said. "At this point in time, I don't believe there is no other option."

Your health is failing, Thel. We don't have time for you to figure a way to subdue the beast. Just kill it.

The AI wasn't wrong. He had been deprived of sleep for several days. That didn't fare well on the body. It could even be deadly.

"I'll sleep when I'm dead," Thel said.

That may be sooner than you think, Prometheus retorted.

Thel ignored the AI's snark.

The conversation only lasted a few seconds, but in that time Phobos had charged and covered half the distance to the Vexnoxtuque killing machine, his claws hooked. Thel brought Prometheus' foot up, connecting with Phobos' unarmored gut, the blow lifting Phobos off his clawed feet. Thel brought the end of the stock of the hard-light sword down on the top of Phobos's head, throwing the beast to the ground. Phobos moaned at the robot's feet, dazed. Thel took a deep breath and let it out.

What is it? Prometheus asked.

Thel shook his head, the giant robot mimicking the motion on the outside, ignoring the question. He knew the AI already knew, but he didn't want to say what was wrong aloud. He was surprised he had made it this far, battling the Titans' children and defeating seven of them. His exhaustion was growing.

His lapse in action was taken advantage of.

Phobos thrust himself upward, tackling the giant robot, his arms wrapping around Prometheus' waist. Thel shouted in surprise as the metal warrior he piloted fell backward under thousands of tons of weight. Phobos stood, hovering over the fallen robot with malicious intent in his blue eyes. He raised a clawed hand, ready to strike down the mech. Thel's mind cleared. He reacted fast, bringing the hard-light sword up, the blade piercing Phobos's falling hand. Phobos threw his head back, roaring in agony. He looked at the blade sticking through his hand, slowly easing it free, whimpering in pain as he did. He finally wrenched it free in a spray of purple, squealing in pain. Thel rolled Prometheus to his feet. Phobos clutched his injured hand with his good one, sneering at the being who dared to inflict pain upon him.

"It doesn't have to be this way," Thel said, trying to reason with the beast.

Phobos' only response was a savage roar.

Or maybe it does, Prometheus said.

"Fine. I'm going to take out his legs, then we'll hit him with a cryo weapon."

And if that doesn't work?

"Then we'll resort to…*that*."

Phobos roared, taking a step forward. Then another. Before Thel knew it, Phobos was charging. Thel held the hard-light sword in front of Prometheus as Phobos slashed his claws out at the robot. Phobos' hand recoiled as he howled in pain, his claws having made contact with the energy blade. Scorch marks dotted his armored skin. While Phobos was distracted with his pain, Thel spun Prometheus, sweeping the Vexnoxtuque's clawed feet out from under him with the robot's own metal leg. Phobos fell on his back with a surprised bark. Thel saw the monster's blue eyes widen as he sent a metal fist into the beast's face.

Thel looked down at the unconscious beast through Prometheus's eyes. He looked at the robot's fist, finding purple flecks dotting the mech's white and red fist along with a few of Phobos' obsidian teeth.

"That was the most violent I had to get with one of them," Thel said, still staring at Prometheus' fist.

The worst of them is next, Prometheus said.

"Zeus…"

Thel turned his attention back to the creature at Prometheus' feet. He administered Phobos a dose of the cryo serum, before dragging him to the middle of the city and burying him there. The city was a mess, practically rubble. He could see bodies mixed in with the destruction. The sight made him cringe.

This is why you should have killed them all, Prometheus said. *The Titans too. I know they never chose to become what they did, but you'd be doing them a favor killing them instead of keeping them alive; imprisoned.*

Thel knew the AI was right.

"We're sticking to the plan...for now," Thel said.

Thel got to work, digging Phobos' grave. A grave that would soon be the place the great Coliseum would be built.

36

Anchorage...

Tsuzar couldn't believe his eyes as the metal face of the ancient robot Prometheus filled the view screen.

Could it be? Did Thel Shuum survive all these years? Has he reappeared to finish what he started so long ago? Tsuzar wondered. He had so many unanswered questions.

Only one way to find out.

He turned to the Hestialite at the console in front of him and said, "Open a comm channel to Prometheus."

The Hestialite nodded, working his long slender fingers over his console's holographic keyboard.

After a few minutes, he called out, "Comm link established, sir."

"Thel, is that you old friend?" Tsuzar asked.

"Who is this?" A voice asked, definitely not Thel. "How are you communicating with me?"

While it wasn't Thel, it was familiar.

"William?" Tsuzar asked. "Is that you?"

"Tsuzar?" the pilot of the robot asked.

"Indeed, my friend."

"Why are you here?"

"We were tracking a group of Plagueonians still loyal to Echidna here. They stole some of our ships. Our informant sent out a beacon, alerting us to their position. But on our way here, we intercepted another, familiar energy signature. Prometheus."

Prometheus' head snapped to the ground as the two Vexnoxtque at his and Marugrah's feet twitched.

"We'll take care of your Plagueonian problem while you take care of the Vexnontuque," Tsuzar said.

"Roger that," Will said.

Tsuzar stood from his command chair, looking over his crew in the control room. "Everyone, battle stations!"

His crew went to work, preparing weapon systems and shields.

It's time to end this civil war and finally have the peace we long for...

Iris and Ares stumbled to their feet, snow pelting their armored hides. Will and Marugrah acted in unison, lashing out at the Kaijus. Iris was quick, avoiding Prometheus' flung fist. Her hand clamped down on the robot's forearm, using the momentum from his punch to swing the giant robot around where she sent a foot into his back and sent him sprawling to the ground.

Will got the mech to his hands and knees, another foot strike connecting with his side, sending him to the ground once more. Iris roared, closing in on a suspected victory, her colorful aura growing brighter.

That's what you think, Will thought, tightening Prometheus' fingers around Faithful's handle.

Once Iris got within a step of Prometheus, Will swung the sword toward the Kaiju. Iris barely registered the move, only getting a graze from the tip of the sword on her thick-skinned side, colorful blood leaking as she jumped back with the help of her massive wings.

Will got Prometheus to his feet, Faithful at the ready. Iris stumbled back with a roar, her eyes glowing, about to fire her eye lasers.

Deploying energy shield, Prometheus announced.

Will raised Prometheus' right arm as the energy projector emerged from a compartment in the robot's forearm, the shield flickering to life, Faithful in the right.

Colorful lasers burst from the cores of her mechanical eyes, striking the energy shield protecting Prometheus with such force that it made the mech stumble back a couple paces. The blast only lasted a few seconds, Iris seemingly unable to keep a constant stream for long. Will flicked off the energy shield, the generator retreating into the compartment it emerged from. The giants stood, staring at each other, snow and ice pelting their bodies.

Will was the first to react, bending Prometheus' knees and putting the robot into a crash course for the colorful Kaiju. A few steps from the behemoth, he swung Faithful. Iris folded her shield-like wings in front of her, trusting them to protect her from the attack. She roared in surprise and anger as the sword cut through her wings, an array of colors spraying from her wounds.

A knight slaying a dragon, Will thought as Iris stumbled back in pain, falling to her knees in the snow covered rubble of what was once Anchorage.

Iris looked up at Prometheus with a snarl before Will shoved Faithful's blade through the Kaiju's chest. He pulled the blade upward, slicing through the beast's neck and head. The two halves of the creature peeled apart, sinews snapping, blood gushing, cleaved symmetrically. Iris' carcass fell forward, drenching the snow and rubble with colorful blood.

Will looked down at the gored beast for a few moments. A pained roar pulled his attention away from the dead Kaiju and to his struggling friend. Ares pulled his sword from Marugrah's shoulder, the guardian monster stumbling back, holding his injured limb. Ares roared, his glowing green eyes full of menace, closing in on his prey.

I don't think so!

Will rushed Prometheus forward, Faithful aimed for the Kaiju's spike covered back. Ares, sensing the robot's approach, twisted to the side, Faithful's blade grazing the beast's side, doing nothing more than carving a thin line in his thick, grayish-brown skin.

Oh shit!

Ares brought his sword around, aimed to lob off Prometheus' head. Two, red, obsidian claw tipped hands grabbed ahold of the blade, green leaking from them, saving the robot from being decapitated.

Finish him! Marugrah said, struggling to keep the Kaiju's blade at bay.

Will nodded Prometheus' helmet-like head, bringing Faithful up, the energy blade punching through the Kaiju's armored chest, exploding in a fountain of flesh and blood from the creature's spike covered back. Ares roared, flailing in pain, knocking Marugrah and Prometheus away, Faithful still lodged in the Vexnoxtuque's chest.

The two guardians stumbled to their feet, watching as Ares continued to flail for a few minutes, soon falling to his knees. Will walked Prometheus up to the Kaiju, rubble crunching under the robot's metal feet. Ares looked up at its executioner with a weak snarl.

Vicious until the end, huh?

Ares tried to raise his arms and attack, but he was too weak, the life draining from his body along with his blood. Will imagined himself frown at the monster in sorrow. None of them asked to be used as weapons. None of them asked for the lives they've lead…None of them asked to be monsters that only knew how to kill.

All he could do was put them out of their misery.

That was something, he came to learn, that Thel-Shuum couldn't bring himself to do.

239

He grasped Faithful's handle with Prometheus' metal hand and pulled the sword from Ares' chest. Thousands of gallons of purple blood gushed from the wound. After a moment of staring at the dying beast, Will swiped Faithful horizontally, lobbing off Ares' head and ending its miserable life. Marugrah stepped up next to Prometheus, looking down at Ares, green blood dripping from the sword wound in his shoulder.

A boom turned their heads to the sky. Kaiju armored ships fell from the sky, trailing yellow flames. The few remaining ships disappeared, the newcomers victorious. The gigantic mothership lowered toward the two defenders that stood in the middle of the decimated Anchorage.

"Good job, William," Tsuzar's voice entered Will's head. "Come aboard. Both of you. We have much to discuss."

Will ushered Marugrah into the Kaiju holding bay, where the six Kaiju from two years ago, Zorax, Cerboura, Drakonah, Vishlari, Plague, and Wraith, along with many more Kaiju they never got to see, were kept. Marugrah all but collapsed into one of the nests meant for Kaiju naps and immediately fell asleep. Will parked Prometheus next to the sleeping Kaiju. Before he left, he noticed the nest farthest from them was occupied, its occupant unmoving. It was only a glance before he was ushered out of the room.

Now, he stood in the control room, which he had been in two years ago, next to Tsuzar. Will turned to the Hestialite, looking the same as he remembered him, but now he wore a set of royal looking armor.

"It is good to see you again, my friend," Tsuzar said, extending his hand to the young man.

Will took the Hestialite's hand, giving it a shake with a "Likewise."

"I see you've been busy," Tsuzar said with a grin. "You've defeated the Titans and their children."

Will nodded. "All but one. No sign of Zeus."

Tsuzar's face looked thoughtful. "They must not have set him loose yet. But they will. The rest of their weapons are dead. Zeus is all they have left."

"How hard can one Kaiju be to take down?"

Will meant it as a joke, but Tsuzar didn't see his humor.

"Zeus is the strongest of the Titans' children," Tsuzar said. "It took everything Prometheus had to push it to Antarctica where it froze and was soon imprisoned."

Will's brows furrowed in confusion. "How do you know what happened if you guys left before they were imprisoned?"

"We left observers on Earth to witness what was to be the end of humanity…and the conquest of another planet. Though, Earth was to be shared with the vampires. But, as you already know, Echidna shares nothing. She'd soon betray Typhon and wipe his race of bloodsuckers out of existence."

Will nodded his agreement. "And what of the Titans' children? How'd they come to be?"

"Very differently from the Titans and the other Vexnoxtuque you encountered two years ago. They were born. A product of reproduction. Though, without the augmentations and conditioning by Echidna and her scientists, I doubt they'd have been as hostile as you've encountered them to be. You've seen what has happened to most of them. Outfitted with alien weapons. But that was only because Echidna didn't see them as effective killing machines after injecting them with a new Vexnoxtuque serum."

241

It looked like there was more Tsuzar wanted to say, but he was interrupted by one of the many Hestialites at the consoles filling the mothership's control room.

"Sir! Vexnoxtuque signature detected!" the Hestialite called out.

"Take us to it!" Tsuzar commanded, looking from the Hestialite to Will. "It's time to finish this once and for all."

Will nodded, agreeing with the Hestialite commander once again. He wanted it all to end. For the people he cared about to be safe from the disasters and enemies of the past few years.

Ashley...

He knew she was a part of the risky mission to retrieve the captured President Scott on the Plagueonian fathership. He hoped she was alright. He hoped all of them were alright. His teammates.

Will watched the view screen as it changed scenery, from the snowy sky of Anchorage to the blackness of space.

Then the Earth slipped into view.

His eyes widened in amazement at the sight. He had no words for how beautiful Earth looked from beyond its atmosphere. He saw Tsuzar smile at him out of the corner of his eye.

"Coordinates locked," a Hestialite reported.

"Prepare for warp!" Tsuzar commanded, sitting in his command chair. He motioned Will to a seat that was set up next to his command chair. Will obliged, sitting down.

"Roger. Warping in 3...2...1..."

And then they were gone.

37

I charge forward ready to leap on Echidna, rip her throat out, bound off her onto Typhon and do the same to the vampire king. However, a silver sword blade bursting from Typhon's shoulder, coated in his black blood, stops me in my tracks. Typhon roars in pain, grabs the person that stabbed him and tosses them at me. They collide with me, my feet sliding over the smooth metal floor, but I don't fall. I look down to see Sasha in my arms. She smiles at me.

"I'm not letting you do this alone," she says.

Distant gun fire reaches my sensitive ears. My team has engaged with the Vrykos and the Order vampires again. As much as I want them to just run and get the hell out of here, I know they won't leave me behind.

I'd never leave one of them behind, either...

I set Sasha on her feet. "Let's kick their asses."

She gives me a smile and a nod.

We turn to our enemies as Typhon snaps off the blade sticking from his shoulder and pulls the rest of it from his back.

"Asshole! My boyfriend gave me that!" Sasha growls, charging the vampire king.

My head snaps to the side, seeing movement. I bound into the air in time to avoid Echidna's fist. There is no way of avoiding the snake that twists around from her back toward me. I roar in pain as its teeth dig into my sides...but they don't puncture, the armor beneath my fur saving me from being bitten in half. I hook my claws and swipe them at the snake's wriggling body, slicing into its flesh. I slice at it again and again, until finally the jaws part and I fall back to the floor. As soon as my

243

feet hit the floor, fingers wrap around my body and I'm tossed through the air. As I sail, I flip head over heels, until my feet strike the far wall and I push with such force I leave an indentation in the gray and gold metal, flying back the way I came like a bullet. I see surprise on Echidna's face right before I collide with her, wrapping my arms around her midsection and tackling the she-beast to the hard, metal floor.

Echidna shouts as we hit the ground, sending her fist into my side three times. My only acknowledgement is a grunt as I open my sharp tooth filled mouth and bite down on the side of her neck. She roars in pain and anger, beating the top of my head with her fist. I don't budge, even as my brain rattles each time her fist connects with my hair covered wolf head. I dig my teeth deeper into her flesh, her warm, black blood filling my mouth. The taste is awful. Like oil and gasoline. Chemical-like.

Probably from all the Vexnoxtuque serums she's pumped into her body.

My primal instincts kick in, telling me to thrash my head. I do, my sharp teeth shredding her thick flesh, more of her chemical blood flowing. She screams in pain, frantically beating her fists across my body. Her snakes wrap around my body, teeth locking onto me, slithering bodies squeezing. The squeezing soon becomes so intense I can hardly breath, forcing me to release my hold on Echidna. The Plagueonian Queen pushes me off her. I roll to my feet just as Echidna gets to hers. She holds her wounded neck, black seeping between her fingers.

"You little bastard!" Echidna growled.

I snort a laugh, enjoying her pain.

She growls, beyond pissed with me.

"I'm going to rip you limb from limb!" she roars and charges, fingers hooked.

I dodge swipes of her claws, most of them missing, some hitting their mark, harmlessly bouncing off my armored skin, frustrating Echidna even more. She swings faster, her snakes lunging at me, jaws agape. I'm able to avoid a few, but I'm soon caught, snatched in the jaws of one of her snakes, and lifted into the air. Pain wracks my body as I'm slammed against the metal floor.

I bounce across the floor, only stopping when I'm able to get my feet under me, my nails screeching against the metal floor as I slide to a stop. Echidna stands feet from me, panting in anger, the wound I inflicted on her neck almost healed.

I need to give her a debillitating wound, one that will take longer to heal...

I analyze her as she pounds toward me, her snake toes wriggling furiously. Royal looking armor covers her torso, biceps, forearms, thighs, and calves, along with a crown-like helmet adorning her head. Unlike the Kaiju, she barely has any 'natural' armor covering her body. Her sides ripple with unnatural muscle formations.

No armor...

I zero in on my target as it grows closer, hooking my fingers. A few more steps, and Echidna is nearly upon me. I watch as she reels her hand back and slashes it at me. I avoid the strike by bounding in the air, landing on her thick arm, and push off. My claws dig into her soft, exposed side, followed by my sharp teeth. Echidna screeches in pain as I bite and claw at her side, bloody chunks flying away from her body. I hear the swoosh of wind that is her snakes slithering through the air as they aim themselves at me in an effort to attack me. Just as the sound gets loud enough, meaning they were close, I jump away, the snakes' gaping maws biting into the body that they were trying to protect. Black sprays, a pain-filled shriek erupting from Echidna. She stumbles back, clutching her ruined side, cursing.

"Damn you," she says. "Damn you!"

I wipe away some of her chemical tasting black blood from my mouth, glaring at the Plagueonian Queen. She gives me a growl, taking a step back. Then another. Before I know it, she has turned tail and is running away, holding her wounded side, making her way around her throne. She stops, turning toward her partner in crime.

"Typhon!" she calls.

Typhon tosses Sasha away and turns toward his retreating partner. He glances at me, gives me a sneer, and follows Echidna. They disappear behind the throne, slipping out a hidden door or passageway that had not been visible to us when we entered the throne room.

Sasha steps up next to me. "What now?"

"Same as before. We get the hell out of here," I say, turning away from the throne our enemies just escaped behind. "I'm pretty sure Echidna and Typhon just locked themselves in the ship's control room, so getting to whatever they are using to control the Kaiju, if that is to be believed, is out of the question."

She nods, bending down and retrieving my belt from the ground, my modified Desert Eagles still.

"You okay?" I ask.

She smiles, appreciating my concern for her well-being. "Yes."

"Good."

We dash across the room, toward our other team members at the throne room door who were engaged with the few remaining Vrykos. The Remnant vampires seemed to have disappeared during Sasha's and my fight

246

against Typhon and Echidna. They cover us as we run out of the throne room and into the hallway

"Echidna, I had no idea…" Typhon started, but the anger-filled glare his partner gave him made him trail off.

"I don't give a damn what kind of idea you had or not had," Echidna snapped. "You never warned me of his strength. You said he was a Lycan, not a Fenriri!"

"I thought he was a Lycan. The last time…"

"Enough excuses, you fool!"

She clutched her side, black oozing from between her digits. Her snakes, usually full of life and energy, dragged across the ground as they made their way down the circular, gray and gold hallway until they came upon the door that would allow them to access the control room of the fathership.

"I want a course set for the nearest major human city!" Echidna commanded, her voice echoing through the vast control room filled with workers and consoles, a command chair sitting at the back of the room.

"Of course, my Queen!" one of the pilots of the ship said, tapping at his console.

"My Queen, you're hurt!" a Plagueonian, wearing the garb of a scientist, said, approaching her.

She looked down at her side, easing her hand away from the wound. It was bad. Her regenerative abilities were slow due to the severity of it.

Heal, damn you! she thought to herself with a growl.

"I want the Hydra serum," Echidna commanded.

"But…my Queen…there is no more. We only had enough to revive you, Typhon, and Plague," the Plagueonian replied.

She cursed, but had another idea.

"What of the blue serum?" she asked.

"We have some, but…you saw what it did to the Hydra," the scientist said.

"Yes. It made it stronger. And that's exactly what I want to be. Now, if you have it, hand it over!"

The scientist bowed, knowing not to argue with her, and made his way out of the control room to retrieve the orange serum.

I'm not done with you yet, Jeremy Walker…

She turned to a Plagueonian at a console. "Once we arrive at the human city, unleash Plague and Zeus."

The Plagueonian nodded.

This world will burn…

38

As they were about to round the corner that lead to the rectangular space that they entered through, Wolf stopped his team, sensing something sinister. He peeked around the corner, seeing a small contingent of Remnant vampires in full alien armor, looking up at the hole in the ceiling, dusky sunlight streaming through. They turn their heads from the hole to the rest of the room. Wolf turned back to his team.

"What is it?" Eva asked, her voice a whisper.

"Vamps. Eight of them," Wolf said, his voice also a whisper.

"That's nothing," Aaron whispered with a wave of his hand. "We just took on a mini-Kaiju. We can take them."

"I know we can," Wolf said, "but I don't want to draw attention to our location until we know just how close or far away Jeremy is."

Aaron nodded, understanding Wolf's reasoning. He watched as his friend's eyes widened, locked behind him. Wolf snapped his head around, finding a vampire behind him, raising its plasma rifle. A blur of red streaked from his peripheral, embedding in the vampire's black, armored chest, yanking it off its feet and tossing it down the hallway they just came from. Wolf's eyes landed on Ezekiel as his tail claw disappeared in a red mist.

"Thanks," Wolf said with a nod.

Ezekiel nodded back.

"Qriznak? Did you find anything?" a voice called.

"So much for not being detected," Ezekiel said, pulling the cloth with the sharp toothed smile stitched in it over his face.

Wolf rolled his eyes and shouldered his FN SCAR. Just as the first hint of another vampire rounded the corner, he took aim and fired, three rounds punching into the creature's head. It fell back, three holes in its head leaking blood, sending the remaining six vampires into a frenzy.

Wolf rolled from cover, firing his rifle, dropping another vampire of the Remnants with a head shot. Eva rolled up next to him, her AF2011-A1 double barrel semiautomatic pistol, given to her by Jake Walker, a former teammate of theirs that died in Rome a year ago in the Titan conflict, at the ready, two .45 caliber rounds exploding from the twin barrels. A vampire's helmeted head snapped back, two holes in its head.

Ezekiel and Ben bound from around the corner next, making short work of the last four before Aaron could make it around the corner, Marudon still cradled in his arms, rifle in one hand.

"Awh, man. You guys get all the fun," he grumbled, lowering his rifle.

"Don't be too discouraged," Ben said. "I can hear more coming."

"Which way?" Wolf asked, raising his weapon.

Ben pointed down the hallway opposite of where they came from. Wolf pointed his weapon down it, unable to see farther than the bend. The rest followed his lead, aiming their weapons down the hall. Wolf instinctively fired a shot at the first hint of movement.

"Hold your fire!" a deep but recognizable voice called.

"Jeremy?" Wolf said, lowering his weapon.

A black furred wolf stepped around the corner, red eyes, boney spikes jutting from its back.

"Who else would it be?" the creature asked.

Wolf sighed and gave his captain a smile. Jeremy, unable to smile in his current form, gave his teammate a nod.

"So glad to see everyone is okay," he said.

"Likewise," Wolf said as Sasha, Josh, Ashley, Mikayla, and President Scott stepped out from behind Jeremy.

Ashley raced over to Aaron, exchanging a few words with the man before she took Marudon from his arms. Marudon, waking from her unconscious state, looked up at Ashley, giving her a weak, sharp toothed smile.

"Did you think we'd just let you leave so easily?" a voice said, pulling their eyes up, to the hole they entered the ship through.

A black, armored figure jumped down from the hole, in a crouched position, a giant, silver bladed sword punching through the metal floor beside him.

"You're not going anywhere," the newcomer said, standing.

The vampire before us wears the basic black, alien armor we've seen since encountering the Remnants at Carters Dome, with one key difference: a crest jutting from the helmet's forehead area. It lifts its massive

250

sword that looks like it belongs in a *Final Fantasy* game, the blade glinting with the last rays of the setting sun. My senses tell me the blade is made of silver.

Where have I seen that before...?

"Who's gonna stop us?" Aaron asks, his weapon shouldered, but not aimed at the vampire...yet. "You?"

The vampire chuckled. "You may have captured me before, but that was because I let you. It was part of the plan. I'm much more formidable than you know."

"Capture...?" Wolf says, realization dawning on his face before turning back to his normal stoic expression. "Valok."

"Ding, ding, ding! We have a winner!" Valok made an exaggerated cheering noise.

"Nice sword," I say. "I met another vampire that carried a sword. It was smaller, though, and jagged."

Valok's demeaner changed, the vampire's full attention on me.

Good...

"I think his name was Volak. Sound familiar?"

I can see Valok's arms trembling with anger. With a roar, he lifts his sword and charges at me. I charge, too, worried my team may fall victim to Valok's rage as he swings his massive sword at me. I bound in the air, missing the giant silver blade of the swung sword, wrap my boney fingers around his helmet, flip and land on my feet. I look to my hands to find Valok's helmet. I turn, expecting to find Valok turning to ash in his armor, but find him unharmed...and pissed off.

Dammit...

The hole in the ceiling is dark, the sun having fully set. I toss the helmet aside, with a snarl.

"I shall avenge my brother!" Valok shouts and charges, sword raised in a two-handed grip like a baseball bat.

I duck, avoiding the swung sword, sending a fist into Valok's armored gut. The vampire stumbles back, his head snapping to the side, swinging his arm out, batting aside another attacker. Ezekiel rolls across the ground before jumping back to his feet. Valok shields his face, an energy shield being projected from a device on his wrist, saving his face from having three holes put in his face. While he was distracted, a booted foot slammed into his back, pushing the vampire to his knees.

"You're outnumbered, Valok. You're not going to be avenging anyone. If you continue to try and fight us, you're just going to end up like your brother: dead," I say.

Valok growls. I can see it on his face that he knows I'm right.

"It's not like you're just going to let me go, so get on with it. Kill me," Valok says, his eyes on the ground.

I just stare at him, unmoving. My team follows my lead, staring at the lone vampire on his knees before us. Valok looks up at us, an expression of defeat on his face.

"Come on!" he shouts.

I know what seeking vengeance for a lost loved one feels like. I spent two years looking for the werewolf that killed Jessica out of a thirst for vengeance. I feel pity for the vampire before me, knowing what he's feeling.

"We're leaving," I say, turning my head up toward the hole in the room's ceiling.

I jump up, grabbing the edge of the circular hole and pull myself up on the cloaked hull. Below, Wolf picks up President Scott. I hold out my hands, Wolf tossing the man upward. I catch Scott by his hands and set him beside me. He stumbles and shouts at being able to see the ground hundreds of feet below us. Ashley and Marudon are next. Then the rest of my team that is human. With them standing on the cloaked ship next to me, wind rushing, threatening to throw us off, the non-human members of my team pull themselves onto the hull, able to make the jump from the floor where Valok still sits on his knees, looking up at us.

"This isn't over!" Valok shouts up at us. "I will avenge my brother!"

I shake my head and turn away from the hull, seeing where we are.

"Holy… They must have moved the ship while we were on board," Wolf says, looking out over the city.

An explosion lights up the night sky, illuminating the city.

A battle had begun in Las Vegas.

THE FINAL
CHILD

ZEUS

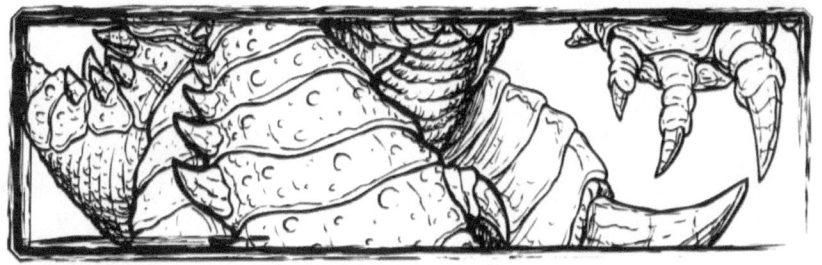

INTERLUDE VIV

Ancient History…

Thel-Shuum shook the dirt from Prometheus' mighty hands. He looked down at the bare earth where he had buried the Vexnoxtuque Phobos.

Ready for the last one? Prometheus asked.

Thel took a deep breath and let it out, steadying himself. His eyelids felt heavy and his body felt as if it were drained of every bit of energy he had. His stomach growled as he had not eaten in a long time. His mouth was dry from lack of water.

Food, water, and sleep, he thought, mentally noting what he'd attend to immediately after he defeated Zeus. *And a lot of each.*

"As ready as I'm ever going to be," Thel finally said.

He looked around at the decimated city. He knew the survivors of the attack would rebuild the city and life would continue on. A hum entered his ears as Prometheus activated the teleportation system. With one last look at the smoldering city, it was gone in a flash of blue light. He was momentarily confused as the light cleared and the same landscape laid before him. The creature standing within the city, however, told him he was in a different city. He towered over everything, even the mighty war machine Prometheus.

Zeus, the god of thunder.

The final child he had to defeat.

Zeus turned toward Prometheus, Thel's heart skipping a beat. His yellow eyes squinted, his mouth curling into a sneer.

I assume you are to blame for the disappearance of my brothers and sisters, Zeus said, his voice deep and authorative.

Thel, no games this time. Kill him, Prometheus said before Thel could respond to Zeus.

"Right," Thel said, clenching Prometheus' hands into fists. "Then we'll take care of the others." He realized his mistake in thinking he was doing them a favor by keeping them alive. No, by keeping them alive he was just continuing their suffering.

He didn't answer Zeus's question, like he had with the others of the Titans' children. Zeus huffed in agitation.

Your silence only confirms my suspicions, Zeus said.

Again, Thel said nothing.

Zeus leaned forward, opened his jaws wide and let out a deafening roar, the white hair dangling from his chin puffing out like an agitated cat's fur.

Thel just raised Prometheus' hand and motioned the giant forward, trying to act as confident as he could. Zeus snarled at him and stomped forward, shaking the ground beneath Prometheus' feet as he did. Thel charged Prometheus forward as well, weaponless. Zeus swiped a massive hand at the robot, Thel engaging thrusters and dodging to the side. Zeus's claw hit the ground the robot was moments ago, rubble, earth, and human bodies flying into the air from the impact. Zeus righted himself, pulling his hand from the crater he created trying to squash Prometheus like a giant bug.

We need to end this quickly, Prometheus said.

"What do you suggest?" Thel asked as Zeus glared at the robot he failed to smite.

The Ion Cannon.

Thel nodded. The Ion Cannon was the robot's most powerful weapon.

"Right then. Ready the Ion Cannon!" Thel said.

Readying the Ion Cannon, Prometheus replied.

Thel avoided another strike from Zeus, rolling Prometheus to his feet. One he got the robot to its feet, he felt the two cannons on Prometheus' back snap together, deconstructing and then reconstructing into a single, long cannon. He reached Prometheus' metal arms back and retrieved the giant weapon. He positioned one hand on the long barrel and one on the handle, a finger around the trigger. The Ion Cannon was three-fourths the size of Prometheus himself. Hover technology on the long barrel allowed the robot to easily hold the giant rifle-like cannon. Zeus's eyes widened, surprised by Prometheus' new weapon. As soon as the look of surprise crossed his face, it was gone. He furrowed his brows and showed his fangs.

Use any weapon you want. None of them shall harm me, Zeus growled.

We'll see about that, Prometheus muttered.

Thel took aim with the Ion Cannon, tightening Prometheus's metal finger over the trigger. Once he had his target in sight, he pulled the trigger back all the way. A crackling stream of violet energy streaked from the barrel toward Zeus. The god of thunder brought his arms up in front of him at the last moment. The stream pushed Zeus back, his clawed toes digging troughs in the earth. The Vexnoxtuque's feet caught on something and it fell onto its back with an earthshaking boom. The attack only lasted for a few seconds before vents on the sides of the Ion Cannon opened, releasing all the pent-up heat and a slide snapped open ejecting the spent Ion round. Smoke surrounded the fallen Zeus, obscuring any view of the beast.

"Did that do it?" Thel asked. "Is he dead?"

Scanning, Prometheus said.

Movement inside the dust cloud caught Thel's attention, getting a gasp out of him. He felt the ground beneath Prometheus' feet shake. Zeus stepped clear of the smoke cloud, his yellow eyes blazing with anger.

"No way… That was the strongest weapon we have and it hardly did a thing!" Thel exclaimed, noticing the burnt and flaking flesh on Zeus's forearms.

Impressive, Zeus said, hunched forward, his arms hanging in front of him, claws touching the ground, blood running down his tan skin. *But not enough to kill me.* He chuckled and righted himself.

The Ion Cannon needs a minute to be usable again, Prometheus reported.

"We don't have a minute," Thel said, returning the Ion Cannon to the robot's back where it deconstructed itself and reconstructed as Prometheus' dual cannons. "We need another plan."

Calculating.

Zeus roared and charged. He covered the distance to Prometheus quickly, more due to his size than his speed, swiping a massive hand at the humanoid machine. Thel was barely able to avoid the strike, the longest of Zeus's claws slicing through the robot's side. The blow sent Prometheus spinning, the machine's legs becoming entangled, sending it to the rubble covered ground. Zeus barked in amusement, stomping toward the fallen mecha. The Vexnoxtuque's shadow fell over Prometheus as the robot looked up at the beast. Zeus raised a massive hand above him, ready to bring it down and crush Prometheus. Thel acted quickly, drawing the hard-light sword, the blade flickering to life, and thrusting it upward as the hand was about to flatten him into the earth. The blade pierced Zeus' palm, just missing the blue disk, and exploded out the back of the Vexnoxtuque's hand.

Zeus threw his head back with a roar of agony, his 'beard' puffed out in agitation. Thel gripped the sword's hilt as tight as the robot could and pulled vertically. There was some resistance, but the sword cut through

Zeus's flesh, slicing free from between the monster's large middle finger and the smaller fourth finger of his hand, splitting it in half from where the blade first pierced the appendage. Zeus stumbled back, squealing in pain, clutching at his split hand with his good hand. With Zeus distracted with the pain, Thel got Prometheus to his metal feet, sword at his side.

"Got a plan yet?" Thel asked the AI.

We need to freeze him, Prometheus said.

"I don't think we'll be able to stun him long enough to hit him with a cryo weapon," Thel said with a shake of his head.

I know, Prometheus said, *but we can transport him someplace cold.*

"But we encountered a few of the other children in cold places. They aren't affected by it."

Right, but remember why they were there. To rest and heal. They would've probably been forced into a hibernative state. That's why they chose cold environments. The cold triggers their hibernation.

"How are we supposed to transport him to someplace cold?" Thel asked.

We teleport him there, of course. Skepticism creeped into Thel's mind. The AI must've detected it, so he elaborated. *It'll drain most to all of our energy for a few moments, but my calculations indicate we will be able to transport Zeus to the nearest freezing environment.*

"Alright, then," Thel said, trusting the AI. "Let's do it."

Zeus was still clutching his mangled hand and squealing in pain when Thel stomped Prometheus toward him. He had already retracted the hard-light sword. It was a mistake. Zeus saw him coming and reached out with his hands, the devices on his palms crackling with electricity. Thel's vision flickered as

263

electricity rippled through the robot. The AI reported no major damage. Thel reached out Prometheus' arms, wrapping them as far as he could around Zeus's thick waist.

Engaging teleportation system, Prometheus reported.

More electricity rippled through the robot's body as Zeus slammed his hands upon Prometheus' back. Thel's vision flickered again, but his grip on the Vexnoxtuque was unwavering. The teleportation system hummed, quickly growing louder. Then they were both gone in a flash of light. The decimated city was replaced by a barren, snowy land. It wasn't too dissimilar from where he fought Athena, Ares, and Iris. Prometheus told him it was different place, however. It was a whole continent of ice and snow.

His vision went black and he began to panic.

"Thes-"

He didn't get to finish his sentence as something impacted with the robot outside and he was overcome with the sense of flying. Another, more jarring impact rocked the robot. With a flicker, his vision returned and he was staring at the sky.

Should have told you we'd have a momentary loss of power, the AI's voice came.

"It would have been nice," Thel snapped. "Especially with our proximity to Zeus."

My apologies.

Thunderous impacts and the ground shaking beneath him told him Zeus was approaching. Thel rolled Prometheus to his feet…in the wrong direction. An impact to Prometheus' back sent him flying. The robot hit the ground face first, sliding through the snow and ice. Thel got Prometheus' arms under him, pushing him to his feet. Thel whirled the robot around, finding Zeus

264

stomping toward him. His body steamed, the enormous amount of heat his body created reacting to the cold air.

The AI was right, though, Thel thought, noticing that with each step Zeus took, his movements became more sluggish and stiff. Zeus stopped, his brows furrowed in confusion. He looked down at his legs with a growl, frustrated at his impaired mobility.

Thel seized the opportunity, propelling Prometheus forward. Zeus noticed his approach a moment before he collided with the Vexnoxtuque, throwing him into the glacier that was behind him. Prometheus stumbled back as Zeus's enormous mass and extreme body temperature carried him through the glacier, which fell atop him. Thel heard Zeus moan, but the creature made no attempt to unbury itself and retaliate. Thel skirted around the crumbled glacier, finding Zeus' head exposed. He breathed heavily, his breath condensating in the near freezing temperature, evaporating. His eyes were wide and radiated with hate and anger.

I...underestimated...you, Zeus breathed.

Thel thrust Prometheus' hand out to his side, about to deploy the hard-light sword when the AI said something that stopped him.

Unknown life-form detected, Prometheus said.

"What are you talking about?" Thel asked, lowering the robot's arm. "Did we miss one of the children? Did one of them become free?"

No, Prometheus replied. *This is something different. Not a Vexnoxtuque. It's something I'm not familiar with.*

The AI was quiet for a moment before speaking again.

There is a distress signal, too. The Atlanteans are under attack by whatever it is.

Thel nodded, looking down at Zeus's exposed head, his eyes closed. He administered Zeus a cryo grenade before melting the surrounding ice to cover the monster,

265

where it almost immediately froze back over due to the extreme cold. To his surprise, and relief, the frozen chunk of ice containing the Vexnoxtuque began to sink into the ground, falling into an undiscovered cave system beneath the continent. Thel covered the hole and turned to the horizon.

"We'll come back and finish the job on the children," Thel said.

Alright, Prometheus said. *I've kept track of the exact coordinates of each of the children.*

"Good job, buddy."

Engaging teleportation system.

After a growing hum as the teleportation system charged up, they were gone in a flash of light.

PLAGUE

39

The bay door opened, fresh air filling the Vexnoxtuque nest along with the sounds of a city, rousing Plague from his slumber. He stood from his nest, stepping out of it and toward the open bay door. A rustling sound turned his attention to another occupied nest; Zeus was stirring.

His mother's scientists had kept the beast sedated since its awakening, knowing the creature would attack them as he and his brothers and sisters saw them as the enemy as they did with their parents, the Titans.

"Plague," his mother's voice came. "Would you be so kind as to show our guest to the door."

Plague made his way to Zeus, unafraid of him as he was still pumped full of sedatives. He grabbed the creature by the shoulders, pulling it from the nest it was resting in and toward the open bay door. Zeus was much bigger than he, so it was a difficult task, but he managed to pull it off with his own enormous strength.

He was stronger than he was before, the new serum that revived him altering his body, though slightly, and making him stronger than ever before. He could feel it coursing through his body. But he was damaged psychologically. The place he was for the last two years, while he was dead, was complete darkness. He'd fought to survive in it. He was chased and toyed with. Now he was out of that place. Ripped away, jarringly. It messed him up.

He shook his head, channeling his old demeanor and ruthlessness.

I'm not going back to that place, he thought.

He looked down at the massive form of Zeus at his feet, then out at the city they'd chosen to set him loose upon. It was like any other human city, alive and lit up

269

in the dark of night. He looked below, seeing a green patch of land, littered with human homes.

A good a place as any, Plague thought and kicked his foot out at Zeus. The larger Vexnoxtuque rolled over the side, landing with a thunderous boom, crushing homes and their occupants. Plague looked down at Zeus. The jarring impact with earth had woken the beast fully. He stood to his full, six-hundred-foot height, smoke billowing around him, looking around. With a mighty roar, Zeus took a step. Then another. He made his way out of the green patch and into the city.

Plague jumped out next, bending his knees as he landed in the rubble of crushed homes, no doubt hiding crushed human bodies beneath. A flash of light in the sky turned his eyes --yes, he had eyes now-- to see the massive mothership in the sky above him.

What is this? Plague wondered.

Another flash of light, this one in the city, beckoned Plague's attention. Two figures stood before him and Zeus, both recognizable: Prometheus and Marugrah.

Once the mothership arrived near the Vexnoxtuque's signature, Will engaged Prometheus' teleportation system, teleporting the robot and Marugrah both into the city below. Will was surprised to find themselves in Las Vegas, Nevada. They stood in the city, side by side, looking over their adversaries.

You're kidding me, Will thought upon seeing the flaming-headed Kaiju that was Plague. *How the hell is he back from the dead?*

Probably the same way Echidna and Typhon are, Will reminded himself.

However, the Plagueonian Prince looked slightly different, mostly in his face. His head was saurian-like, with furrowed brows and blazing orange eyes. The rest of him was basically the same. Armored skin. Armor plated back. Flaming hot hands and tail, the bones within visible. He had more spikes, though.

His attention turned from Plague to the other, bigger Kaiju in the city that he knew to be Zeus. It stood two-hundred-feet taller than the robot he piloted and Marugrah who stood beside him. Shaggy, white hair hung from its fearsome face, below his maw filled with sharp teeth, the first Kaiju Will had seen that had hair. Three rows of jagged spikes ran down his armored back. His arms were thick and armored, ending in five fingers, one longer and thicker than the rest, ending in boney claws. Circular devices, like those he remembered the Titan Hyperion had all over his body, were attached to his palms, these blue in color. He stood on powerful, armored legs, a spike protruding from his knees, ending in four clawed toes. His chest looked like an armored ribcage. His skin was tan in color, his eyes burning yellow, like lightning.

Snarling turned Will's attention to his side, where Marugrah stood. The guardian monster had his eyes locked on Plague, the Plagueonian Prince staring back at the Maruian.

It's decided then, Will thought, making sure Marugah heard it.

The slight nod of Marugrah's fearsome saurian head told Will he heard. With an earth-shaking roar, Marugrah charged, fingers hooked. Will turned his attention to Zeus, the god of thunder stumbling forward, seemingly out of it.

What's wrong? Will wondered, watching as the beast shambled forward, looking dazed and confused.

It appears to be drugged, Prometheus said.

"Maybe Echidna kept it drugged while he was on the ship, so he wouldn't attack them," Will said.

271

It's a possibility, Prometheus replied. *The Titans' children are not allied with the Plagueonians.*

Will just nodded, the robot's head mimicking the action.

It being drugged makes it easier to take down, Prometheus said, getting another nod out of Will.

Will's mind raced, thinking of what to attack Zeus with first.

Zeus's thick skin will absorb the rounds of the railgun, Prometheus said, reading Will's mind. *The swo— I mean Faithful would be an appropriate start.*

"I hate it when you read my mind," Will said with a scowl. "But I trust your judgement. Deploy Faithful!"

Roger.

The sword's hilt shot from the compartment in Prometheus' palm. Will snatched it from the air, the hilt unfolding from its compressed form. Will engaged Faithful's energy blade, it flickering on like green fire, as if the blade was made of the fires of Olympus.

Zeus's head flicked toward Prometheus, his eyes widening a touch. He shifted in the robot's direction. Within moments, Will was facing Zeus head on, a snarl reverberating from the beast's throat.

"It recognizes you," Will said to the AI.

Of course it does, Prometheus said.

Will raised Faithful as Zeus let out a roar that shook the massive robot. He took a step forward, his movements slow and weak still. Will felt confident as he rushed forward, Faithful at the ready. Zeus had the size advantage, but at the moment, Will had the power advantage. He aimed low, swiping Faithful at Zeus's legs. The energy blade sliced through skin and armor, purple blood spraying as Zeus roared in pain. With the Vexnoxtuque's jaws open wide, Will noticed two blue disks in his mouth, one on top and one on the bottom.

272

Zeus swiped his clawed hand down at Prometheus, Will rolling the robot to the side, avoiding the strike. Will swung Faithful out again, striking the beast's ankle in an explosion of flesh and blood, dropping him to one knee. Zeus snarled and roared, lashing out again, faster, anger waking him up. Will couldn't avoid the strike, Zeus' clawed hand smacking Prometheus in the chest, sending the mech flying.

Prometheus skipped across the city, coming to a rest in Southridge, a district of homes, all crushed beneath his metal body. The thought made Will cringe.

The people in the houses…they're all dead…

A rumble pulled Will's attention away from the morbid realization. He looked up to find Zeus stomping toward him, killing even more people with each foot step.

This isn't going to be as easy as we thought…

40

Soon after exiting the Plagueonian fathership and witnessing the beginning of the battle between Prometheus, Zeus, Marugrah, and Plague, I called for pickup, the cloaked VTOL that brought us to the ship picking us up. Now, aboard the futuristic ship, gliding over the city, we watch the battle below, Savernst included, who sits cross legged at the back of the cargo bay, by the closed ramp.

There must be something we can do…

The inside of the cargo area, with ten seats, five on either side, is covered in a series of large, flexible screens, projecting the world outside around them in real time via cameras embedded in the ship's hull. Currently, our attention is directed down, at the city below.

Marugrah opens his maw, his green, crackling flames erupting from within, washing over Plague. It's an ineffective move, however, as Plague's mutation allows him to withstand enormous amounts of heat, parts of his body super-heated and flaming already. Plague lashes out with a flaming hand, the bones within faintly visible. Marugrah squeals in agony as the hand finds his face, burning his armored flesh. Marugrah stumbles to the side, clutching at his injured face. Plague takes advantage of the situation, sending a clawed foot into Marugrah's gut, sending the Kaiju to the ground. Buildings are crushed beneath the Kaiju's massive body.

People too, I can't help but think.

"Get me in touch with Cole," I say to the pilots.

"Roger. Patching you through now, sir," one of the pilots says.

"Cole here," the CCU director responded, his voice voice coming through my headset.

"Cole, it's Jeremy," I say. "I hope you're cooking up a plan to respond to the Kaiju attack here in Vegas."

"Military response hasn't really been effective against a Kaiju in the past," Cole says. "But they do help distract the bad guys long enough for the good guys to get the upper hand."

I smile. "You sound like you have a plan."

"Of course I do. Area 51 has mobilized troops to respond to the attack. They've been leading in researching weapons to use against Kaiju, with some help from DARPA, so they may have a few surprises."

My smile turns into a grin. "Roger that."

Cole disconnects and I connect to the pilot. "Level out here."

"Roger that," the pilot says.

My eyes turn back to the city below. Marugah sits on his knees as Plague closes in on the guardian monster.

"Does this thing have weapons?" I ask.

"We have a chain gun hidden in the craft's underbelly," the pilot replies.

"Open fire on the flaming one!" I order.

"Roger that!"

The pilot swoops the VTOL around behind Plague, the co-pilot activating the ship's weapon systems. The gatling gun emerges from the craft's underbelly, bright orange tracer fire lighting up the night as the gun opens fire on Plague's armor plated back. Plague cranes his head around with a jaw twitch I assume to be a snarl, his eyes squinting in confusion at finding nothing in the sky behind him, the gatling gun having fallen silent as the Kaiju turned toward us.

The eyes are new, I think, remembering photos I've seen of the creature from two years ago. He, like Marugrah, had undergone changes, it seems.

My distraction idea works, Marugrah recovering and standing up behind Plague, arms to his side, fists clenched. Spikes emerge from the chambers on his forearms. Plague turns around slowly, sensing that Marugrah was back on his feet. Marugrah raises his arms, thrusting them, and the spikes protruding from his wrists, forward. The spikes puncture flesh, spraying purple, one in Plague's side, one in his shoulder. Plague threw his flaming-head back, and though I can't hear it, I know he's roaring in pain.

A chuckle turns my attention to Savernst at the back of the cargo bay, her head turned down. She's enjoying Plague's pain. She looks up, seeing me looking at her. She turns her attention up, toward the mothership floating in the sky.

"I need to get up there," Savernst says, her gaze shifting from the ship to me.

The trepidation must show on my face.

"There is something on board that can help the Maruian and the Mechinike," she says.

"Like what?" I ask.

"A weapon. It's been in development for a long time. It was finished before I went undercover. At first, we were going to destroy it, but then the Plagueonians attacked us. We decided to keep it, in case they somehow got hold of a Vexnoxtuque."

"And you're sure it can defeat them?" I motion down at Plague and Zeus.

She nods.

I watch as Prometheus is sent flying by the larger Zeus, skipping through the city. Plague spins, his burning tail catching Marugrah in the side, the Kaiju crying out in pain.

They can't keep this fight up for long...

"Fine," I say. I put the headphones back over my ears, having taken them off to converse with Savernst. "Set a course for the mothership."

"Um, you sure that's a good idea, sir?" the pilot asks, his voice unsure of the order.

"Tsuzar will welcome you," Savernst says.

"Tsuzar helped us two years ago, in the fight against Echidna," Ashley says into her head phones. "He's an ally."

"I'm sure," I say.

"Yes, sir," the pilot says, turning the VTOL toward the mothership.

"Uncloak, too," Savernst says. "So, they see us coming. I'll get in touch with Tsuzar."

I nod and relay the order. The pilots are skeptical about boarding an alien ship. Considering what I just went through, I'd usually agree, but Savernst helped us escape. I doubt she'd turn on us. Not to mention Ashley

276

trusts her, and her leader, Tsuzar. If she trusts them, I'm going to trust her judgement.

I watch out of the windshield, which really isn't a windshield, really a screen like the inside of the cargo bay, as the mothership grows larger, much larger than I expected it to be.

"Tsuzar welcomes you," Savernst says. "He's opening the docking bay for you."

A door near the middle of the underside of the whale-shaped ship opens, beckoning them inside. My heart races as we grow closer, soon entering the ship full of aliens that almost wiped the human race off the face of the planet two years ago.

41

After docking in the bay meant to hold ships, we were escorted through the ship, pilots included, ending up where we now stand, all thirteen of us, including Savernst. The room we entered, the ship's cockpit, is vast, rows of consoles, each occupied by a Hestialite, filling the center of the room. A ramp leads to a lower level at the front of the room, two Hestialites at what look like controls for the massive ship. At the back of the room, a chair much like Echidna's throne sits, a Hestialite wearing royal-looking armor occupying it, giving him the look of a high-ranking officer.

That must be Tsuzar, I think.

Tsuzar stands from his seat and spreads his arms wide.

"Welcome," he says, looking over the team. "It's good to see some familiar faces."

Ashley, Marudon cradled in her arms, half awake, Aaron, Wolf, and Eva, all that is left of the original team from two years ago, minus Will, offer greetings to the leader of the Hestialites.

"Where is the rest of your team?" Tsuzar asks. "Angel, Brice, Walker?"

They hang their heads, Wolf being the one to speak. "They're…dead. Lost last year in the fight against the Order and the Titans."

"Oh. My apologies."

Wolf looks up at Tsuzar. "They died noble deaths. Besides, now we have new friends, including our new captain, Jeremy." He motions to me.

I step forward with an awkward wave. "Nice to meet you."

"Nice to meet you too, Jeremy."

I motion to the rest of my team, pointing to them as I speak their names. "This is Sasha, Josh, Mikayla, Ezekiel, Ben, Joel, and John."

"Pleased to meet you all."

A few awkward seconds pass by before I speak again.

"Savernst says you have a weapon," I say, getting right to business. "A weapon that could help defeat the Kaiju below."

Tsuzar looks at Savernst, then back to me. "Such a weapon does exist, yes. What about it?"

"I want to use it. Prometheus and Marugrah won't be able to hold out against them forever." I motion to the floor as I say 'them', meaning Plague and Zeus. "They weren't fairing too well when we entered your ship."

Tsuzar nods, understanding what I'm getting at. "I understand. Will is your teammate and friend. You're worried."

"Not just Will. Marugrah too. He helped us defeat the Titans last year, and he's helped us defeat the Titans' children thus far. He's as much of an ally and friend as the rest."

Tsuzar nods, smiling. "I consider him the same. He played a big part against the Plagueonians two years ago."

He stares at me for a few moments.

"Fine," he finally says. "I'll take you to the weapon myself." He turns to Savernst. "You're in charge while I'm away. Make our guests at home. And get Marudon some medical attention." He motions to the rest of my team.

Savernst nods and they trade spots, Savernst at the command chair, Tsuzar beside me.

"Follow me," he says and we exit the room via a door on the opposite side.

I take one last look at my team before the doors close, Sasha giving me a worried look. I give her a confident smile, letting her know I know what I'm doing, the doors closing. We continue down a hallway like we traveled down while in the Plagueonian fathership. We stop at the end of the hall, a door before us. Tsuzar turns to me.

"I feel I should be the one to use this weapon," he says. "I understand you wanting to help, but it could drive you to darkness."

I study Tsuzar's face, his eyes pleading.

I understand his side of the story. His race was under the rule of a tyrant for thousands of years, just waiting for the right opportunity to revolt against her. He succeeded, but the fight isn't over and he feels it's his job to finish it. But this is my planet and my friends are in trouble. I need to help them.

"I'll take the risk," I say.

Tsuzar frowns and nods, turning toward the elevator and presses a holographic button to call the elevator.

"I understand where you're coming from," I say. "But it's not just your fight. This is my planet and my friends are in danger."

A smile stretches across his face as he says, "Indeed. I'll give you covering fire from above."

I nod, giving the Hestialite a smile of my own.

The elevator opens and we step inside. The doors close and I barely register that we are descending. The alien elevator is a much smoother ride than the earth variety. We ride in silence for a few long moments before the doors part and we enter a dark room. Lights on the ceiling snap on, bathing the room in light.

It was large, super large, with giant compartments. Like giant rooms.

And one of them is occupied.

Tsuzar motion towards it and says, "This…is the weapon…Saibosuta."

"Wow," I say, looking up at the creature.

"Impressive, I know," Tsuzar says.

"It's…a Kaiju!"

"Sort of. It's more of what you would call a 'cyborg'. Half alive and half machine."

"And it's a weapon?"

"Indeed. It's a bit like Prometheus. It needs a pilot to function."

That's not completely true, I think, remembering how Prometheus took control of itself and attacked Marugrah a year ago. I keep that to myself, though.

"That's what you meant by 'it'll drive you to darkness'. I'd be piloting a Vexnoxtuque, a creature gone mad," I say.

Tsuzar's only response is a nod. He turns to me.

"You still want to go through with this?" he asks.

I nod. "Of course. I'm not going to just sit by and do nothing."

"Well then…let's get you settled behind its controls."

We make our way to a lift next to the Kaiju nest, taking it up to a doorway that leads us around to the creature's back. A compartment opens at the base of Saibosuta's neck, a chair within with a helmet of some sort hanging above it. A bridge extends from the cockpit to the platform we stand on. Tsuzar motions me across.

"Just sit in the chair and put on the helmet. You'll automatically be connected to the creature's nervous system, acting as its brain. It's lobotomized so you'll have full control," he tells me.

I sigh and make my way to the cockpit of the giant monster. I sit in the chair, taking one last look at Tsuzar before the door closed, faint light illuminating the small square space. I look up at the helmet hanging above me. I reluctantly reach up and pull the helmet down, placing it over my head, covering the top half of my head.

Then, everything went dark…

42

Zeus was fully awake now, attacking with bloodthirsty ferocity. Will could hardly keep up with his fast slashing claws, which was surprising for the creature being so large. Zeus' claw caught Prometheus' shoulder, sending the massive robot spinning, the robot tripping over its own feet and falling to the ground, crushing more small-scale buildings.

"Dammit," Will growled.

Will used the thrusters on the robot's waist and chest to lift Prometheus off the ground and get him back on his feet. A roar from Zeus announced the Kaiju's approach. Will spun Prometheus, channeling the momentum into Faithful. The crackling green blade of energy struck flesh, cleaving a gash in Zeus' gut. Zeus

roared in pain as purple blood sprayed from the wound.
Will swung the sword around, Zeus catching the blade
in his hand. The flesh steamed and bled as Will tried to
wretch the blade free from the Kaiju's grasp. Zeus
pulled, Faithful slipping from Prometheus' metal hands,
sending the sword flying through the city, cleaving
through the Stratosphere Tower and embedding in the
building behind it, what looked to be a fancy hotel.

Shit!

Will resorted to fists, throwing punches into the
Kaiju's injured gut. Purple flecked the robot's fists as
they connect with the gash on Zeus' stomach. Zeus
roared and squealed each time Prometheus' fists
connected with the wound. Zeus kicked out, tossing
Prometheus away. The robot flipped through the air,
Will using the thrusters to stabilize the mech. Will was
able to land the robot on its feet, sliding through the city,
finally coming to a stop.

Orders? Prometheus asked.

"Get the tasers ready," Will said.

Roger that.

Compartments in both of Prometheus' arms snapped
open, devices flipping out from within, extending to the
sides and locking in front of his fists like brass knuckles
with prongs on the front instead of spikes. Electricity
sparked between the prongs.

Zeus roared, stalking forward, claws hooked. Will
stood his ground as the Kaiju approached. Will reeled
back the mech's arms and shot it forward. Electricity
shot into the gash as the prongs made contact. Zeus
squealed in pain as Will threw punch after punch,
electricity shooting into the god of thunder's body.

Doesn't this bring back memories? Plague asked, a
mental chuckle echoing through Marugrah's head.

Death and destruction is what I remember, Marugrah replied.

Plague chuckled again.

Marugrah snarled.

You're still the same as always, Marugrah, Plague scoffed. *Arrogant and impulsive. It's a wonder you were able to defeat me twice before.*

Enough talking, monster! Marugrah roared and charged at his enemy.

Rubble crunched beneath his massive feet as he stomped his way across the green patch of land, the homes it once held crushed when Zeus fell upon them, decimating them. Marugrah collided with Plague, pushing the Kaiju back, his feet sliding as he tried to stop Plague's advance. Buildings were decimated as Marugrah pushed Plague through homes that were untouched by Zeus. Marugrah pushed, throwing Plague into the y-shaped Las Vegas Hilton, immediately regretting it as he felt hundreds of lives inside the building wink out of existence as the Kaiju crushed it.

As I said, Plague said as he shook the rubble from his body and began to climb to his feet. *Impulsive. You're trying to defend humanity, yet you also destroy it in the process.*

It's the price that must be paid to save many more, Marugrah said solemnly, remembering something that Cole said two years previous.

Plague's laugh echoed in Marugrah's head.

People are going to die no matter what. Whether it be by my hand, your hand or their own. It's inevitable, Marugrah said.

Yes, humanity is a destructive race of fools. I don't understand why you protect them, Plague said.

Because…I have faith that they have the ability to change.

You're as big of a fool as they are! Plague charged, burning fingers hooked. Marugrah sidestepped the charging Kaiju, raising his foot and tripping the Plagueonian Prince. Plague quickly rolled back to his feet, facing Marugrah once again.

They will never change, Plague growled. *They're like us that way. We're monsters meant to destroy. I know you feel the bloodlust creeping up on you. They were designed to be food, but the fools that are the vampires used their own DNA to make them; making them destructive. All they know is to destroy, like us!*

You're wrong! Marugrah said. *I am no monster. Never was. I'm nothing like you! I can make my own choices. Lay my own path. Determine my future. You know nothing but war and destruction. We only knew it because of you! It's the same with the humans. They only know it because of the vampires.*

Plague laughed. *You damn fool.*

Marugrah brought his fists up, taking a fighting stance, the spikes still protruding from the chambers on his forearms. *Maybe, but I'm the fool that is going to defeat you for the third time.*

Plague brought his own burning fists up. *We'll see about that.*

The two Kaiju warriors charged at each other, Marugrah avoiding a punch from Plague aimed for his face, swiping his wrist spike low, slashing the Prince across his unarmored side. Plague screeched in pain, bringing his knee up, connecting with Marugrah's armored gut, the pain dull, but jarring. Marugrah stumbled back, barely registering that Plague had spun, the burning end of his tail connecting with Marugrah's side, scorching his flesh. Marugrah threw his head back and roared in pain.

You're dead, Maruian, Plague said confidently.

"We're dead," **Will** said as Prometheus laid on his back, Zeus stalking toward them.

The taser gauntlets had worked for a time, but Zeus was resilient when it came to pain, pushing past it and retaliating.

Incoming projectile, Prometheus said, turning Will's attention skyward. Something was falling from the sky, heading straight for Zeus.

The hell is that? Will wondered, trying to zoom in on the object, but it was moving too fast.

Zeus must've sensed its approach, too, turning around and looking up at the falling object seconds before it collided with him and sent him to the ground on his back with a thunderous boom, a cloud of smoke washing over him and the object that collided with him.

Not smoke, Will realized as he got Prometheus to his feet. *Steam.*

After a few moments, the steam cloud evaporated, revealing the object to him, standing atop the massive form of Zeus, its eyes locked on Prometheus.

Will took a step back, raising Prometheus' fists, the tasers still deployed.

The creature was mostly covered in armor, the purple speckled, crimson red flesh of its neck, mouth, bottom jaw, stomach, between the shoulder and fore arm, right hand, and the toes on its left foot all that showed. The gray and gold battle armor greatly resembled that of a Plagueonian. Upon closer inspection, the creature's left arm and right leg were robotic, sporting the same color scheme of the battle armor. Three green eyes sat on its face, one on the front, one on either side of its head. Various vents covering the Kaiju's body vented steam, the creature seemingly producing untold amounts of heat. It raised its hands in a 'calm down' gesture.

"Will, it's me," the voice of his commander entered his ears.

"Jeremy?" Will asked, surprised, lowering Prometheus' fists.

The creature before him nodded its head, holding its arms out to its sides, palms skyward.

"Meet Saibosuta."

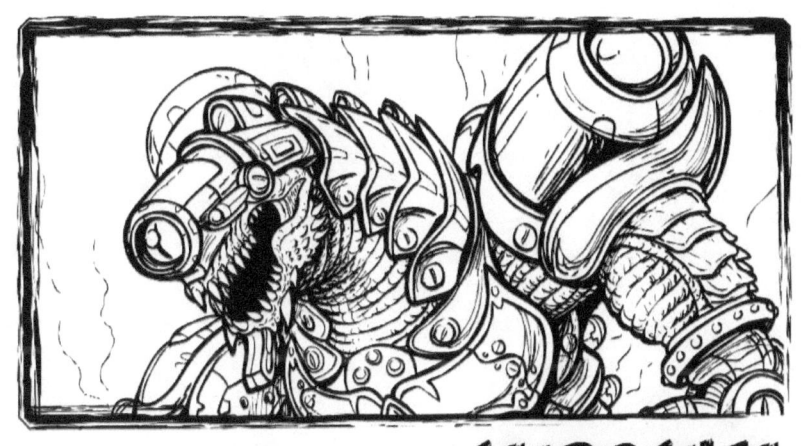

SAIBOSUTA

43

The beast I landed on, Zeus, shudders beneath
Saibosuta's feet, a growl reverberating from the Kaiju's
throat. I jump away, sliding the cyborg up next to
Prometheus. Zeus got to his feet, looking from me to
Prometheus. I see confusion from the sudden appearance
of the newcomer in his glowing yellow eyes.

"Saibo got some cool features going for him that could
help us?" Will asks.

I focus, searching for any special abilities Saibosuta
may be hiding. I smile when I find one. The three
fingers on Saibosuta's robotic arm clench into a fist,
seemingly deconstructing back into the arm, revealing a
proton cannon. I raise the weapon up and say, "Like
this?"

I hear Will chuckle, Prometheus' helmet-like head
nodding at me.

Zeus' anger filled roar turns our attention back to the
god of thunder. He charges, mouth wide, electricity
sparking between the disk devices in his mouth. As the
electric currents from both devices meet in the middle, a
ball of energy forms, electricity shooting from within
like a lightning beam. Will and I dive to opposite sides
as Zeus' attack strikes where we were standing. I roll
Saibosuta to his feet, crushing buildings and cars
beneath his massive feet, bringing the arm that has
transformed into a cannon up. A yellow beam of energy
shoots from the cannon, burning a path of black into
Zeus' armored side.

Zeus turns to me, his white hair swaying back and
forth, his mouth open, lightning shooting from his
mouth. I'm unable to avoid the attack. Chunks of
Saibosuta's shoulder armor was blown away, sending
the creature spinning. I'm able to stop Saibosuta's spin,

finding Will descending upon Zeus, having leapt in the air, Faithful back in his hands, pointed downwards, at the Kaiju's spike covered, armored back.

Zeus roars in pain as the energy blade scrapes down his back, carving off skin and armor, and cleaving off a few of his spikes. I aim for the gash on his stomach, firing the proton cannon at it. Armored skin and purple blood fly away from Zeus' stomach as the energy beam contacts the wound. Zeus stumbles back, a clawed hand to his gut, trying to hold his intestines in his body.

I focus again, Saibosuta's robotic arm transforming once again, the hand returning, turning into a buzz saw, the fingers acting as the blades, spinning. I slash the arm out, the saw ripping through the armored skin of his arm. Zeus pulls his arm away with a roar of pain, his colorful insides falling in a bloody heap at his feet. Zeus looks down at his intestines, his eyes wide, his jaws trembling in pain and shock.

"Now!" I say.

Prometheus steps around Zeus, swinging faithful downward, severing the organs from the Kaiju's body. Zeus roars in pain once again. I will the robot arm to transform from the saw to the cannon, firing a proton beam into Zeus' eviscerated gut, the beam exploding out the creature's back. With the Kaiju's spine severed, his legs fall out from under him as he falls face first into rubble. We look down at the twitching god of thunder as the life slowly fades from him.

"It's almost sad," Will says.

I crane Saibosuta's head toward Prometheus, whose armored head is still turned down, looking at Zeus.

"How so?" I ask.

"None of them asked for what was done to them," he replies. "They might have been peaceful if not for Echidna and her scientists experimenting on them."

290

I look back at Zeus, his body gone still. He's dead. He might have been strong, but for some reason, he was sluggish. Almost…hindered. He was unable to keep up with two enemies, ending in his demise. While Will may think he didn't deserve it, and maybe he didn't, he was still a monster. He has killed untold amounts of people and needed to be put down either way.

"It needed to be done," I say.

Prometheus' head nods, imitating Will. I nod Saibosuta's head back at him. I turn, shifting my attention to the other battle happening in the city, hundreds of feet away. Will follows my lead.

Marugrah stumbles back, clutching his side. His foot catches on something and he falls, landing on his back. Plague struts toward him in a confident manner, moving in for the kill. Will and I glance at each other, through the robot and monster we pilot, and nod. We rush forward, side by side, not caring that we were crushing buildings along the way, all of them evacuated. Plague stops, just feet from the fallen Marugrah, his eyes widened in surprise.

An explosion from above stops us in our tracks, our eyes snapping skyward. Plague's and Marugrah's too. An object falls from the sky, landing between Will and I and Plague and Marugrah, a cloud of dust obscuring whatever it is.

"I have a feeling this one isn't an ally," Will says.

"Same," I say.

As the dust clears, a horrifying beast is revealed. *Another Vexnoxtuque…*

The monster stands up straight, his arms to his side.

"Ah…," a deep voice echoes in my head. "I forgot how it felt to be in this form."

I clench Saibosuta's hands, his robotic arm back to normal. "Who are you?"

The monster shifts its horrendous face toward me, tilting it to the side. He chuckles and bows. As he straightens back up, he says, "I? I am Thorath, a general in the Plagueonian army." His mouth drops open, tentacles unfurling from within.

I hook Saibosuta's claws.

"A little antsy are we?" Thorath asks with a chuckle.

"I never was one for talking with my enemies. I prefer to let my fists…err…claws do the talking," I say.

"Fair enough," Thorath says, charging.

"I've got this ass clown!" I say to Will. "You go help Maru!"

I see Prometheus nod and watch him skirt around as Thorath collides with Saibosuta, the two of us grappling. The two tentacles on Thorath's back, ending in armored diamond shaped structures snake around toward me. As the fleshy centers begin to open, I bring Saibosuta's armored knee up, plunging it into Thorath's gut. The fleshy centers close, Thorath stumbling back, a gnarly hand to his gut. His brows furrow, his eyeballs waving angrily via tendrils.

I roar at Thorath, surprising myself at the volume and ferocity of it. Thorath flinches back, just as surprised.

I charge.

44

"Ma'am."

Echidna turned, finding the scientist she sent away standing beside her, a case in his hand. She reached a shaking hand toward the case, but once she reached where it was, it was gone. She whirled to the being that took it, her anger spiking, it already high at the death of Zeus.

"Typhon," she growled.

He had the case open, looking inside. He plucked a vial from within, holding it up, the blue liquid within swishing. He handed it to Echidna, her brows furrowing at the gesture. He confused her.

Then he pulled out a second vial filled with the blue liquid and said, "I knew if you found two vials, you'd try to take them both."

He wasn't wrong.

She took the vial in her shaking hand, the pain in her side intense, her healing abilities all but useless. In the time it took for the scientist to retrieve the vials, it had healed a tiny bit, blood still gushing from her side.

I'm going to die again..., she thought.

She shook her head as the memories of what she went through the last two years in the realm of darkness entered her mind.

No, I'm not going back!

She jabbed the diamond tipped needle into her arm, depressing the trigger, the blue liquid surging into her body. It felt cold, overtaking her arm and spreading throughout her body. She glanced over at Typhon as he depressed the trigger, the blue liquid surging into his arm. He looked over at her.

"We do this together...partner," he said.

If only you knew my true intentions...

She chuckled internally.

As far as the vampire knew, they were working together to take over Earth which they would then divide equally. However, she was using him and his vampires. Once they succeeded, she and her Plagueonian army would turn on them and wipe them out.

She pulled her hand away from her injured side, finding it fully healed.

A searing heat overtook her body, a scream tearing from her throat.

"My Queen!" the Plagueonian scientist that brought the serum to her called, running up to her. "Are you alright?"

She screamed again, her arm lashing out, striking the Plagueonian scientist and sending him flying across the control room.

Another scream tore through the air, this one from Typhon.

Terror swept across the fathership's control room as Typhon and Echidna began to change into horrific versions of themselves.

Will felt bad about leaving Jeremy behind to take on the Kaiju that introduced himself as Thorath. He was like Plague, a Plagueonian-turned-Vexnoxtuque, which meant he was just as deadly. After seeing the way he handled the beast known as Saibusuta, Will had faith his Captain would be just fine.

Will made a beeline for Plague, who had resumed closing in on the fallen Marugrah. The pounding of Prometheus' metal feet drew Plague's attention. He ducked as Will thrust Faithful at him, sending a burning fist into Prometheus' metal gut. Will brought the butt of Faithful's stock upon Plague's flaming head, aiming to daze the Kaiju.

Plague wrapped his arms around Prometheus' waist, lifting the mech off its feet and dropping backwards. Prometheus' metal face found the rubble covered ground, Plague letting go of Prometheus' waist and rolling to his feet. Using the thrusters mounted on the robot's back and chest, Will got Prometheus to his feet.

You back for revenge for me taking your princess? Plague asked, his mentally projected voice full of snark.

To Will's surprise, Prometheus was the one to respond.

Yes, the AI said, *I...we...will get revenge for both Thel-Shuum and Dal-Un!*

Plague chuckled.

During their banter, Marugrah had gotten to his feet, standing behind the alien prince. Plague, sensing the Maruian Kaiju behind him, slowly turned, coming flaming face to saurian face. Will slid Prometheus up behind Plague, grabbing the Plagueonian Kaiju's arms, pulling them behind him, planting a metal foot on his armor plated back. Plague roared in pain, struggling to free himself.

Marugrah clenched his fists, spikes slowly sliding from the chambers on his wrists. Plague's struggle became frantic. Marugrah's brows furrowed, his lips lifting, revealing his sharp teeth, his growl filling the air. He raised both his arms, thrusting them forward, the jagged spikes finding the softer flesh of Plague's sides. Plague threw his flaming head back, wailing in agony. He leaned his head forward, opening his jaws wide. A swooshing sound sounded from his throat, the flames in front of his mouth shooting forward, washing over Marugrah's face.

Marugrah stumbled back, clutching at his seared face. His spikes slipped out of Plague's side with twin slurps, black blood gushing from the wounds. Plague chuckled. Will pulled on his already caught arms, getting a grunt of pain from the beast. Will heaved upward with Prometheus' leg, throwing Plague off his feet and into the air. Will used the momentum to swing the Kaiju up and over the giant robot he controlled.

Will turned Prometheus as Plague hit the ground, shaking it like an earthquake, sending rubble and dust flying into the air. Marugrah stepped up next to him, looking battered and tired.

Makes sense, Will thought. *He's been fighting nonstop against the Titans' children...*

Marugrah roared, angry and fierce, his long tail ending in a spiked club twitching.

He's using anger to energize himself...

Plague stumbled to his feet; dazed. He shook his flaming head, squinting his eyes in anger.

Marugrah dropped to all fours, taking a flanking position. Will did the same, taking a spot on the opposite side of Plague. Plague looked back and forth frantically, unsure of what to do.

"Now!" Will said, charging Prometheus forward, Faithful at the ready.

Marugrah aimed low, going for Plague's leg, while Will aimed high, swinging Faithful at Plague's armored chest.

They both missed.

Plague jumped back, Marugrah's face hitting the rubble covered ground, getting a mouth full of concrete, dirt, and grass. Prometheus stumbled forward, the momentum of the swung sword carrying him forward, where he tripped over Marugrah.

Plague laughed.

You fools. You'll never beat me being as uncoordinated as you are, he said.

"He's right," Will said, connecting with Marugrah.

Will got Prometheus to his feet, helping Marugrah up. Marugrah nodded at him, understanding.

What do you propose? Marugrah asked.

"Well..."

Will laid out his plan to Marugrah, who nodded.

You two done? Plague asked, his flaming head tilted to the side, a burning hand on his armored hip. A raised brow completed the sassy gesture.

"Did he...hear our conversation?" Will asked.

296

No, Prometheus replied, *I blocked his telepathic signal. Only Marugrah heard it.*

Will sighed in relief. "Good."

Indeed.

Plague stood up straight, cracking his knuckles.

"Sassy bastard," Will mumbled.

Marugrah grunted his agreement.

Will and Marugrah charged, side by side. Marugrah had his wrist spikes deployed, Prometheus having Faithful at the ready.

A more coordinated double team, huh? Plague scoffed. *How cute.*

"Remember the plan," Will said.

Roger, Marugrah replied.

Will swung Faithful high, aiming to lob off Plague's head, but, as predicted, the prince of the Plagueonians ducked. While Will had distracted Plague, Marugrah had snuck around behind him, using his tail to take out the back of his knees. Plague roared as his knees gave out on him, the Kaiju falling forward. Will spun Faithful around, thrusting the sword downward, the energy blade slipping through Plague's armored back. It exploded out his chest. Plague roared, its tone high and pained.

Y-you damn f-fools, Plague growled, his voice quivering with pain.

An explosion pulled Will's eyes upward. Twin fireballs rained from the sky as a shimmering shape started drifting to the side. The giant shape soon revealed itself to be a giant, armored, Kaiju-like ship.

You guys are in trooouuuubbbblllle, Plague said in a sing-song voice. *She's coming...*

"Who's...coming...?" Will asked.

Echidna.

ECHIDNA

45

An explosion turns Saibosuta's head upward. Through his eyes, I see the shimmering shape of the Kaiju-like fathership we infiltrated. The bottom of it, near the front had exploded, twin fireballs falling from the sky.

What the hell? I wonder.

"It's her," Thorath says, his attention skyward as well.

Her...?

Does he mean Echidna? How could that be her? She's only ten feet tall. The fire balls falling from the sky are huge, much bigger than the Plagueonian Queen.

The image of the MegaHydra flits through my mind.

The blue liquid we found... Could they have more? Would she be stupid enough to inject herself with it?

Of course she would. She's a tyrant. She wants power. Turning into a Kaiju would be a big change in power level.

The first fireball arrives in the city, decimating the Atomic Testing Museum and the surrounding buildings, leaving only a giant crater filled with smoke and flame.

The second fireball arrives next, landing in the heart of the city with the same result, a crater filled with flame and smoke left in its wake.

From within both craters, giant forms stir. I tense, feeling the darkness radiating from their souls, filtering through the Kaiju I'm piloting. It sends a shiver through my actual body, Saibosuta following suit.

"You can feel it, can't you?" Thorath asks. "Their energy. Their power."

A growl slips from Saibosuta's mouth, under my direction. Thorath chuckles, clearly amused with me.

Not the response I was looking for...

My attention turns toward the crater in the heart of the city, the smoke dissipating, a massive form standing within. A breeze carts away the last of the smoke, revealing the dark gray beast standing within. Its head is horrible, reminding me of some sort of demon, armored and horned. Furrowed brows above blazing purple eyes. A skull-like nose. Its maw drops open, filled with sharp teeth. Jagged armor plates run down the Kaiju's back, ending at its ass. Three wriggling, spiked tendrils ending in snapping maws filled with sharp teeth protrude from each of her sides. Strong, armored arms hang at the creature's sides, ending in four clawed fingers. It stands on stocky, armored legs ending at feet with four tendrils ending at snapping jaws. The basic shape of the creature is the same, though, and tells me exactly who I'm looking at.

Echidna.

Kaiju Echidna, just what I need, I think with a roll of my eyes. Well, I imagine I rolled my eyes, at least.

Another roar turns my attention in the opposite direction, where the Atomic Testing Museum once was, another beast revealed. Its head is almost like an armored bat, with long pointy ears framing its horrific face. Long fangs are surrounded by smaller, but just as deadly, teeth. Its armored brows are furrowed, anger radiating from its red eyes. Spiky armored plates run from the base of its head, down its back, ending at its tail bone. Two giant spikes protrude from the Kaiju's shoulders. Two armored arms hang at its sides, its armored hands with five gnarly fingers ending at wicked claws, clench into fists. It stands on armored legs, ending in five toes, three on the front, two on either side of the back, each ending in sharp talons. Its chest is armored, decorated with swirling designs. The most disturbing part of the creature is the 'snakes', like those on Echidna, that cover its body. They protrude from its arms, legs, chest, back, and three act as its 'tails'.

Is that...Typhon?

It must be. Great. Kaiju Echidna and Typhon...

"Think we can take them?" I ask Will, barely avoiding Thorath's swiping claws.

"Well, there is three of them and three of us," Will says.

"Three?" I throw a punch into Thorath's gut, pitching the beast forward. I bring Saibosuta's knee up into Thorath's chin, the Kaiju stumbling back; dazed. "You take care of Plague?"

"He's not moving, so I'm pretty sure the bastard is dead."

"Good." Thorath roars and charges. A quick glance to either side reveals Echidna and Typhon closing in, their roars echoing through the Las Vegas night air, sending shivers down my spine.

"You can't hope to beat us all," Thorath says, sounding confident. "One of us alone is powerful, but three of us together, we are unstoppable!"

Saibosuta grunts with my scoff. "We'll see about that."

The tentacles pop up from behind Thorath, the rings within the diamond shaped structure at the end vibrating, the fleshy centers opening, releasing twin sonic booms that send shockwaves of pain through Saibosuta's body. Saibosuta squeals with my pained shout. I stumble back, Saibosuta's hands to his head. Two more booms rock Saibosuta's body, the Kaiju squealing in agony with me.

Thorath roars, the earth shaking beneath Saibosuta's feet. I look up to see Prometheus, Marugrah by his side, looking at their feet where Thorath lays. Prometheus' helmet-like face turns toward me.

"You okay?" Will asks.

I nod Saibosuta's head. "K-kinda. That hurt."

Will chuckles. "I could tell."

303

I look to either side of us. Typhon and Echidna are halfway to us, stomping their way through the city, uncaring of the death and destruction they are causing. Echidna stops, looking down at the body at her feet. She kneels, taking the body in her hands. Plague's body. She cradles it, one hand behind his flaming head and one on his armor plated back. Her eyes furrow, a wail slipping from her fanged mouth as she throws her head back.

"Well…shit. Now she's super pissed," I say.

"Which means she's going to act on instinct. Anger will cloud her mind. Make her predictable. Believe it or not, that's a good thing," Will says.

Marugrah nods his agreement, knowing firsthand what anger does to a Vexnoxtuque's mind. He looks down at Thorath, who had begun to stir, stomping on the Kaiju's head, knocking him out again.

A presence turns me around in time to avoid a clawed fist being thrust at my face. I grab the fist and kick out Saibosuta's robotic foot, kicking Typhon's out from beneath him. He roars as he goes down, landing face first next to Thorath. A roar turns me back to Echidna who has broken into a sprint, anger radiating from her purple eyes.

The ground shakes beneath our feet, stumbling the charging Echidna. I look to the distance, finding the fathership crashed, its hull blazing with yellow flames. It seems the crew tried to land the ship, but all they managed to do was crash. I can only hope they all died. Our Plagueonian and Remnant problem solved for good.

She looks from the ship to Zeus' corpse not too far from where we stand, her gaze finally landing on us, glowing with sinister intent.

"It's all falling apart!" she roars, thrusting a finger at us. "And it's all because of you three!"

I'm pushed forward, Typhon getting to his feet while we were distracted. I stumble forward, turning back to the vampire Kaiju, finding Thorath standing next to him, having also gotten to his feet, throwing away both Marugrah and Prometheus.

"Fear not, my dear Echidna," Typhon says. "We still have a chance to prevail!"

I clench Saibosuta's hands. There is no way in hell I'm letting these bastards win. For Saibosuta's size, the cyber Kaiju is quick. Saibosuta's metal hand finds Typhon's gut, pitching the vampire Kaiju forward. As he does, the many snakes covering his body snap at me, missing by mere feet. I spin Saibosuta, the Kaiju performing a roundhouse kick, sending Typhon crashing into Thorath before he could react to my attack, both alien behemoths falling to the ground in a tangle of limbs. I hear Echidna roar, outraged with my attack on her allies. I turn in time to see Marugrah grappling with the Plagueonian-turned-Vexnoxtuque.

The battle begins.

Battle Las Vegas

46

Sasha was glued to the view screen that displayed the battle raging below them. It started with Plague and Zeus and it would end with Typhon, Echidna, and Thorath. Marugrah, Will, and Jeremy were holding their own, but Sasha had a feeling something was going to go wrong. She couldn't help but feel nervous for her boyfriend. He had just ran off to pilot a giant monster without even consulting her first. She knew he could be impulsive, especially if he felt it was for the greater good.

That also means protecting me, she thought with a faint smile, a hand to her stomach.

After Jeremy had left with Tsuzar, Marudon was taken away by what she could only assume to be Hestialite medics to attend to her wounds. The rest of them were given chairs, alien in design, but recognizable, to sit in and weird alien food that actually tasted pretty good. It was a good twenty minutes before Tsuzar returned…without Jeremy. Sasha stood from her seat, her empty food tray next to her chair. Tsuzar, knowing her unasked question, motioned to the view screen.

She watched the battle unfold until the moment they were at now: a three on three fight. Marugrah was grappling with Echidna, growling and snapping their jaws at each other. Her six tendrils ending in snake-like jaws swooped around behind the maroon Kaiju, their teeth digging into his flesh in various places. He threw his head back, roaring in pain. He brought his head back down, leveling his emerald eyes at her. Her violet eyes widened in surprise at the intensity of them. He tightened his grip on her hands and spun. Momentum lifted Echidna off her feet. Marugrah let go, hundreds of teeth ripping from his maroon flesh as Echidna was sent

309

flying through the city, skipping like a stone across water.

The camera changed, switching to Will, piloting Prometheus, fighting Thorath. The mutant Plagueonian Kaiju stumbled back from a punch to the face with a hiss, the tendrils in his mouth writhing in agitation. Tentacles popped up from behind Thorath, ending in what looked like tentacular clubs, like something on a squid. Though, unlike a squid, the club lacked suckers and instead had rings of armor surrounding a fleshy center. The fleshy center opened, unleashing a sonic blast upon the robot. Prometheus stumbled back, clearly in distress from the attack. The three-barreled cannon on Prometheus' back snapped up, firing a barrage of laser blasts at the attacking Kaiju, cutting off Thorath's painful attack. Prometheus stomped forward as Thorath righted himself. Prometheus deployed what Sasha knew were called 'tasers', the devices locking themselves over the robot's fists. He threw a punch at Thorath, electricity sparking against his armored flesh. The Plagueonian Kaiju roared in pain. Prometheus threw another punch. And then another. Each time, the Kaiju took a step back, wailing in pain, electricity sparking off his armored flesh.

The camera changed focus again. The snakes covering Typhon's body snapped at the cyborg beast that she was just informed was known as 'Saibosuta'.

That's the creature Jeremy is piloting, Sasha thought anxiously. She didn't like the idea of her boyfriend inside a giant rage machine.

Seeing Sasha's distress, Ashley, sitting in a chair next to her, grabs her hand, giving it a squeeze. She gave Ashley a smile. The two had grown close since meeting the previous year. Same with Jeremy and Will. Now the two were fighting side by side, piloting giants.

310

While we sit here and watch, she thought helplessly. She knew Ashley felt the same.

"Kick his ass, Jeremy!" Josh shouted at the screen as Jeremy made his move.

Saibosuta's mechanical arm transformed, seemingly deconstructing and reconstructing into something new. It resembled Prometheus' hard-light sword, complete with a crackling blue energy blade. He slashed his blade arm at Typhon, cleaving away one of the lunging snakes covering the vampire king's body. Typhon roared in pain as black sprayed from the severed snake. Typhon stumbled back, fists clenched, jaw twitching in anger. Saibosuta stomped forward, slashing his sword arm at Typhon, cleaving away two more snakes. Typhon stumbled back again, claws hooked, shaking with uncontainable rage. Typhon roared and lunged at Saibosuta. The cyber Kaiju reeled back his blade arm, about to stab Typhon through the chest when his cybernetic limb was caught by a flaming hand.

"Jeremy!" Sasha cried as Saibosuta's robotic arm was pulled from the creature's body and Typhon plowed into him, sending him toppling to the rubble covered ground.

TYPHON

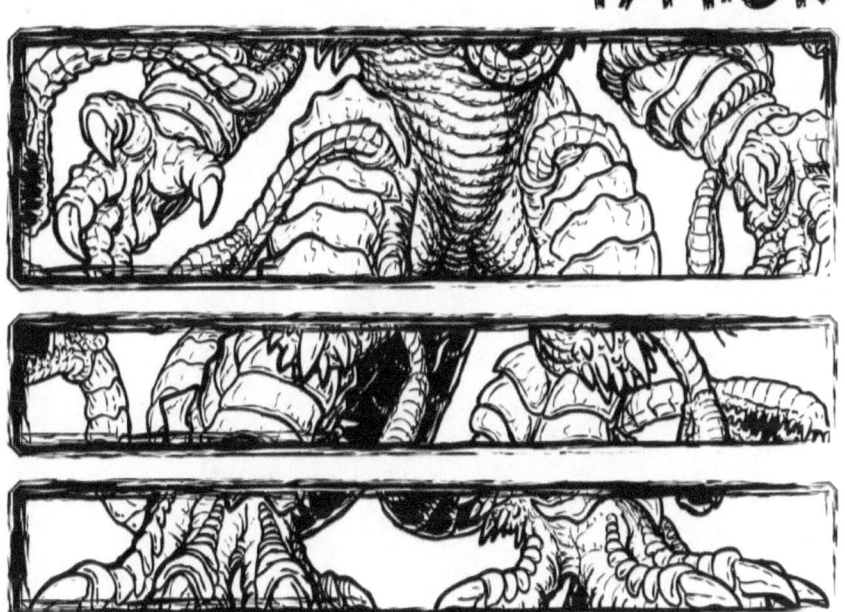

47

Pain rockets through my body as Saibosuta's cybernetic arm is pulled from his body. I don't get a chance to see who attacked me while I was busy with Typhon as I'm tackled to the ground by the vampire Kaiju. I claw at Typhon with Saibosuta's remaining arm. I feel his claws slice into Typhon's flesh, his blood spraying against Saibosuta's armored skin. Typhon roars in pain, raising his body up enough for me to get Saibosuta's legs under him and push the snake-covered Kaiju off the cyber-beast. As Typhon is sent flying, I roll Saibosuta to his feet…coming face to flaming face with Plague.

How…? I think.

Plague thrusts out a clawed foot, connecting with Saibosuta's gut, sending us pitching forward in pain. Plague twists, his flaming tail connecting with Saibusuta's side, sending pain rocketing through us as we fell to the ground once more. Plague chuckles above us.

I then realize I've been referring to Saibosuta and me as 'us'.

Pathetic, Plague says, his voice entering my head telepathically. *I sense you within that abomination, human.*

I roll Saibosuta to his feet, barely avoiding Plague's stomping foot.

"How are you still alive? Didn't Prometheus shove a sword through your heart?" I ask, honestly baffled.

Plague chuckles, amused by my confusion. *The serum that was used to revive me was made using Hydra DNA. The DNA bonded with mine, granting me regenerative abilities. It's slower than the Hydra's, but it's still there,* he explains.

Always with the Hydra, I mentally groan.

Plague clenches his fists. *Enough talk*, he growled. *We're going to rip you from that abomination!*

We?

I turn Saibosuta to find Typhon standing behind me. With a smirk, Typhon sends a fist to Saibosuta's face, making us stumble back…right unto Plague's flung fist. We stumble, our foot catching a piece of rubble and sending us tumbling to the ground. I turn Saibosuta's head upward, finding both Typhon and Plague standing above me, looking down at us menacingly. They pounce, tearing into Saibosuta's body as we scream in agony.

Tendrils wriggled in Prometheus' metal hand. Thorath squealed in pain as Will increased the pressure on his tendrils. Another squeal, this one not from Thorath, but from another creature. He turned, finding Plague and Typhon standing over his fallen ally, blood spraying, tossing limbs and organs over their shoulders.

"Jeremy!" Will cried, kneeing Thorath in his gut and tossing the Kaiju aside. He broke Prometheus into a run, grabbing Plague by his armor plated back and threw the beast away. He spun Prometheus, the robot's leg connecting with Typhon's side, throwing the Kaiju away. He frantically scanned the mangled mess of flesh and metal that was Saibosuta.

"Life signs?" he asked the AI.

Scanning, Prometheus reported. *The Kaiju is definitely dead, but I am detecting a life sign. Human…Well, not exactly, but you know.*

"Jeremy," Will said. "How do I extract him from…this?"

My scans indicate a hatch located at the base of Saibosuta's neck.

Will flipped the corpse over, quickly finding the hatch. Before he could order Prometheus to open the hatch, it opened, Jeremy popping his head out. He looked up at the giant robot that saved him, giving it a wave. He looked to be fine, despite pain obvious on his face. Will sighed in relief.

Relief washes over me in waves, along with pain, as I look up at the giant metal face of my savior. I disconnected the neural connection with Saibosuta before Typhon and Plague started eviscerating the cyber Kaiju. During their assault, I was tossed around the 'cockpit', knocking my head a few times.

The relief fades as twin shadows fall over Prometheus.

"Behind you!" I shout.

Prometheus turns, getting a fist to his metal face. The robot stumbles to the side from the blow as Typhon, the one who threw the punch, and Plague advance on him.

"Get out of here!" Will's voice booms through the air.

I hesitate for a moment before Plague's flaming head turns toward me. I quickly climb from Saibosuta's cockpit, descending from the dead Kaiju toward the ground. An impact shakes me loose. I catch a glimpse of Plague's flaming fist smashing the cockpit, the punch meant for me.

The ground is unforgiving. I'm sure if I were human, I'd have died from the impact, my spine, and most of my bones, shattered. I'm not human, though, and it just hurts like a sonuvabitch. My skin is probably bruised and scraped to hell. I shrug it off, stumbling to my feet. My mind swirls from the knocks I took inside Saibosuta's cockpit. I push past it the best I can when I see Plague sight in on me again, a snarl erupting from his flaming, sharp-toothed maw. I do the only thing I can: I run.

I avoid chunks of concrete from decimated buildings along with other debris, hopping over it or swerving around it. Smoke is thick in the air, irritating my lungs and making me cough. The ground shudders beneath my feet as Plague pursues me.

Why am I running? I think to myself. *I can't outrun a Kaiju...*

I'm about to give up when something ahead of me catches my eye. I'm filled with hope and pour as much speed as my wobbling legs allow me. Plague is still hot on my heels. I know by how close his footsteps sound. Just feet away.

A yellow light illuminates the dark sky ahead of me, the beam slicing through the blackness, aimed behind me. I slid to a stop, turning in time to see the laser strike Plague's armored chest, throwing the Kaiju back with a roar. I waste no time, turning back in the direction of the ship and take off as fast as my battered body can manage.

I didn't have to go far, since the ship came to me. It was like the mothership, whale-like in shape, but smaller. A dropship, if I had to assume its purpose. It swings around, the doors on the side opening. Familiar and welcome faces beckon me toward them. I hustle to them, jumping in the ship and all but collapse inside. I'm wrapped in a strong yet gentle hug. I return the embrace.

"I'm glad you're okay," Sasha whispers in my ear, her voice cracking, trying to hold back her emotions.

I frown and lower my head. I hate to make her worry about me. I did accomplish eliminating Zeus, but now Will and Marugrah have four other Kaiju to deal with.

"I'm sorry," I say to her.

She looks me in the eyes, tears streaming from hers. "Just stop being so impulsive. Consult your girlfriend before you go and do something stupid like that," she chuckles, wiping the tears from her eyes.

I smile and nod.

A presence beside us calls for my attention. I turn toward it, finding Tsuzar.

"You're alright," he says, surprised.

I give him a nod, grimacing. "For the most part. No psychological damage like you feared."

"Hmm," is his only reply.

Eva and Hlad help me to my feet, the three of us, along with Sasha, the only members of my team that seemed to have accompanied Tsuzar on my rescue, looking out the hatch.

The battle below isn't promising.

Typhon and Plague are teaming up on Prometheus, the robot barely holding its own. Marugrah was still scuffling with Echidna, Thorath sneaking up on him.

"We have to help them," I wheeze, coughing.

"And we will," Tsuzar says, stepping up next to us. "We must return to the mothership first."

48

Faithful was the only thing keeping the encroaching Kaijus at bay. Will swung it wildly in front of Prometheus. Typhon and Plague snarled and snapped their jaws at him. Two small cannons popped out from the sides of each of Prometheus' shoulder pylons, pelting the beasts with yellow beams of energy. The creatures seemed unaffected by the attack.

"Eth…need some options here!" Will said frantically.

Enough with the 'Eth' nickname, the AI snapped.

"We don't have…look, I'm sorry, okay?"

There was a moment of silence, Typhon taking a tentative step forward. Faithful's blade slashed him across the chest. He roared in pain, stumbling back.

Apology accepted, the AI finally replied. *And I prefer Thes as a nickname. It's what*...he *called me. Thel-Shuum.*

Will smiled. "Alright, *Thes*, what do you say our options are?"

The AI was quiet for a moment, thinking, running through every available option they had and determining which was best for their current situation.

Will, Prometheus finally came, *we need to get some space between us and them.*

Will smirked. "Roger that, buddy."

Marugrah roared as tendrils wrapped around his throat, their spike covered underside digging into his armored flesh. Echidna takes advantage of the situation, rushing forward and sending a clawed fist into Marugrah's armor plated gut. Marugrah pitched forward in pain, spittle flying from his sharp-toothed maw. He fell to his spiked knees, the tendrils releasing him.

Echidna and Thorath hovered over him as he looked up at them, holding his gut. Echidna threw a punch, connecting with the side of Marugrah's saurian head, sending a couple teeth and blood from his mouth. He landed on his hands and knees, getting a kick in the side from Thorath, his claws digging into his soft skinned side. He remained on his hands and knees despite the force of the blow.

Echidna's mad cackle reverberated through Marugrah's head.

You're strong, but not strong enough to defeat the both of us, she said, peering down at him with her blazing purple eyes. *If you were smart, you'd join us. Help us to conquer this putrid planet and its occupants.*

Marugrah's only response was a snarl.

Echidna kneeled in front of him, lifting his head, her eyes meeting his. *If you did*, she said, *I could take you back to your home planet. You could live there again.*

Marugrah's eyes softened. Memories of his life on Maruia flashing through his mind.

That's right, Echidna said. *You could be our guard of Maruia as we finish our military base that was planned for the planet.*

Marugrah's brows furrowed as anger coursed through his body in waves. *My planet...was destroyed for...a* fucking *military base???* Marugrah snarled.

Echidna chuckled in amusement, triggering Marugrah. He thrust his snout forward, his almost indestructible skull crashing into Echidna's armored face, sending her toppling backward with a shriek. Thorath pounced, digging his claws into Marugrah's sides and lifting the creature from the ground. Marugrah went rigid as he was lifted over Thorath's head and sent flying through the air. He hit the ground, sliding through the city, decimating buildings hundreds of feet away. He tried to push himself up, failing. He was tired, barely able to move. He'd been fighting for days against the Titans' children, swimming hundreds of miles. The full force of his exhaustion was getting to him now. He couldn't use rage to energize himself anymore. He could only watch as Echidna and Thorath stomped their way toward him.

His eyes widened in surprise as yellow laser bolts rained from the sky, striking the advancing Plagueonian Kaijus.

We arrive at the mothership in time to help Marugrah. The dragon-like Kaiju was flung across the city by

321

Thorath as we enter the control room, Hlad and Eva still helping me walk. They lower me into a chair, Sasha stepping up beside me, our eyes on the view screen projecting the battle. Tsuzar slides behind some controls, pressing buttons before taking hold of twin joysticks. He jams down the triggers, raining yellow laser bolts down on Marugrah's attackers.

I smile as Thorath and Echidna are pelted with bolts of energy, pushing them to the rubble covered ground.

A Hestialite approaches me, a device in their hand. A twang of hesitation washing over me before I remember these guys are our friends.

The Hestialite, thin and slender, like Savernst, raises the device. "It's an x-ray scanner," she says with a friendly smile at my apprehension.

I nod. She sweeps the device over my body, looking at its screen thoughtfully.

"I believe it would be best to get you to our medical bay," she says.

I sigh, but nod. Sasha and the Hestialite helps me to my feet as they escort me out of the control room and to the med bay. Before we exit the control room, I take one last look at the view screen, Tsuzar still firing away at Thorath and Echidna below us. I smirk at the sight.

The trip through the ship to the 'med bay' is short and before I know it, I'm in an alien-looking, but familiar bed. I look over to the other occupant of the room, which is huge, able to house a good forty patients, Marudon. She looks comfy as she sleeps. I notice all the gashes she had when we rescued her are gone. A sound pulls my attention upward as a hollow, pill-shaped device descends toward me. I almost panic until the Hestialite that brought me here speaks.

"This device will heal your wounds. I noticed a cracked skull, a fractured arm, and a few broken ribs causing internal bleeding during your scan," the medic says.

"Jesus," Sasha says, looking at me with worry.

I don't even feel half the wounds the medic describes. I feel lightheaded and numb. The pill device settles over the bed, darkness surrounding me. I hear it whir, activating.

Tiredness grips me and I drift off to sleep.

49

"Ready?" Will asked.

Ready, Prometheus replied.

Will clenched Prometheus' fists, the metal limbs deconstructing and reconstructing into cannon-like devices. He aimed them at Typhon and Plague as they closed in on Prometheus. He activated the devices, twin sonic booms slamming into the beasts, forcing them to the ground with wails of agony as their eardrums burst from the loud booms of sound.

"That should give us the time we need," Will said as Prometheus' hands returned to normal.

Roger that, Prometheus said, getting to work.

The cannons on Prometheus' back shifted, snapping together, deconstructing and reconstructing into something new. He pulled it from the robot's back, inspecting it. It was a single, long cannon that resembled a giant sniper rifle, minus a scope. It was massive, too, almost as big as Prometheus himself. The only way the robot was able to hold the weapon was thanks to the hover technology built into the weapon's underside.

He lifted the Ion Cannon, aiming it at Plague as he stumbled to his clawed feet. Will depressed the weapon's trigger, a crackling beam of purple energy erupting from the barrel, cutting through the air. Plague wailed in agony as the beam cut through his side. The beam lasted for only a few seconds, disappearing to reveal a large chunk missing from Plague's side. Vents on the weapons side released the pent up heat, a slide snapping back, ejecting the spent Ion round, chambering a new round upon closing. He fell to his knees, blood gushing from his side. It seemed to be a fatal blow, but Will stabbed him through the chest with Faithful before, skewering his heart and he somehow survived. In fact, Will noticed, the wound seemed nonexistent.

Hydra DNA? Will wondered.

He didn't dwell on the thought too long, watching Plague fall to the ground, seemingly lifeless. He shifted his aim toward Typhon, unconscious from his sonic attack, when a familiar roar caught his attention. He looked to find Thorath, somehow free of the laser barrage Echidna was caught in. He had made his way to the fallen Marugrah, too exhausted to move, hitting him with twin sonic attacks from the tendrils on his back.

Will shifted his aim to Thorath's head. When Prometheus reported the weapon was ready to fire once again, he pulled the trigger. The sound of the firing Ion Cannon caught Thorath's attention, turning his head toward it before the purple beam disintegrated his head. Thorath's body fell to its knees before the beam cut out, falling sideways to the ground, blood jetting from the dead Kaiju's stump of a neck.

Marugrah looked at the dead Kaiju in surprise, looking to Prometheus. Will nodded Prometheus' head at Marugrah, who nodded back at the robot.

Two down, two to go, Will thought, turning the Ion Cannon to Echidna, still caught in the laser barrage raining from the mothership in the sky. She laid on the ground, struggling to right herself as the bolts of energy struck her armored flesh, the force of them keeping her on the ground.

Heat vented, Ion round replaced, Will tightened Prometheus' finger on the Ion Cannon's trigger. A pinprick of light erupted at her core, barely visible, as Will pulled the trigger. Before the beam reached her, the light enveloped her and then disappeared. The laser barrage cut out, the operator probably as confused as Will was at the disappearance of their target, a crater left from the Ion Cannon where she was. Will lowered the Ion Cannon, baffled. Jeremy reported the same thing happening to Kronos a year ago.

What the hell is going on? Will thought, frustrated at not knowing.

The Ion Cannon was yanked from Prometheus' hands, jolting Will from his anger. He turned the mech toward the creature that yanked the weapon from him, an armored fist connecting with Prometheus' metal face. The robot stumbled back as Typhon roared in anger. He took a step towards Prometheus, stopping, looking down at his chest where a pinprick of light erupted suddenly. Typhon's eyes widened in surprise. Will watched in disbelief as the white light overtook Typhon before disappearing, the Kaiju gone. Bright, white light caught Will's attention once more as Plague disappeared.

All Vexnoxtuque...eliminated? Prometheus said, just as confused as Will.

"I don't believe they're dead," Will said.

Why do you say that?

"That light...it's the same as when we *teleport*."

You don't think...?

"I do."

Will turned his attention toward Marugrah, the Kaiju still laying on the ground. He strode toward his friend as the mothership lowered to collect both of them.

I open my eyes, feeling better than I ever had. I smile when I see my team gathered around me. Sasha. Josh. Eva. Hlad. Jones. Aaron. Ashley. Will. Ben. Ezekiel. President Scott. Even Marudon, who is in Ashley's arms. Tsuzar and Savernst are here, too. They greet me warmly. I frown, realizing that Will is in the room and not in the giant battle mech that is Prometheus.

"The battle is over?" I ask.

They all nod.

I perk up. "That means we won?"

They hesitate.

"Technically, yes. But there is something else going on," Will answers.

I sit up, Sasha putting a hand on my shoulder. I give her a warm smile and turn to Will. "What do you mean?"

"Remember what you told me about Kronos? How he disappeared in a flash of white light?"

I nod, my eyes widening in realization.

"Yeah," he says, "Echidna, Typhon, and Plague all did."

"What the hell is going on?" I wonder aloud.

Will shook his head. "I wouldn't have thought about this without seeing it with my own eyes, but it looked as if they were teleported. Prometheus is scanning for teleportation energy signatures. I have a feeling he is going to come up positive."

"You think they were teleported?" I ask. "Teleported where?"

"I couldn't tell you that." He frowns deeply, Ashley putting an arm around him.

"This just keeps getting better and better," I say, shaking my head.

"Well, I have some more news for you," Sasha says, turning my attention toward her standing beside me.

"And what is that?" I ask, skeptical. I notice she has a hand resting on her stomach.

"I'm pregnant," she says, sending my head spinning.

I sputter and stammer, unable to form words or a sentence. She giggles at me.

"It feels good to finally get this out there," she says with a sigh and a smile. "I meant to tell you earlier, but I never got a chance to."

Everyone around us offer their congratulations, even Tsuzar and Savernst. I, however, am at a loss for words. She looks down at me, still in an alien hospital bed, her smile fading.

"Aren't you going to say something?" she asks.

"That's...this...wow," I say, her smile returning with a laugh. I look up at her with a smile of my own, happy she wasn't hurt during our infiltration of the fathership. There were so many instances she could have been.

"Marry me," I finally say.

Epilogue I:

It's been 3 months since Las Vegas. President Scott
returned to the White House, thanks to a ride from the
Hestialites. The Hestialites returned to space, their long-
fought battle over, but not before dropping off our giant
robot back at the island designated to stash him and
Marugrah, who disappeared into the ocean's depths.
Their civil war with the remaining members of the
Plagueonians was finally over. Cole ordered a team to
sift through the wreckage of the fathership. Reports have
indicated there no survivors. Both Plagueonians and
Remnant member bodies were found, all of them dead.
They will no longer be a problem for us. Cole has had
the bodies of the Titans' children carted away to who-
knows-where…besides him. The damage the Kaiju
caused is extensive, both to the cities they attacked and
the people they killed. Hundreds of thousands of people
are dead.

But all of that is behind us now.

I adjust the tie to my suit nervously as I stand at the
altar. The pianist begins playing 'Here comes the Bride',
directing my attention down the makeshift aisle, lined
by my team and friends from the CCU in chairs, all
dressed up like I am. Sasha is there, looking just
gorgeous in her white wedding dress. Her arm is looped
in Will's --it's how we arranged it as her dad is dead and
she has no immediate family. Not to mention mine
thinks I'm dead. With the way I am now, a monster, I'd
like to keep it that way.

All I can do is smile like an idiot as they make their
way down the aisle.

We decided to have the wedding in Central Park, in
New York City, which has been completely restored
since the battle that took place here against Plague two

years ago. The sun is high in the sky. The air is warm. Birds chirp. It's as perfect a day I could have asked for to have a wedding on. Before I found out Sasha was pregnant, her baby bump evident now, I was against marriage, the last girl I proposed to having been mauled by a werewolf. But now…I feel as if this is the best decision I've made in my entire life.

As they reached the altar, Will passed Sasha off to me. I can't help but give the man, my best friend a hug. Will stepped back and went to sit next to Ashley. Sasha and I smile at each other, turning to the man standing behind the altar, the man that is going to marry us.

Josh.

"Before we start," he says to everyone sitting before him, "I just want us to have a moment of silence in honor of my sister. I know she approves."

I smile, giving him a nod. Everyone bows their heads, sitting in silence for several moments.

"Okay," Josh says, lifting his head, breaking the silence. "Let us start, eh?"

We commence with the ceremony, ending with Sasha and I sharing an intimate kiss. The people watching us applaud. I turn to them, feeling happier than I ever thought I could.

Except for Marugrah, all known Kaiju are dead. While Will's theory that Kronos, Echidna, Typhon, and Plague were teleported somewhere, I can hope we never see them again. There is also the case of the Atlantean destroyer. People have been searching for the sunken city for as long as stories have been told of it, so as long as the city remains hidden, we don't have to worry about that one. If it is even alive.

The world can finally rest in peace without the fear of a Kaiju attack.

Epilogue II:

Echidna stumbled back. One moment she was on Earth, being pummeled by laser bolts falling from the sky, the next she was in a dimly lit, foreign terrain. She started to panic, thinking she had been taken back to the darkness.

"Echidna, darling, don't you just look...horrific," a voice said, attracting her attention.

She looked back and forth. Typhon stood to her right, looking as confused as her, but the voice she heard wasn't his. To her left laid Plague, motionless, a hole carved into his side. The voice wasn't his either.

"Oh my," the voice came again. "He doesn't look well."

"I'll heal," Plague mumbled.

A figure, no more than fifty feet tall, much smaller than herself, stepped up to Plague.

"Not fast enough," the figure said. "You've lost a significant amount of blood. If you die, I would have wasted valuable teleporter energy to save you."

Tentacled creatures slithered up to Plague, carting him off.

"Where are you taking him?" Echidna asked, panicking.

As the horned figure turned to her, she recognized who he was.

"Surtr?" she asked, stunned.

He spread his arms to his sides. "Awh, you remember me. I'm flattered." He grinned, showing his sharp teeth.

Typhon just looked flabbergasted. Echidna looked unsure herself.

Surtr crossed his arms, one robotic from the forearm to his hand. "Right. You see, we've not actually met. Well, not this version of you. I've been to multiple dimensions. Met multiple Echidnas. All of them are dead. They died trying to take over Earth. If I hadn't saved you, you'd have succumbed to the same fate."

Echidna shook her head, opening her mouth to speak. Surtr raised his robotic hand before she could.

"Look, maybe it'll just help if I get to the point to avoid confusing you further. I'm amassing an army. A legion," he said.

"And you saved us to join your...legion?" Echidna asked.

"Ding, ding, ding," he said.

Echidna was quiet for a moment before speaking again. "And just what is your end goal?"

He smiled. "Why the destruction of humanity, of course. In all dimensions."

If Echidna could smile, she would have.

"You in?" he asked.

"Of course," Echidna replied.

Typhon said nothing. Echidna elbowed him. He grunted at her.

"If she's in, so am I," he said.

"Good," he said and began walking.

They followed him to a cliff overlooking a valley of sortsl. Within it swarmed hundreds of giant bodies. Most of them were unknown to her, but a few of them she recognized. They were Vexnoxtuque. Including the Titan Kronos.

Their legion.

NOTE FROM THE AUTHOR

Thank you for reading the third installment in my Jeremy Walker series! As you can tell by the second epilogue, his adventures aren't over just yet! A great evil is plotting against him.

I really enjoyed writing this story. It is the largest roster of monsters I've written thus far. It was a challenge, for sure, but I think I did well in pulling it off!

As always, I'd like to thank my proofers: Emily Jenkins and Elizebeth Cooper! Thank you two so much for helping make my book better!

I'd also like to thank Ray Fromm for contributing his awesome artistic talents to drawing the main beasties! They look amazing, my man!

If you like the book, please leave a review on Amazon or wherever you bought this book!

—Z.C.

CREATURE DESIGNS

The following are the creature designs for the sixteen Kaiju (Marugrah, MegaHydra, Athena, Artemis, Plague, Poseidon, Hestia, Ares, Thorath, Iris, Hades, Echidna, Typhon, Zeus, Phobos, and Saibosuta) and Prometheus drawn by the awesome Ray Fromm!

MARUGRAH

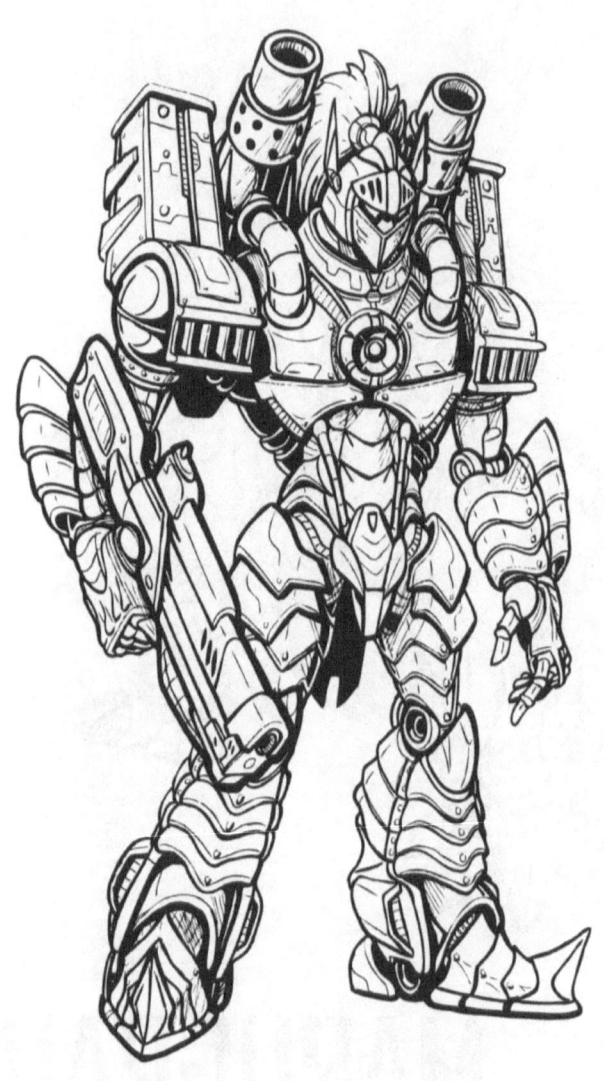

338

PROMETHEUS

339

MEGAHYDRA

ARTEMIS

HESTIA

342

ATHENA

HADES

343

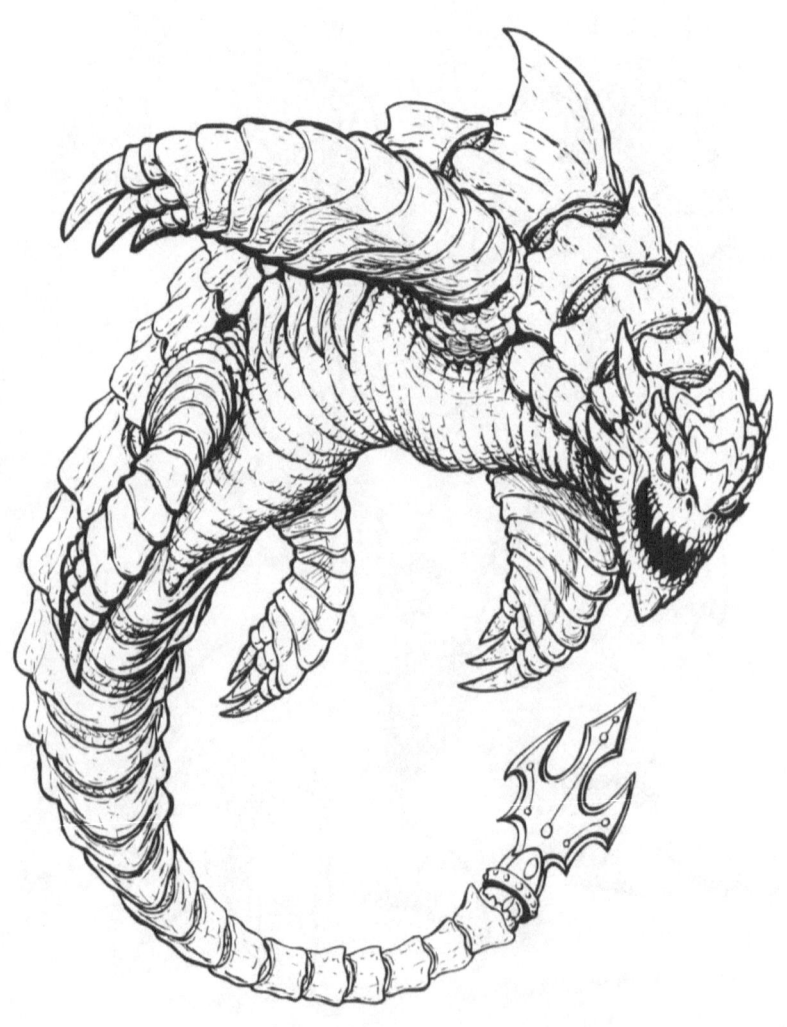

344

POSEIDON

345

ARES

346

IRIS

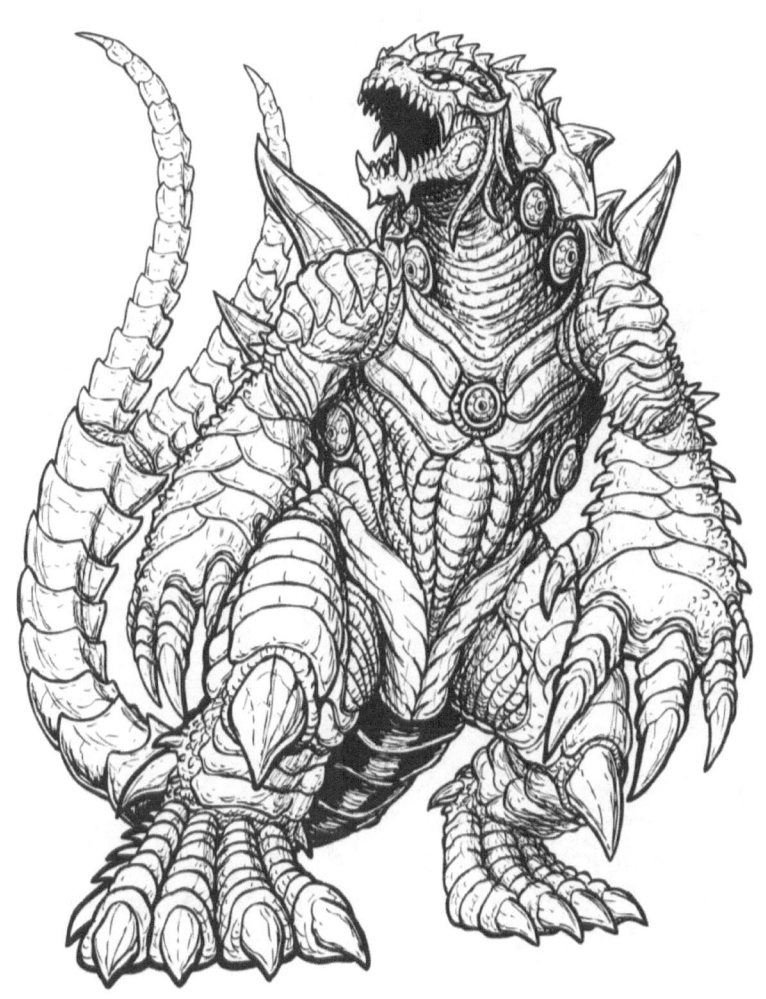

PHOBOS

ZEUS

349

THORATH

350

ECHIDNA

351

PLAGUE

352

SAIBOSUTA

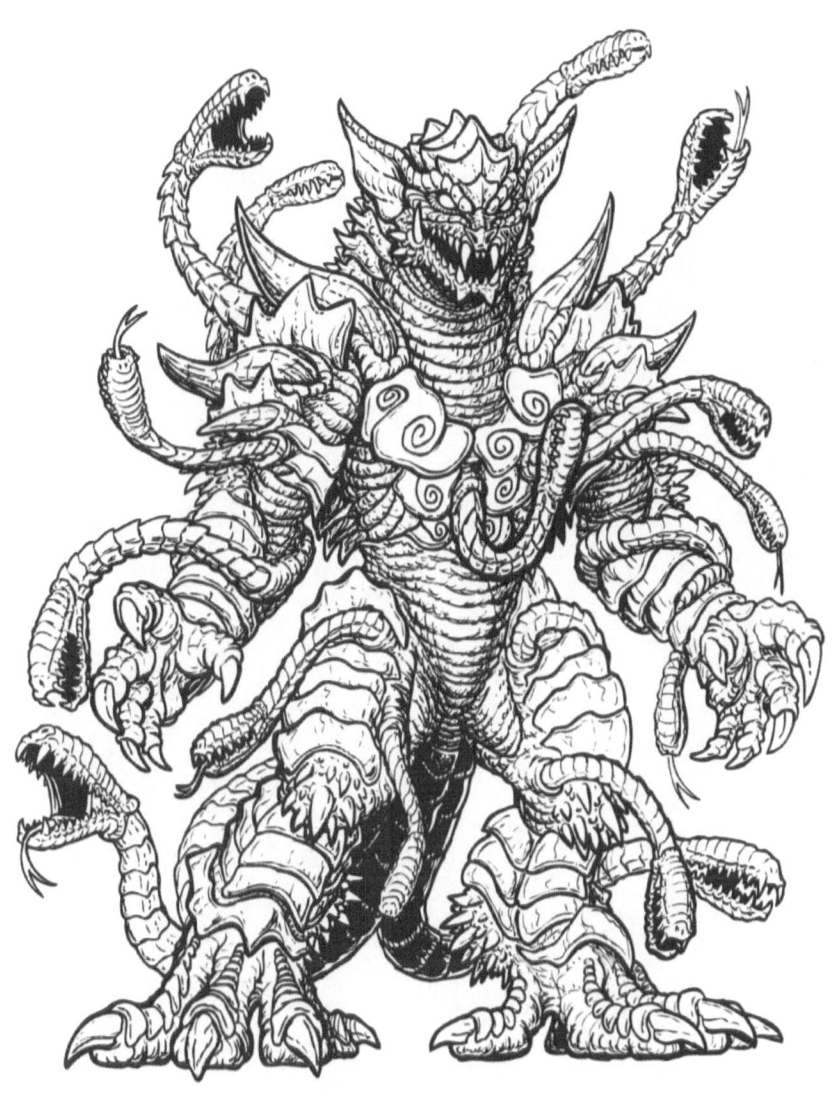

353

TYPHON

COMMISSIONS FORM GABE THE KAIJU ENTHUSIAST:

The following are commissions of Marugrah, Prometheus, Plague, and Zorax I had done from Gabriel Gregory, AKA: Gabe The Kaiju Enthusiast!

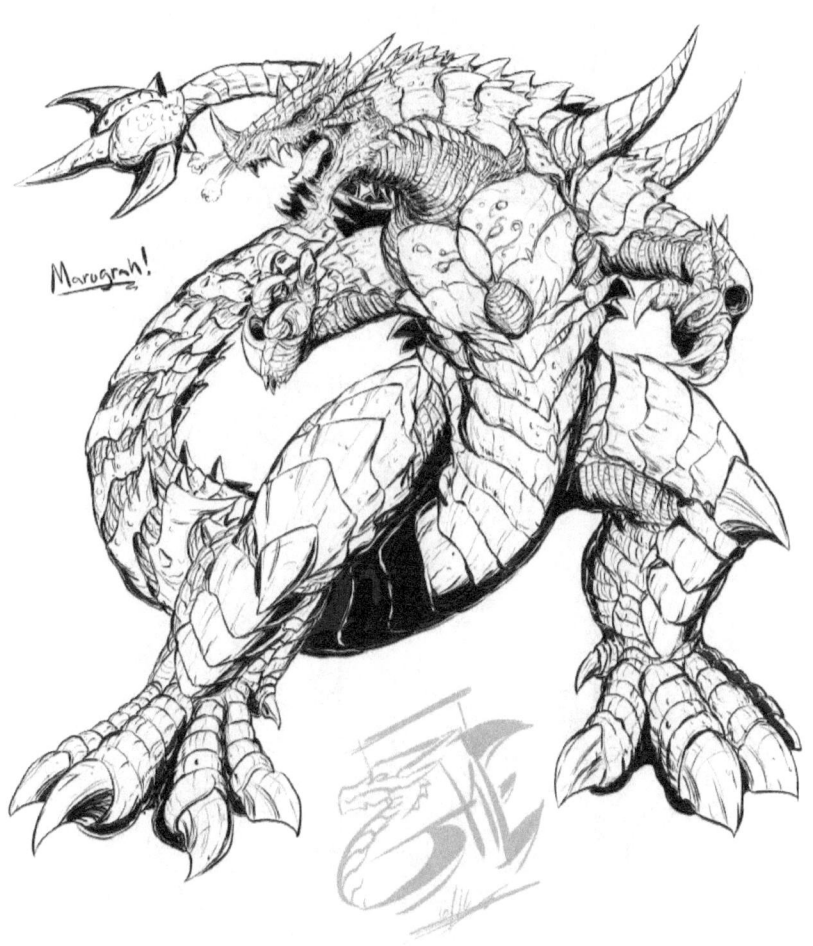

Marugrah!

Prometheus

360

www.ingramcontent.com/pod-product-compliance
Lightning Source LLC
Chambersburg PA
CBHW030552180626
46816CB00005B/1512